For the Love of a
WOMAN

Christina James

This is a work of fiction. Names, characters, places and incidents are either the product of the author's imagination or are used fictitiously. Any resemblance to actual persons living or dead, business establishments, events, or locales, is entirely coincidental.

For the Love of a Woman

Published by Valerie Harris
Copyright 2011 by Valerie Harris
Cover by Angela Anderson, Angela Anderson Design
ISBN: 978-1-938799-04-4

Layout by www.formatting4U.com

Dedication

For Courtney and Scott, may you chase your dreams and do whatever it takes to make them come true. Always believe in yourself and others will too. Don't be afraid to let your heart choose the road that's right for you.

Chapter One

Mitch drifted off to sleep, warring with the visions behind his eyelids when the dream took hold.

Transported back to that horrible day, terror gripped him by the throat, defying his attempts to suck in air with desperate breaths. Fear's icy fingers crawled along his sweat-dampened skin like a slimy worm slithering across a rain-slicked ground. But Mitch couldn't let fear win. If he did, death would surely follow. He could only fight his way out of the nightmare.

Moving quietly along the liquor store's dark hallway to the backroom where the girls were held captive, Mitch relied totally on his specialized police training to guide him to the hostages. His eyes scanned the darkness, adjusting to the lack of light. His ears strained for any sound but found only silence. The ominous scent of death—the smell of spilled blood— made his heart pound painfully within his chest.

Mitch's mind filtered a thousand vicious curses as he inched forward, desperate to reach the girls who depended on him for their lives.

Time passed too slowly as he ignored his own pain and crept onward into the darkness, maybe to his death.

His gun steady in his hand, his senses on high

alert. The second he viewed the figure lying on the ground, motionless in a dark pool of liquid, his world changed forever. And not for the better.

Mitch woke abruptly in a cold sweat, his skin chilled and clammy. The way his heart pounded, he felt like he had just run a marathon. He pinched the bridge of his nose and shook the sleep from his foggy mind. Sitting behind the steering wheel in his truck while using the seat's headrest as a pillow only cramped his muscles. Taking a nap on the side of the road wasn't conducive to a decent rest. A quick glance at the clock showed he'd been asleep for just under an hour. And he felt worse now than when he pulled over to rest his bleary eyes.

Turning the ignition, the engine roared to life and Mitch pulled his truck back onto the rural highway. He was tired, hungry, and lost somewhere in the damn Smoky Mountains. Running from a past that haunted him to a future he couldn't see would have been better with a direction in mind. Small drops of water splattered on his windshield, just a hint of the storm brewing in the east.

He had driven with no particular destination. But for the first ten hours on the road, he had an idea of where the hell he was. Not now. Now, huge green fields dotted with grazing cows and horses seemed never ending. Deep forests with tall, leafy trees and ragged undergrowth abutted the fields. And still there was no sign of civilization. The two-lane backcountry route was an infinite winding road. Like being stuck in a maze with no way out. Similar to what his memories did to him, keeping him stuck in the past, stuck on one day with no way out.

The once deep blue skies held dark gray puffy clouds and threatened rain. His six-foot-two inch frame ached from being cramped behind the wheel for so many hours. His fault really for driving with no purpose. A glance in the rearview mirror confirmed that he looked as bad as he felt. His eyes were bloodshot, the tiny red lines making the whiskey color of his eyes dark and menacing. Gray half-moons had set in under his eyes, causing him to look old and withered. Scratchy dark stubble covered an angular jaw that gave his chin an angle of defiance, jutting out just enough to square his face. His thick, light brown hair cried out for a haircut.

The "ding ding" alarm sounded just as big fat raindrops hit the windshield. The tiny picture of a red gasoline pump on his dashboard warned of low fuel. He burst out laughing, laughing so hard that it hurt. It was either laugh or punch the windshield and that would just let in the heavy rain now lashing out from mean skies.

Ding, ding.

"All right, for Christ's sakes. I'll get you some go-go juice as soon as I find some sign of life around here," he complained, while straining his head to look into the distance through the rain-spotted windshield.

Slowly, Mitch drove through the downpour. Scanning the distance, there was no sign of people anywhere. The mountains were a huge mass of land and he cursed himself for not paying attention to his whereabouts.

His arms tensed, holding the steering wheel, while his thoughts wandered to the recent events that had left him in this current predicament. He still

3

couldn't believe that he had really left his home, his life, his job. Everything. Just ran. There was nothing left for him now in Boston. Only haunting memories and a job with the police force that was out of reach. His conscience weighed heavier and heavier each day. He only hoped the distance from Massachusetts would help ease the pain. Wherever the steering wheel turned, he'd go but not for long without some gas and sleep.

There might be enough gas for another few miles...maybe. He smirked when he saw the old green and white sign on the side of the road indicating the Town of Courtsville two miles ahead. With the rain pelting the windshield, he sure was glad to find civilization again.

Lightening streaked across the sky, spotlighting the distant mountains. Thunder crackled with deafening roars. The wind shook his truck, blowing through the trees and slanting them toward the roadway. No way in hell did he want to get stranded in a friggin' thunderstorm with no food or water and no damn aspirin. He didn't know what hurt more, the pain between his eyes or his knee.

"Just like in the movies," Mitch complained, squinting to see through the stream of water pouring over the windshield. Small hailstones bounced off the glass like ping pong balls. On the roof, it sounded like drums.

He slowed, squinted, and almost drove right by the one-island gas station. There were no lights on. No sign of anyone working. What the fuck? To his relief, when he pulled up to the pump, he glimpsed a dim light in the window of the small shack. The front door opened as a tall, white-haired elderly man in overalls holding an umbrella stepped out.

Mitch rolled down his window. "Fill 'er up, please," he directed, unfastening his seatbelt to get his wallet.

"You ain't from around here, are ya?"

"No, sir." Mitch caught bright blue eyes watching him. He wasn't looking for conversation. Just some fuel.

The man started to pump the gas. Mitch was rolling up his window when the guy reappeared.

Mitch stared at him in bafflement. "What?"

"Can't very well talk to the hose while she fills ya up, so thought I'd talk to you."

"About what?"

"Don't know."

Small towns. Is this what people did? Make idle conversation just to hear themselves? "Well, I don't have much to talk about. Been on the road too long." As proof, he yawned, unable to stop himself.

"You got far to go?" the man asked, holding the umbrella as the rain slowed to a light drizzle. Thunder still echoed in the distance. At least the storm had passed.

"Not sure. But I could use dinner and a night's sleep. Can you tell me if I'm anywhere near either?"

"Not gonna get far in this truck," the man announced, angling his head toward the hood. "Nope. Not more than two miles I'd say."

Now he had Mitch's attention. "Why?" Mitch followed the man's glance. A large plume of white smoke bellowed from under the hood. "Son of a bitch!"

5

Before Mitch finished another line of curses and managed to get out of the truck, the old man was already standing in front of the hood.

"Pop it," the man commanded.

Mitch complied, reaching under the steering column and pulling the black lever until he heard a pop. He walked slowly to stand by the old man who used his hand to brush away the smoke.

"Yup. Just as I thought. You cracked the radiator. Ain't no antifreeze or water left in 'er." He shut the hood. "It'll get you about two miles but not more without stalling or worse, blowing the engine."

"Shit!" Mitch stood with his hands on his hips and studied the shack. There was no sign of a garage, but he had to ask. "Can you fix it?"

"Wish I could help you there, my friend, but I only sell gas. There's a good mechanic in town."

"Can I get to him without causing more damage?"

"Sure, I guess. But won't do you any good. He's closed up shop by now. It's poker night."

Mitch wasn't even going to ask. "What do you suggest then? What if I filled the radiator with some water?"

"Won't do any good. It'll just piss out of the hole. Your engine's so hot, probably been on the road some time now. You'd stall or blow your engine after two miles. That's my guess."

Mitch wanted to kick the truck. But he just stared at the ground trying to think of something. Every situation had a way out. Or at least he once thought so. Had once been trained to think so.

The old man left Mitch's side to take the hose out

and replace the cap. "That'll be thirty three even," he said, returning to Mitch.

Mitch pulled out his wallet for the cash.

"You a cop?" the man asked when he noticed his badge in his wallet.

Mitch didn't know why he kept the thing. How many times had he thought about chucking it out the window the last ten hours, but could never bring himself to do it? No. That badge had been earned with his blood and guts. He may no longer be a cop, but he'd hold onto it.

"Not anymore, sir."

The man pointed to his leg. "Got injured on the job?"

"Yeah."

"Too bad. We could use a new sheriff in these parts."

Mitch smirked. "Sorry. Not interested."

"Now that's a damn shame," the old man said, the hopeful smile he held a moment ago now gone. "Tell you what. You look like an honest man. For a cop, that is."

"Ex-cop," Mitch reaffirmed.

The man waved his hand in the air. "Okay, ex-cop. Anyway, why don't you come home with me? The missus will take good care of you, give you a meal, fix up a bed for you for the weekend, until you get your truck fixed."

Mitch stared, not use to such hospitality. "That's very kind of you, sir."

"Name's Joe McFadden. Folks around here call me Ol' Joe. Not because of my age. Hell, I've still got a lot of years left. But because I've been in town for generations. Well, not me, but my family."

Mitch laughed. "I get the picture. I do appreciate the offer, but I have to decline. Can you give me directions to the mechanic? I'd like to see if I can catch him."

"I'm telling you it's pointless. He's closed up by now. But suit yourself. I doubt you'll even make it to town. You'll only end up having to sleep in this cramped truck all night. Probably wouldn't be a smart thing to do with that bum leg of yours. But get a pen and right down these directions."

Mitch did as instructed.

"You sure you want to risk driving instead of coming home with me? Your truck can be fixed first thing Monday morning when Maddy opens his shop."

"I'll be fine. Thanks again."

Mitch pulled out onto the road and followed Ol' Joe's directions. He'd beg the mechanic to fix his truck and offer him extra money if need be. But no way was Mitch bunking down with strangers, especially someone who would offer him food and comfort. He'd just left that behind with his family for Christ's sakes.

Per the instructions, he'd watch for the yellow tower and follow the road into town. Once his truck was repaired, he'd get directions to the nearest motel. In the morning, he'd drive again until he figured out what he wanted to do with his life now that his career was over.

Chapter Two

Twenty minutes later, Mitch sat stoned face inside his truck, cursing himself for his stupidity. Why he chose to ignore common sense and drive a defective truck into the middle of no man's land was beyond him. Now that he'd managed to pull his stalled truck over to the side of the road and halfway into a ditch, he sat and waited. Surely someone had to come by and he could grab a ride to get some help. He should have made sure his cell phone was charged. Now with a dead truck, that wouldn't be possible.

After an hour had passed and daylight was turning into evening, Mitch let loose a string of curses and then grabbed what he needed from the truck for what would probably be a long walk. Every muscle protested the sudden physical activity. He needed food and water. Who was he kidding? What he really wanted was a cold beer.

If he understood Ol' Joe's directions then he was about a mile from town. How the hell he would make it that far on his bum leg he didn't know, but it would certainly be slow going and take at least an hour. If he were still in his prime, he'd have made it to town much sooner. But since he walked with a cane, there was no hope of speeding up his travel.

After walking for an eternity on the quiet, dusty country road, a house appeared on the right. Mitch thanked his lucky stars and walked into a circular driveway. Maybe he could pay the owner for a ride into town. The white clapboard could use a fresh coat of paint. Some shingles needed replacing where rot had formed. But the owner probably knew that.

The large and plentiful windows made the house seem like a mansion. It was a simple house, not a lot of frills or fancy lawn ornaments. There was a huge wrap-around porch with two rocking chairs strategically placed to look out on the surrounding fields and woods. Small flowers dotted the front yard. A couple of rose bushes bloomed with red, pink, and yellow flowers. Azalea bushes covered in hot pink blooms framed the walkway to the house. It was very welcoming, just enough charm for the front of the house.

As Mitch neared the porch, he caught a whiff of the perfumed air. A garden hose was neatly wound around a hook on the side of the house and under it sat cut firewood. The chimney, he noted as he approached the front stairs, looked as if it were about to crumble down on some poor slob's unsuspecting head. As long as they didn't fall on his head. He'd had his fair share of trouble this year and wasn't looking for more.

Mitch gripped the cane as he walked to the stairs. He hated the damn thing. Made him feel like an old man. Made him feel helpless. The cane brought attention to him, more so than the limp or the scar on his shoulder blade that could be seen when he wore his sleeveless T-shirts. He'd have to buy more suitable clothing to hide the scar so no one would feel the need to "ooh" and "aah" or ask him questions.

It was none of their damn business how it happened.

Mitch stopped to catch his breath—just to take in the area he told himself and not to steady his legs. Glancing around, he noticed three horses in a pen in the distance. They grazed lazily, their long tails swaying back and forth. A small red barn sat a short walk from the house. That roof also looked like it could use a new layer of shingles, and the door hung lopsided in its framc. Nothing a little adjusting couldn't fix. If he owned this place, he would've kept up on the maintenance.

As he walked again, Mitch gripped the cane and let it take most of the pressure off his knee. Just like the doctors and nurses told him to do. He bet he could get good distance if he threw it across the wide-open fields. Then he'd never have to look at the stupid thing again. And he wouldn't be constantly reminded of everything that was taken from him. Wouldn't be reminded of his failure. Wouldn't be reminded of...

His breath hissed out like a tire going flat in a hurry. Stop it! Stop thinking back. Look forward.

He gritted his teeth as he climbed the wide front stairs. The house sure had seen a lot of traffic by the sound of the loud creaks, like wood splitting. How many secrets did this house hold? All old houses had some.

The name on the door read *The Hamptons*. Mitch hoped the Hamptons were home and didn't mind letting him borrow their phone for a tow truck. Then he'd find a place to get a decent meal and a good night's sleep.

Unable to find a doorbell, Mitch knocked hard on the doorframe. When he got no response, he tried again. And again. Finally, frustrated and tired, he opened the screen door slowly.

"Hello?" he called.

No answer.

The wind whipped at his back, sending a slight chill through his bones but not because it was cold. He hated entering quiet places where the unknown waited. Like that fateful day in Boston.

He stepped in and shut the screen door behind him. "Hello?" he called again. His eyes searched for any movement.

Stepping forward, Mitch steadied himself to give his legs some desperately needed recuperation after that long walk. "Just my luck, deserted. Hello?" he said loudly now. Who goes out and leaves their doors unlocked?

"In here," a woman's voice yelled out.

"Where is here?" he asked in the direction of the response.

A slender woman in her early thirties appeared in the doorway wearing slim fitting gray sweats and an oversized black T-shirt. She dried her hands on a dishtowel as she stepped closer to him. Her long blond hair was pulled back neatly in a tight ponytail. She wore very little makeup, maybe a touch of eye shadow and eyeliner. Otherwise, her creamy white skin was flawless except for a few fine lines at the corners of her eyes.

Those eyes. They were as blue as the sky. Big, wide, gorgeous eyes stared back at him. A man could easily get lost in their depths. There was a familiar look to them, like he had looked into those eyes before, but the woman was a stranger to him. He would've definitely remembered this beautiful creature.

"Sorry. I was in the kitchen fighting with the stove." She kept her gaze on him but stopped a few feet away from him. She was about seven inches shorter than him. "Did your truck finally break down?"

He stared at her dumbfounded. "How'd you know that?"

"Before my phone went out due to the storm, my father called and told me to expect a stranger on my doorstep within a few hours. You were determined to drive your truck when you shouldn't have." She wiped the back of her hand across her forehead.

"Yeah, well, I did give it a hell of a try. So Ol' Joe is your father?" That explained the eyes.

"Uh-huh. Says you turned him down when he offered you a place to stay for the night."

"I didn't want to impose. Your father was very nice to offer but, from where I come from, that kind of hospitality is unheard of and, no disrespect to your dad, but I felt uneasy staying with a stranger."

"Looks like you should've taken him up on his offer." She walked over to the window and looked out. "Dad said you'd be walking up the road before long."

He grinned tiredly. "He was telling the truth."

"Now what are you going to do?" she asked, returning to his side, those eyes studying him thoroughly.

"If I could borrow your phone, I'll just call a tow truck and get out of your way. My cell needs to be charged. Something I didn't realize until my truck

13

died."

She laughed, the soft sound tightening his gut. "I'm sorry. I shouldn't laugh. It's rude. But it's just that, well, we don't have the kind of services around here that you're probably used to."

"You telling me you don't have a tow truck?"

"No, of course we do. It's just that the tow truck operator is the, um, mechanic, and he's off duty until Monday morning."

Mitch took a deep breath and willed himself not to lose his temper, a temper that was on the verge of exploding since he'd started walking from his truck. "You're joking, right?"

"No, I'm not. Your truck will have to stay where it is for now. At least until Maddy can get to it on Monday. Don't worry, it'll be safe. No one will bother it."

Mitch clenched his teeth to keep a string of curses from escaping. "Can you at least tell me if there is a motel in town that I can get to? I'm not interested in sleeping in my truck for the weekend."

She folded her arms and bit down on her lower lip, her nervous eyes watching him. "I'm afraid you've stumbled into a town that doesn't have such amenities. That's why my dad offered to let you stay with him since there really is no other place around here."

"Any way to get in touch with the mechanic? Hell, I'll pay him double to fix my truck now."

She laughed, an action that lit up her face. "I don't think Maddy's wife would appreciate you dragging him away from his family for any amount of money. Around here, money doesn't talk as loud as it does in the city."

"I didn't mean to insult anyone. I'm just saying that I'd be willing to pay the man for his trouble, especially if he were doing me a favor."

"Sorry, but you're out of luck. He won't do it simply because if he did it for you he'd have to do it for everyone else, and his wife would never allow it. Weekends are for rest."

"Yeah, well, if this town had a motel then I could get some rest." He ran his hand through his hair, fighting the urge to tear it out. Damn town probably didn't even have a barbershop either. "What do you suggest I do, Ms. Hampton?"

"Marlena. But call me Marly."

The sultry sound of her voice, the way her eyes watched him intensely, stirred his gut, creating the feeling a man gets when he notices a woman. But he didn't want to notice this woman. He wanted to get back on the road and that seemed damn near impossible. "Okay. Marly. Any ideas because I'm fresh out of them?"

"You can take my dad up on his offer to stay with him and my mom. They're good people. You'll get the rest you need and he'll be in touch with Maddy so your truck can be fixed first thing and you can get on your way."

"Guess I have no choice."

"Sure you do. You can sleep in your truck."

Mitch grinned. "No, thanks. If you could call your dad and see if the offer still stands, I'd appreciate it."

"Sure." Turning to a small desk in the entryway, she picked up a cordless phone and began to dial then hung back up. "Afraid the phone is still dead and so is

15

my cell last I checked."

"Of course it is. I wouldn't have it any other way," he complained, suddenly really regretting hitting the open road.

"Losing land line and cell phone service happens a lot around here due to the weather. Don't panic. Should be up soon. Worse case, I'll drive you over to Dad's in a few hours. I heard you were hungry."

As if on cue, his stomach growled. "You heard right. I could definitely eat."

"I can't brag, but I make a decent dinner. You're welcomed to stay."

The offer was enticing. She was so friendly, a breath of fresh air from the hard-ass, pushy women he was used to. "I wouldn't want to impose, really."

"I wouldn't have asked if I didn't want you to stay. You're hungry and exhausted from the looks of you."

"Gee, thanks," he teased, not able to keep a smile from forming.

"Sorry, just telling it how I see it," she said, smiling back, her fingers toying with the dishtowel she still held. "And since you have no wheels and the closest restaurant is like seven miles away, then I guess you're stuck with my cooking unless starving appeals to you."

"That it doesn't. I'm willing to pay for the food."

She stood close to him with her hands on her hips. "My, my. I almost want to believe you're serious, but then that would mean you're trying to insult me."

"No," he stumbled for words, looking down into those heavenly blue eyes. "I'm not."

"Good. Then it's settled. Afterwards, I'll take you

to my dad's. And we'll have no talk about money. I'm sure I can find something for you to help with while you're here." She smiled warmly. "Just give me a few minutes to get my stove working."

"Sure."

Mitch watched her face change, like a light bulb went on in her head. "Actually, I would like to impose on you for something, if that's okay?"

He cocked an eyebrow. "Absolutely."

"Can you look at the stove?" Without waiting for him, she turned and walked from the room. He had no choice but to follow.

His gaze focused on her slender frame. Of course, his eyes weren't too tired to follow the sway of her hips. The small but curvy little bottom was certainly a sight for sore eyes. It had been too long since he'd noticed a woman. She wasn't even dressed up and she had his mouth watering.

Those long legs and smooth curves teased his sexual appetite, something that hadn't mattered lately. Slowly, he walked behind her, enjoying the view even knowing she was probably off limits. The sign out front had said, *The Hamptons*. Was it normal to be jealous of something so easily?

In the kitchen, reality struck Mitch like a lightning bolt. Why was he being such a dumb ass, fantasizing over this lovely lady when he roamed the States looking for a reason to explain his existence? Must be lack of sleep.

Marly's voice broke into his thoughts. "The storm knocked out the lights. That happens a lot around here, too. We lose all the modern day comforts like electricity and communication. And when the lights go on again, I have to re-light the pilots by hand, but today I just can't get it going and I'm losing patience."

"I'll give it a try but can't promise anything. My specialty is not stoves." He rested his cane against the kitchen counter.

"Do what you can if you don't mind. It's got to be better than what I'm doing."

The stove was old but fit in with the style of the kitchen just fine. There was a small wooden table with four chairs by a window. Lace placemats and a vase of yellow flowers that had seen better days were neatly placed on the table. Cherry wood cabinets lined one wall and another wall held shelves with knick-knacks. It was a very quaint space, big enough to move around for cooking and cleaning but cozy enough to enjoy a quiet dinner.

Marly leaned closer to Mitch. She smelled of lemons and herbs, the scents tickling his nose. Strange combination. Maybe she had cleaned with something lemon scented, and the pork chops marinating by the stove were the source of the herbs.

He studied the stove, not really knowing what to do. When he began to light the pilot on top of it, Marly grabbed his arm.

"No, not there. There." She opened the oven door and pointed.

"Okay." He studied the inside. "Just how did you do this before?"

"You have to light the pilot through that small hole while turning the knob and, when the flame hits the gas, it'll light."

"That doesn't sound too comforting for the guy sticking his head in the oven."

She laughed, the sound tightening his gut into a knot. Her hand fell onto his shoulder, the touch raising the hair on his arm in awareness. "I wouldn't put you in harm's way. I've done this hundreds of times and never got burnt. The flame goes down into the stove not up."

His skin burned now, but not from the fire, from her touch. The only reasonable explanation was the lack of a woman's touch over the last few months. "Yeah, well, the way my luck has been lately, I don't want to chance it."

"Trust me. You'll be fine."

Something in her tone convinced him she meant what she said. So he got back to business. He used the top burner to light the long wooden stick match. The smell of lit matches immediately stunk up the room as he placed the burning stick over the small hole in the bottom of the oven and turned the knob until he heard hissing gas.

"Now move it around a little," Marly instructed, leaning over Mitch's shoulder. He nervously obeyed, expecting an explosion at any moment. "No, go this way." He obeyed. "Try to move it so that the tip goes into the hole just enough."

With all his strength, he concentrated on the task, but couldn't help thinking of sexual images as she talked about tips and holes and moving around. She was driving him crazy. This was insane!

He glanced up at her. "Do you want to do this?" he asked, with a little more annoyance than was necessary. If truth be told, he was more annoyed with himself than with her. Hell, she was only telling him how to light the damn stove and he was getting a friggin' hard-on.

"Sorry," she said quietly, removing her hand from his shoulder. "I'm a hands-on type of person. I don't like delegating duties. I prefer to do them myself."

"Well, since you've so nicely delegated this to me, would you mind giving me some room to work with?"

"Fine," she agreed, but only moved back an inch.

Turning back to the stove, Mitch wanted to get it done so he could eat then get the hell out of there before his dick was tortured anymore. He needed to get as far away from Marlena Hampton as possible. He was far too comfortable around her.

Wiggling and turning the stick proved harder than it looked. Just when the match had gotten too short and threatened to burn his fingertips, he heard a 'poof'. Marly straightened, clapping.

"You did it. Now we can eat." Into the stove went the pork chops and a casserole dish containing scalloped potatoes.

The sight made his stomach growl. "How long until we eat?" Mitch asked, grabbing his cane and walking back toward the doorway, placing as much room between him and Marly as possible.

"About an hour." Filling a pot with water, she placed it on top of the stove, lit the pilot and turned to him. "Mitch, tell me something."

"Okay."

She walked slowly to him, stopping in front of him, her head angled up to look in his eyes. "I haven't let a serial killer or escaped convict into my home, have I?"

Mitch studied her face—the high cheekbones,

small pointed nose, and tiny beauty mark along her jaw. Her eyes searched his. "Not any more. I gave that stuff up years ago," he teased.

He totally expected Marly's face to drain of all color, but she surprised him with a big smile while laying her hand on his arm. Those slender fingers with long manicured nails dug slightly into his skin. The funny sensation was even more distracting. He was just tired. Just overtired.

"Do you want a shower before dinner?"

Oh, God, the woman was killing him. He strategically placed the cane in front of him to hide the ever increasing bulge in his jeans. He could easily picture her in the shower with him.

"That sounds like heaven. Let me grab my bag. I left it by the door. At least I was smart enough to grab a change of clothes before leaving the truck behind."

"You would've been smarter if you had listened to my dad."

He sent her a quelling look. Her hands flew up, palms out. "Okay, that was a low blow, but I can't help it. Your stubbornness has obviously wiped you out, walking around on that bad leg. And don't try to deny it. Come on. I have an empty apartment over my garage where you can shower."

He only offered a grunt and turned to follow her into the living room. They passed the seven-foot long flowery couch with two armchairs of the same pattern. There was a decent size television, although it was an older model, and a small stereo system in the room. A few end tables had lamps and pictures on them. Mitch studied the picture of a man in military uniform. Must be her husband.

The woman wasn't free. Besides, if she were, what the hell would he do with her? He had a bum leg, a fucked up life, and was on the road to nowhere.

So he channeled his thoughts to dinner and sleep. He grabbed the duffel bag and followed her out the front door and down the steps to a large garage. Forcing himself to keep up with her pace even as his knee screamed only added to his misery. She had only given his cane and leg a cursory glance. Either good manners or a lack of curiosity kept her from inquiring about his injury because Marly struck him as the type of woman who wouldn't think twice about asking what's wrong.

Hadn't he hated that from people? Was he disappointed that Marly didn't bother to ask about his injury? No, that wasn't it. He was just surprised since every person he had run into after the accident had always asked the inevitable question, "Why do you need a cane at your age?" A nightmare. That's why.

Mitch rested for a moment at the bottom of the stairs that led up the side of the garage.

"Do you make it a habit of staring off into space?" Marly asked, with just a note of annoyance in her voice as she leaned against the door jam waiting for him at the top of the steps.

"I'm sorry." Mitch rubbed his hand over his face. "Told you I was tired." Pushing past the pain, he climbed the stairs and followed her into the small apartment.

Marly opened two windows. The place was sparsely decorated with a couch, small television, and coffee table. A tiny kitchenette boasted a countertop with a stool and mini fridge.

"The bathroom is through that door. I'll grab you a towel so you can take a hot shower while dinner cooks." She didn't wait for a reply but walked into the kitchen area, opened a cabinet, and returned with a large fluffy towel. He could use a hot shower just as much as he could use sleep.

Mitch had to hand it to Marly. She sure could make someone feel at home.

He accepted the towel. "So is that a nice way of telling me I smell and should clean up?"

"What?" She laughed. "No. If I thought that, I'd tell you that you smelled."

He smirked and placed the towel under his arm.

"There's regular soap in the bathroom so you don't have to worry about using anything girlie."

His smile came so easily that it stunned him. When was the last time a smile graced his face? Months and months. But it felt good.

"That's a bonus. Will your husband be home soon?"

She had been heading to the door but turned to stare at him. "Why do you ask? Thought you weren't a serial killer?"

"Just don't want to be surprising a jealous husband."

Those bright blue eyes dulled with sadness. "You won't have to worry about that. I no longer have a husband. But the love of my life, Jeremy, will be home soon so I will make sure he's aware that you're here so there are no surprises." She walked away again, hesitated, and then turned back to him. "I don't recall you giving me your name?"

He stepped closer, steadying himself with the

cane, not missing the change in her composure, the grief outlined on her face, the paleness of her once rosy cheeks. "Mitch Allen."

Her gaze caught his and held for a moment. "Go take your shower," she said, barely louder than a whisper. "I've got mashed potatoes and veggies to make. You're not afraid of veggies, are you?"

"Nope. If you put it on my plate, I'll eat it."

"Good. Now go take your shower. I'll yell up to you, Mitch Allen, when dinner is ready."

Those sweats and T-shirt didn't do her curves any justice as he watched her walk away. And he couldn't help but wonder what kind of secrets Marly held that made her go from friendly and happy one minute to sad and vulnerable the next. Why the hell he should care was beyond him.

Mitch remained at the top of the stairs until Marly walked down and out of sight, pleased with watching her very sexy body move. But he wouldn't want to piss Jeremy off by getting caught checking out his girl so Mitch decided that, although a hot shower sounded real nice, he would begin with a cold one to shake the little urge creeping through his body for the very interesting Marlena Hampton.

Chapter Three

Marly quickly moved around her bedroom. Standing in a fresh bra and panties, she combed her hair and touched up her makeup, not a lot so that it looked obvious but enough that she looked presentable. It wasn't every day that a gorgeous man graced her dinner table. And Mitch Allen could definitely be classified as gorgeous. And sexy. So very, very sexy.

That tall, rugged, dangerous look in a man had always been a weakness for her. Mitch Allen played the part of a real man to the hilt. He may be exhausted beyond words, but his golden brown eyes still danced with emotion as he faced his current predicament— being stranded. Wasn't he adorable earlier as he fought to control the temper that blazed in his eyes when he realized just how stuck he was until Monday?

Standing in her kitchen, his thick, disheveled hair the color of wet beach sand had just begged for her to run her fingers through it, maybe grab a fistful and tug…hard. His jaw, so powerful and stern, needed a shave to remove the brown stubble. Marly fantasized how that stubble would feel as it scratched along her skin while Mitch's mouth kissed her thoroughly. The thought sent a shiver from her head to her painted toenails. A glorious shudder she hadn't felt in years warmed her.

And now look at her racing around her bedroom between roasting pork chops and mashing potatoes to pretty herself for a man she barely knew and would be leaving in a few hours to go bunk at her parents' house. So what? This was exciting! It was exhilarating to have an adult over for dinner. And it was even more interesting that the adult was a mysterious, gorgeous 100% male. Even his limp was sexy, although she was positive he'd disagree.

She finished dressing and steadied her breath before she stepped into the hallway. Time to see if the handsome stranger was still hungry.

****

After soaking up the shower for twenty minutes, Mitch changed into clean jeans and a flannel shirt. He didn't have the energy to shave. He really didn't want to take the chance of cutting his throat since he was so tired.

He looked out the window and noticed the storm had passed and evening was settling in. The sky had tried to brighten even as it began to darken with dusk. It was certainly beautiful country out this way. Forests circled the huge fields surrounding the property.

"Mitch? Dinner will be ready in a few minutes if you want to head downstairs," Marly spoke through the screen door.

He hadn't heard her approach, not even a creak from the stairs. His skills and training were better than that. He silently cursed himself for slacking and faced her. She had changed her clothes as well and now wore a pair of faded jeans that fit her snug enough to show off her delectable curves. A plain white T-shirt and sneakers completed her attire. Why she looked sexier than any woman he could remember, he hadn't a clue.

Lack of sleep. Too much driving. Yeah, definitely could lead to these impure thoughts.

"It's a nice view, don't you think?" she asked, pointing toward the window.

Mitch kept his gaze on her face. "It certainly is from where I'm standing."

She smiled, her thin lips spreading across her face. "It's much better at sunrise. Come on downstairs with me so I can get dinner out of the oven before it burns or before Jack can eat what's already on the table."

Jack? Who the hell was Jack?

Mitch followed Marly down the stairs and into her house, fighting a scowl thanks to the pain in his knee.

His nose led the way even as he followed Marly into the living room. "Smells great."

"It'll taste great, too. Why don't you relax on the couch until dinner is on the table?" Marly yelled out to the yard, "Jeremy, dinner."

"I could help you," Mitch offered.

"No need. Just go sit and give me a few minutes to get situated here."

He obliged her, especially since the couch and its big cushions looked mighty inviting. Sitting down, he wasn't disappointed. He rested his head back and shut his eyes for a moment. He folded his arms across his chest and, for the first time since he set out from Boston, he relaxed. His body melted into the cushions, and the headache he'd been battling for hours subsided. His stomach gave a loud growl as his nose once again picked up the mouth-watering scents emanating from the kitchen. Mitch enjoyed the moment and gave his body a much deserved rest.

His senses picked up on something, something close by. A dark shadow covered his eyelids. Was someone there? Mitch's eyes opened instantly, his fists automatically clenched. He'd let his guard down and now his lapse in judgment had put him in danger.

Mitch remained calm, as his police training had taught him. His dangerous eyes met curious, deep brown eyes that were wide as saucers and, at present, watching him intensely. Mitch surveyed the tall, lean boy standing in front of him, staring at him, his brows clenched in disapproval.

"Who the hell are you?" the boy asked with more bravado than was necessary.

Mitch bit back a smirk. "Who the hell are you?" he demanded the same, but in a much lighter tone.

"I asked you first."

"So you did."

"So who the hell are you?" the boy repeated, keeping his position.

"Mitch Allen."

"So. That doesn't tell me why you're here in my house."

"You asked who I was and I gave you an answer. If you want to know why I'm here then just ask. I'm not a mind reader," Mitch said, adding a little muscle to his voice so the kid wouldn't get it in his head to keep acting like a bad ass.

"Fine. Why the hell are you here?"

Mitch eyed the boy. "Do you always swear so much? Or am I just lucky to be blessed with your mouth today?"

A red stain crept into the boy's cheeks. He didn't speak but continued to watch Mitch inquisitively.

Mitch sat forward and, to the kid's credit, he didn't back away but stood his ground. Man and boy eyed each other until the boy spoke again.

"Why are you here, Mitch Allen?" the boy asked nicer.

"Now that's better. Your mom invited me to stay for dinner. My truck broke down up the road and can't be fixed until Monday."

Marly walked in on their conversation. "Okay, dinner is done. Come sit down, you two." She turned and left them alone again.

Mitch looked back to the boy. "Don't you think it would be polite to share your name with me?"

"Jeremy. My name's Jeremy Hampton."

Mitch used his cane to help him stand. He extended his hand to Jeremy. "It's nice to meet you, Jeremy Hampton. Does your mom really cook as well as she says, or am I in for a torture session?"

That one question did the trick of breaking the ice between them. Jeremy grabbed his stomach and broke into a gut-busting laugh. Mitch smiled too and walked into the dining room after the boy.

"What's so funny?" Marly asked, placing glasses at each place setting. "Have a seat there," she said to Mitch, pointing to the cherry wood chair at the side of the oval shaped dining table.

"Nothing," man and boy replied together, stared at each other, and laughed again. Marly dismissed their silliness, busying herself with passing the serving dishes around for everyone to help themselves.

A sound like a herd of elephants came from the kitchen. Mitch watched as the dog roared into the dining room. Marly stopped him in his tracks. "Oh, no you don't, Jack. You go eat in the kitchen. Go. You know better. Go."

The dog dragged himself out of the room with his head hung low. He looked like a mix of Collie and Lab, with dark brown and golden fur.

Jeremy took a seat next to Mitch. The boy was tall and thin but not too thin. He sported a full head of shaggy brown hair. Kid needed a haircut. His eyes were almost like his mother's, big and wide, but they were a deep brown instead of clear blue.

Mitch took his turn placing food on his plate while listening to Jeremy.

"Aw, Mom, I don't like this kinda food. I want to go play."

Mitch smiled. He remembered those carefree days of boyhood when eating dinner was a pain in the ass and meant you had to stop making war with the aliens or something.

"Jeremy, I see that you've already met Mr. Allen. He's going to be a guest of Grandpa's this weekend," Marly said, as she placed a pile of veggies on his plate, earning a snarl.

When Marly went back to the kitchen, Mitch looked at Jeremy who made faces at the veggies. "I don't much care for the mister stuff. So just call me Mitch."

"Cool. Are you dating my mom?" he asked, excitedly.

Marly returned with steaming rolls. "Jeremy! What are you talking about? Mr. Allen had car trouble while passing through town and Granddad is going to help him out."

"If he's eating dinner here then why can't he stay here with us instead of at Granddad's? It'll be more fun here."

Mitch caught Marly's gaze and smiled. Oh, it would definitely be more fun here. Especially if the lovely woman was single. From the blush on her cheeks, she must've thought the same thing. But it would be a major no-no to get involved with Marly for a weekend.

"Because he's staying there." Marly's tone was firm. "Now please pour some lemonade for our guest."

"Aw, man. Why's he get to drink first? I'm dying of thirst." He caught his mother's stare and instantly stopped. "Okay. When I get done eating, can I play video games? Huh?"

"Sure, if there's enough time after you've soaked in the tub seeing as you're wearing half the yard."

"Aw, man, that's not fair."

"So you tell me every time. Now remember your manners and eat please." Marly sipped her drink.

"Why such a big dinner tonight, Mom?"

"Why not? We have a guest and you skipped lunch."

"I hope you didn't go through any extra trouble because of me," Mitch said, devouring his food. He didn't realize how hungry he really was.

"Nonsense. I enjoy cooking. Weekends are really

31

the only time I get to make a decent meal so you lucked out arriving tonight."

"But Friday night is supposed to be pizza night," Jeremy complained, staring at the food in front of him.

"You had pizza last night."

"So. I could eat pizza every night."

Marly sighed. "I know you can. That's why you have me to make sure you eat well. Eat those vegetables, Jeremy. They're good for you."

He shook his head. "I don't care if they are. They taste nasty."

"You could do a lot worse," Marly said, patiently.

Mitch surmised this ritual between mother and son must happen every night when veggies were on the menu. Got to give the kid an 'A' for effort.

Mitch continued to dig into his food with the eagerness of a bear. It was heavenly. The chops were juicy and tangy from the herbs and the potatoes lumpy, just the way he liked. He hated potatoes that resembled soup.

"This dinner is wonderful, Marly. I'm glad I stumbled upon your house."

"Thank you. My dad says I got his cooking talents and my mom's looks."

Mitch drank his lemonade. "Well, your mom must be very beautiful."

Marly laughed while Jeremy made a sour face accompanied by "eeww."

"Don't be rude, Jeremy," Marly warned.

Mitch ignored her and turned to the boy. "How old are you, Jeremy?"

"Eleven."

"Eleven, huh? Well, a kid with your height and

build must have the girls chasing you already."

He toyed with his veggies. "Nope. Girls are dumb."

Mitch leaned over to him and spoke in a whisper. "Your mom's a girl and I don't think she's dumb."

"Mom's not a girl!" he said and laughed.

"What's that supposed to mean?" Marly asked, shocked.

"You're a woman not a girl. I mean, the girls I go to school with are dumb."

"You won't think that for long, kid," Mitch said.

"Do you like girls?"

Marly almost choked on her lemonade. "Jeremy! We don't ask personal questions like that."

"Why not?"

"Well, because, it's not our business. That's why."

"I love girls," Mitch replied, scooping up the last of his potatoes. "But I didn't always.

Girls can drive you crazy, always wanting to talk and see lame movies. You know—girlie movies. But some girls will like the same things you do and they're the ones that are fun." He winked at Jeremy.

"Okay. I think you've asked enough of Mitch. Finish eating because then it's bath time, Jeremy. Now."

"Mitch, when you were a kid did they have video games?"

Mitch eyed the kid suspiciously. "I'm not that old. Of course, I had video games and I'm really good at them. No one can beat me."

Jeremy snorted. "Ha! I can beat you."

"Not a chance."

"Mom! You've got to let Mitch stay here so we can play video games." He turned his attention back to Mitch. "I have the new alien game. It's really cool. I'm the only one of my friends who can get to the fourth board. I can teach you how to play."

Now it was Mitch's turn to snort. "There'll be no need to teach me anything. Like I said, I'm a pro at video games."

The phone rang. "Look what's working again," Marly said, before excusing herself to answer it only to come back a few minutes later looking upset.

"Everything okay?" Mitch asked, risking being nosy.

"Yeah. It's fine. Just a neighbor that drives me up the wall. At least the phone is working again. I dialed my dad, but his phone must still be out. I'll try again in a little bit. Jeremy, go take your bath now since all you're doing to your vegetables is pureeing them. Go."

"Okay, but, Mom, please can Mitch stay? I want to see if he's that good at the video game. Please, Mom?"

"I don't know, Jeremy. I think it's best he stays at Granddad's."

"Let's let Mitch decide," Jeremy said defiantly. "Would you rather stay here or at Granddad's?"

Mitch stared at Marly for a minute, enjoying the wide-eyed look of a deer facing headlights. "I think you need to listen to your mom, kid. It was nice meeting you."

Jeremy sulked away, his shoulders sagging and his head bent low.

"Wow," Mitch said when he was out of sight. "Kid plays a great guilt trip."

"That he does. You know, I didn't mean to, I mean, well. Oh God! This is embarrassing. It's not that I don't want to offer you a room here, it's just that, well, it may not be appropriate that's all."

"I understand. Is that a nice way of telling me you won't be able to keep your hands off my body should I stay?" He grinned wickedly at her, hoping to ease her embarrassment by making light of the situation her son innocently thrust them into. For the first time in a long time, he was actually enjoying a person's company.

Her cheeks colored and her mouth opened in shock. "That's a pretty big ego you have going on there."

"Nah. Not really. Just trying to shield my male pride from rejection."

"Please don't take it personal. But I haven't had a man around here in years and I think it would be too awkward. You're a complete stranger and, while I'm a trusting person, I'm also sensible. You could be a madman or something. I have a young son to protect. Otherwise, I'd be tempted to let you stay."

"Would you now?" he asked, enjoying how he flustered her. If he had to guess, she was a wild woman waiting to be unleashed.

Marly couldn't keep eye contact. "I can see I'm causing both of us a great deal of embarrassment."

"I didn't say I was embarrassed at all."

"Then I'm embarrassed enough for both of us. And I don't even know why we're discussing this. It's not like you have nowhere to stay tonight. I mean, my dad offered you a place."

"I don't care where I sleep at this point. I just need to rest." And sleeping in a beautiful woman's house was certainly not a good idea for a man who hadn't bedded a woman in months. "I thank you for dinner. Can't remember the last time I had a good home cooked meal or had an appetite."

"My pleasure. I do enjoy cooking, but as you could probably tell by my son's antics at dinner, he's not yet acquired the taste for good home cooked meals. With him, hamburgers and pizza would win over me any day."

Mitch attempted to rise and help clear the table until Marly placed her hand on his shoulder, keeping him in his seat. "You stay put. I'll put some coffee on and bring out dessert. That is if you have room for chocolate cake."

"Well, you are twisting my arm, but I'll make room. Let me help you."

"Nonsense. You're a guest. Besides, it's probably not a good idea to carry plates around with a cane."

"Understandable." Truth was, he'd forgotten about his bum leg for the last blessed hour.

Jack snuck in from the kitchen and hid under the table, sniffing the floor for scraps. Mitch was surprised Jeremy hadn't chucked his veggies under there. That's what dogs were for, to get rid of the food you didn't like.

"Hey, Jack," Mitch said, scratching the dog's head as he licked Mitch's hand. "You know, if Marly catches you in here you'll probably be banished again."

The dog continued his search for food until Marly came back in with two steaming cups of coffee. Quietly, Jack scurried from the room.

Through the dining room window, the last light of

the day could barely be seen as night seized the evening. With the storm long gone, the smell of wet earth and wood swirled through the open window on the tails of a gentle breeze that blew the curtains away from the windowsill. Without realizing what he was doing, Mitch inhaled deeply, shutting his eyes to enjoy nature's aroma. The strong scent of coffee quickly teased his nose as Marly placed the mug in front of him on the now cleared table.

"Here you go," she said, then turned away to move to the stairs. Craning her neck upward, she hollered. "Jeremy, how come I don't hear the water running?"

The stomp of feet echoed in the hallway above. The slam of the bathroom door showed that the boy was as happy about the bath as he was about the vegetables.

Marly moved around quickly, bringing cream, sugar, and chocolate cake to the table. Then she was off again to return with a knife, serving spoon, dessert plates, and forks.

There was a time when Mitch had moved fast. A pang of jealously struck him hard in the chest as he watched Marly walk around so effortlessly. Working really hard with his physical therapy routine hadn't provided the results he'd expected. So he did the only reasonable thing a grown man used to his independence could do. He cancelled the remaining PT appointments in favor of his own structured exercise regimen, which he now admits fell short of the professional treatment afforded him in his PT sessions.

"I apologize if my son embarrassed you at dinner

or put you on the spot. He always says what's on his mind."

Mitch drank his coffee black with one sugar. Years of working long hours in the field performing investigations or enduring the agony of hostage negotiations taught him to drink his coffee without cream to keep it warm the longest. Marly offered him a small plate with a slice of heavenly chocolate cake. His eyes liked what he saw and his stomach agreed once he had the first bite and wasn't disappointed by its richness.

When Mitch glanced up, the sight of Marly licking frosting off her finger as she plated her own piece caught his interest. The primitive urge of lust smacked into him like a freight train. He watched in awe. The woman licked her finger until it was clean, ignorant to the damage she caused Mitch who sat, mouth agape, throat closing, and loins aching.

That was something else he'd missed since his accident. Sex. Recovery didn't allow for getting laid, especially when he worked on repairing his mangled body. God, he could use sex as much as sleep right now. But since he lacked the energy to complete the act, Mitch forced his wandering mind back to reality.

Marly sipped her coffee, her eyes studying him. She didn't make him feel uncomfortable. Hell, lately he was used to people staring at him. He just didn't like to be scrutinized.

"Courtsville is pretty far off the beaten path," Marly started. "What brought you this way, if you don't mind me asking?"

Mitch stared at his half empty coffee cup. Misery forced him out this way. "I got lost in the storm."

"Oh? Well, where are you headed? I'll let you know how lost you are."

"Anywhere."

"Anywhere? What's that mean?" she asked and licked the frosting from her fork, her tongue moving on one side of the shiny metal then giving the other side the same treatment.

God, how much more would he be forced to endure? Did she have any clue that she was slowly, excruciatingly tying him into knots? "It means I have no destination. I'm just driving."

Marly studied him while she sipped her coffee.

Why did her stare weigh so heavily on him? "What?" he asked, holding his cup to keep from pulling her into his lap, for him to cradle and kiss. Jesus! He had it bad.

"Nothing. Just trying to figure out if you really are a serial killer. Or what exactly brings a young man through Courtsville where the population has always been 2,946 unless someone is born or dies. We haven't had any new people settle in these parts since the Sheldon's bought the house with the built-in florist shop. Don't know that they do much business, but they get by well enough to stay here."

"I promise, I'm no serial killer. I got sick of the way my life was going, so I left."

"Left? Just like that? You don't strike me as the type to up and leave. From the looks of you, I'd say you're a damn hard worker. You're in really good physical shape. Don't look at me like that. Of course, I mean except for the cane. The rest of you is toned and strong. From talking to you these past few hours, you seem sharp-witted and personable. I'd venture to guess that you're someone who puts his back and sweat into his work. You couldn't have found it easy to up and leave."

Talk about nailing it on the head. She was real good at reading people. He didn't like for someone to read him so easily, especially a sexy woman he secretly lusted after. "It's complicated."

Marly listened attentively, but Mitch wasn't about to spill his guts to this woman he barely knew. He was shocked to realize how much he wanted to though. She was easy to talk to and so far wasn't judgmental.

"I'm sorry, but I'm really not interested in talking about it."

Marly didn't flinch. "Okay. But sometimes it helps to talk about things than to hold them in. I found out a long time ago that it takes more effort to hide your feelings than to share them."

Mitch frowned. "I'll keep that in mind. Since we're playing twenty questions, what's your story?"

The question caught her off guard. She paled, wide eyes staring at him like she saw a ghost. "What makes you think I have any story to tell?"

"Come on. Everyone has a story. Just making polite conversation." Her floral perfume was light and teased his nose.

"I'm afraid to disappoint you, Mitch Allen, but my life is pretty boring and there's no story of interest."

"What about Jeremy?"

She glared, her eyes darkening to a cool blue. "What about Jeremy?"

"His dad. You said you didn't have a husband, but obviously Jeremy has a dad. What about him?"

"He's dead. End of story." The flash of pain in her eyes ran deep.

"I'm sorry," he offered, knowing there wasn't much more to say to such a blatant admission.

"You had no way of knowing," she whispered, a wounded voice surrounded by a steely exterior.

Jeremy and Jack came bounding down the stairs. The boy was dressed in thermal pajamas, his hair wet, and Jack ran circles around him. Jeremy jumped up and down.

"Mom, Granddad said Mitch could stay here. He said he had Uncle Seth check him out and he's good. Mitch, you can sleep here."

Mitch smirked at the kid who was excited as if he planned a sleep over with one of his school buddies. Looking back at Marly, his smirk turned into a grin with the pink flush creeping into her cheeks and her utter bafflement as she stared at her son. "Uncle Seth?" Mitch inquired.

"My brother the lawyer," she said and turned to Jeremy. "When did Granddad say this?"

"Just now. I called him. Told him that Mitch was cool and, even though he was old, he knew how to play video games." Mitch winced. The kid made him sound ancient. "Granddad said Mitch was a decent guy and he'd be okay to stay. But he wants you to call him, Mom. He thinks you'll say no."

"Which I thought I already did. And I'll talk to him about having Uncle Seth check people out for me."

"But, Mom, please. What's Mitch gonna do at Granddad's all weekend? At least here he can play video games with me." The boy turned to Mitch.

"Wouldn't you like to play with me, Mitch?"

The kid's pleading pulled at heartstrings even as Marly appeared to reconsider her initial decision. "Now, I think that's up to your mom. I'm a stranger, buddy. She doesn't know me from a hole in the wall. While I'm not a bad guy, according to Uncle Seth and Granddad, she's right to use caution in opening her house to a stranger, especially a man." Mitch glanced over at Marly who watched him with caution. "My feelings won't be hurt if you want me to stay at your father's."

She glanced from Mitch to her son and back again. "Fine. You can stay, Mitch, since I really don't believe you're a serial killer or something." Jeremy pumped his fist in victory. "Now hold on, kiddo. Just because I allow Mitch to stay doesn't mean you can play video games all weekend. He needs to rest since he's been on the road a long time and you'll have chores to do."

"Sounds fair," Mitch said, when the boy readied to protest, no doubt about the chores.

"Yeah, fair," Jeremy conceded.

"The room above the garage will do just fine," Mitch said, scratching the dog's head when he popped out from under the table.

"No need for that. The bed upstairs in the guest room will be more comfortable for your leg. Jeremy, it's bedtime. Brush your teeth and hit the bed. Good night," Marly said, standing to kiss her son and sending him on his way.

"Night, Mitch. Come on, Jack," he said, motioning for the dog to follow, which the obedient hound did.

Once Jeremy was out of earshot and Marly sat again, Mitch spoke. "Marly, are you sure you're comfortable with this arrangement?"

She sighed. "Yes. Call me crazy, but for some reason I trust you. Besides, my dad knows you're here and will hunt you down if you harm me in any way."

"Believe me, even if I was a troublemaker, I don't have the energy right now. I promise to be a perfect gentleman."

Their eyes met, hers bewildered pools of blue. For a moment, he stared at her luscious mouth as she bit down on the bottom pink lip. He instantly regretted his promise to act like a gentleman when thoughts of bedding this delightful woman consumed him.

"You look wiped out." She stood, studying him from head to toe. Why did it make him feel uneasy? She had done it so matter-of-factly. "I'll show you to your room if you're finished."

Mitch stood and stretched as Marly carried their dessert dishes and mugs into the kitchen. Even exhausted, he felt relaxed after spending time with her. Who knew this crazy day would end so well?

Marly sashayed past him into the living room, her soft floral perfume teasing his nose again. "Going up and down the stairs probably isn't very good for your leg and I apologize. But the bedrooms are on the second floor."

"I can manage." Following her with his cane, he gripped the railing for support while they climbed the stairs. Marly's very sweet ass swaying in front of him provided a delicious view. The ache returned to his loins, making it uncomfortable to walk. Concentrating on each step kept him from falling on his face.

43

At the top of the stairs, Marly turned left and stopped in front of a doorway. "Here you go, Mitch. This is the room." She stepped aside to allow him to enter. "The bed is a queen so it should accommodate your height. I can get you extra blankets if you need them."

More blankets? With her so close, he expected to burst into flames any second. "No. What's here will do. Thank you, Marly. I really appreciate this."

She smiled from the doorway—a warm, friendly smile that tied his stomach in a knot. Christ, he needed to get away from her. Her soft scent intoxicated him, giving him vivid thoughts of her naked body draped in nothing but delicate, red rose petals.

Standing with her arms crossed, she didn't enter the room. "My pleasure. Hope you sleep well. I'd like to promise that you can sleep in tomorrow, but I'm afraid Jeremy and Jack rise early. I'll do my best to keep them quiet so you can catch up on your rest."

He grinned. "Don't worry. I'm an early riser. Besides, all I need is a couple of hours sleep and I'll be re-charged," he lied, knowing he hadn't gotten a good night's sleep since his accident.

"Marly?" He waited for her to look at him. "Good night."

"Good night, Mitch Allen."

She closed the door, leaving him alone in the room with his vivid imagination and unfulfilled desires. He shrugged off his T-shirt and pants and crawled under the sheets in only his underwear. When his head hit the pillow, he prayed for sleep to come quickly. The urge to sneak down the hall to Marly's room and seduce her was unbearable.

And seduce her he could. He knew when a woman wanted him. Marly wanted him. But after talking with her, she wasn't the type of woman to fall into bed with just any man.

So he closed his eyes and rested his head on the crook of his arm, falling to sleep with thoughts of Marly.

****

In her own room, Marly nervously dressed for bed in an old oversized T-shirt and sweats. What was she thinking to allow Mitch to stay the night? She had been distracted by her son's excitement of a prospective video game opponent. Wanting to please her son was no reason to lose her good sense and allow a strange man—correction—a gorgeous strange man to bunk down in her house for the weekend. Her fingers itched to run over every muscle in his arms and wide back.

With a deep sigh, she forced her desires for Mitch to the back of her mind and dialed her father. "Hi, Dad. I hear you like to have people checked out for me."

The chuckle on the other end caused her to smile. "Now, honey, before you bite my head off, I had your brother check him out because I offered him to stay with your mother and me and expected him to reconsider. I thought Mitch would be a pleasant houseguest for you and not cause any trouble. I can't help that my grandson talked you into letting him stay there."

"I must be out of my mind."

"Nah. You just have a big heart. And looks like Jeremy has someone to bully with those video games."

"Oh, if you only could see how excited he is. But it feels weird having a man in the house again."

"He's in the house?" her father asked with a shocked tone. "Why not have him stay over the garage?"

"With his bad leg? That wouldn't be very hospitable."

"I suppose not. If it don't work out then he can stay here tomorrow night. Good night, honey."

"Night, Dad."

With exhaustion settling deep into her bones, she wanted nothing more than to finish her bedtime routine and hug her pillow. She ran her hairbrush through her long, blond locks, applied cream to her freshly washed face, and turned over her sheets before shutting off the light and crawling into bed.

It was odd having a man in the house. A man hadn't slept in the house for years, not since her husband. Even if Mitch was down the hall in another room, he was still too close for her comfort. She couldn't help the attraction for him. He was young, she guessed in his early thirties. A virile, single man, rare around these parts. Pickings of available men in Courtsville were slim at best.

Marly rolled onto her side, unable to get comfortable. Truth was, she wasn't the least bit interested in sleeping, even though she had awoken at six that morning like every workday. She rolled onto her back again and stared at the ceiling. Was Mitch already asleep? Oh, the town gossips would have a field day with this one. Her, a single mom, with a strange, handsome man asleep in her house. She smiled, thinking of all the tongues that would wag come tomorrow afternoon since news of Mitch's accommodations was bound to fly around town by then.

Well, at least Jeremy will have someone to play his video games with, someone who, from the sound of it, knew how to play. It will be good for Jeremy to have some male company. God knew she hadn't a clue how to play video games and wouldn't learn any time soon. She could never maneuver the controls like Jeremy taught her so many times.

After double-checking the alarm clock, she rolled back onto her side and willed herself to sleep. She'd get up early to cook breakfast for Mitch and Jeremy before their video game competition.

Chapter Four

The heat of the bullet seared Mitch's skin, leaving a tender trail along his shoulder. But he couldn't think about his wound now. Not if he wanted to live. Not if he wanted to save innocent lives.

Gunfire surrounded him. Screams echoed in the darkness, enveloping the hallway.

He had to get to her. He had to save them.

Silence came too quickly, too soon. He inched along the wall, listening to his own breath escape in little puffs. Sweat beaded on his forehead. Warm fluid ran down his arm as the blood escaped his wound, making him lightheaded.

Dizzy. He was so dizzy. He shook his head, willing himself to concentrate or die. He blinked his eyes to steady them against the darkness. Staring straight ahead, he searched for figures, outlines of the bodies he needed to save. Inch by inch, he moved forward.

In his restless sleep, he fought for consciousness. Mitch tangled himself in the bed sheets, gripping them with the fear overwhelming him in his dream.

Straining to hear something, he wished to hear anything to prove they were still alive. Hurrying through the black hallway, he moved forward one foot at a time. His hand gripped his gun so hard his fingers felt numb.

He'd be ready to fire a shot if the suspect came into sight. And Mitch would have only the one shot. He would damn sure make it count.

Then, without warning, it happened. He saw the motion coming at him and fired his gun. But the crack of the bat hit his knee anyway and he collapsed in a heap to the floor, the pain knocking him out. As the room went black, he heard the last of the gunfire.

They hadn't saved her. They hadn't saved her like he promised he would.

Mitch woke abruptly, sat straight up in bed, and glanced around the unfamiliar room. He jumped up, ignoring the fire in his knee, attempting to make sense of where he was. Checking his waist for his weapon, he didn't find it. No. He remembered now. He had given up his weapon. The same way he'd given up on himself.

Mitch sank onto the bed, his shaky hands rubbing tired eyes. One night of sleep was all he wanted. One night without nightmares. One fucking night. Was that too much to ask for? Probably, since he'd been asking for over six months now.

Was Marly asleep? Glancing at the clock, the chances were good that she wasn't up at three in the morning. Not wanting to wake his hostess, Mitch climbed back under the sheets.

He was afraid to shut his eyes. Afraid to see the past. Ashamed to see his failure.

He squeezed his eyes so hard they hurt. Using his palms, he kneaded his temples to ward off the headache forming. To hell with it! Wincing at the sharp pain in his knee as he kicked off the sheets, he got out of bed.

He needed something cold to drink. A beer would be great, but he doubted Marly was the type to keep alcohol in her fridge with a young son around. Ice water would do if that was all he could find. And he'd be sure to be really quiet. No need to disturb Marly or Jeremy. Then he remembered Jack. Shit! Would the dog start barking his foolish head off if he heard Mitch walking around? Time would tell, since Mitch was desperate for a drink.

Tugging on his jeans, Mitch left the room, bare-chested and barefoot. He walked along the hall, remembering the lay out. The floorboards creaked a bit, like a typical old house. His eyes glanced back and forth for any movement. But there was none. He was alone in the hall. No dog. No Marly. No Jeremy. They were all still sleeping. He was alone.

The thoughts threatened to re-enter his mind. Thoughts of that fateful night.

The hallway. The darkness. His failure.

Mitch forced himself to stop dwelling on the past and remember that he was hardly in the same kind of hallway. Marly's hallway was pleasant, lit by moonlight peeking through a small window. She had used minimal decorations, enough to add charm. There were pictures of the beach and mountains adorning the walls. A small table sat in the corner by the stairs. The pale blue vase on it held bright yellow flowers. The air smelled of lemons and flowers. Mitch inhaled deeply, willing himself to stay in the here and now and not let the crude memories seep back into his mind.

As soon as Mitch took his fifth step down the

stairs, he realized he'd forgotten his cane. Not wanting to go back for it, he just made do. With slow, painful steps, he climbed down the stairs knowing that stubbornness had won over intelligence. The sharp pains shooting up his leg reminded him with each stride. The cane would've relieved some of the weight on his bum leg.

Along the wall, he found the light and switched it on, shutting his eyes for a moment against the brightness that swept into the room. In the fridge, he found orange juice, apple juice, and grape juice. He went for the grape juice, swigged down a glass, and readied for his second serving when movement flashed across his peripheral vision.

Mitch swung around with agitation. Marly jumped back, hands raised in defense. "Easy. It's only me, Mitch."

He blew out the breath he had held. "Sorry. You shouldn't sneak up on people like that," he complained, relaxing his posture.

"I don't call walking into my own kitchen sneaking up on people," she responded with a stern tone.

Mitch grunted and swallowed the juice, replacing the container in the fridge. "So I guess I woke you."

"No." She stood beside him at the counter. "I always wander the house at three in the morning."

Smart ass. It was an endearing side of her. He liked it. "Sorry to wake you. I usually don't wander either, but I got thirsty. I tried to be quiet."

"I have mother's ears," she said, tugging at her ear lobe. "You must've worked up a thirst from all that sweating you're doing."

51

Mitch didn't realize his skin was covered in a light sheen of perspiration. He turned so his back rested against the counter.

Marly moved in front of him. Checking him over from head to toe, her gaze briefly stopped on his face. "I don't keep the house hot enough to cause that. Are you feeling okay?"

His lips curled into a smug smirk. "If you're asking in a nice way if I'm on drugs, just ask. It's your house."

She moved closer to him and studied his eyes and face. "No. I'd know if you were. You're too handsome to be a junkie."

"We know your eyesight is going because I wouldn't call me handsome."

She grinned, her eyes twinkling. "You didn't. I did. Want tea?" Without waiting for an answer, Marly sashayed to the stove and heated the kettle, pulling two cups from the cupboard. "Have a seat. No sense standing around."

Sitting at the kitchen table relieved the pressure on his leg. His knee was extremely grateful.

"What do you have against using the cane?" she asked, her tone borderline scolding.

"Nothing." Remembering he was shirtless, he leaned his elbows on the table and crossed his arms, hiding half his nakedness and scar.

"I noticed you didn't bring it down with you."

"Didn't know that was a house rule."

The glare she tossed him held warning. "It is now. I don't want you falling down and breaking your neck. If you want to be macho, do it on your own turf. Not mine."

"I'm not being macho. Just forgot the stupid thing."

Soft blue eyes stared until he gave in. "Okay. You win. By the time I realized I'd forgotten it, I was halfway down the stairs and wasn't going back for it. I thought I could do without the stupid thing since I wasn't going far. And don't worry, I won't sue you if I take a header."

She laughed slightly. "Good. Because I'm afraid I don't have anything to lose since the house and land still belong to the bank."

The whistling of the kettle cut through the kitchen. Marly shuffled to the stove. In no time at all, she returned with two cups of steaming tea.

She wore a light green, old flannel robe. That Mitch considered the look sexy as all hell only meant he'd been out of a woman's arms far too long.

"You do that a lot, don't you?"

He stared. Could she read his mind? No. Impossible. But, a little embarrassed, he spoke. "Do what?" He cleared his throat.

"Daydream. Stare off into space."

Phew! That's all she caught onto. Good. "Sorry. Guess I'm just more exhausted than I thought."

"Shouldn't be driving like that."

"I'm not driving. I'm here."

Her eyes watched him closely. "But you're not getting sleep. You're walking around at three in the morning. Is the bed comfortable enough?"

Be more comfortable with you in it. Geez! Where the hell did that come from?

"Yeah. It's fine." He sipped the tea. "So it's just you and Jeremy here, huh?" Best to change the subject. Get her away from his sleeping habits.

When her gaze dropped and she stared into the tea, sadness washed over her face. With a quick recovery, she looked back at him trying to be casual.

"Yeah. Jeremy's dad was killed in action in the second Gulf War."

"I'm sorry to hear that." Mitch did the math. "He died when Jeremy was a baby?"

She nodded. "Jeremy was only a month old. Rick was due back in another month. If you don't mind, I'd rather not talk about it. I hardly know you and you shouldn't have to listen to my life story."

"Did you hear me complain?"

She didn't answer, but the wounded look in her eyes said so much.

"I didn't mean to pry. I'm sorry."

"You did nothing wrong. It's late." She rose and dumped her tea in the sink.

"Actually, it's early." He cracked a thin smile hoping to put her at ease. "I think we should go back to bed."

Her body froze, her back against the sink, her hands clenching the edge. Color rose to flush her cheeks, which was sexy as all hell, as she stared at him.

"Alone, of course," he explained. "That came out wrong. You know what I meant."

"Must be that lack of sleep again," she said, attempting a smile.

Or lack of something.

She pushed away from the sink. "Come on. I'll make sure you don't break your neck on the way up."

On the stairs, she walked beside him. He did his

best to manage the steps at a decent pace. But his eagerness only had his knee begging for mercy.

She must've sensed it and lightly placed her hand on his elbow. "Easy. We're not in a marathon. Not worth doing more damage racing me up the stairs."

"I'm doing just fine." He shook his elbow to loosen her grip, but she didn't let go until they were in front of his door.

"Thanks for the tea," he said, not knowing what else to say to the woman he'd known only for a few hours but who made him feel more comfortable than anyone else.

She turned, walked down the hall, and stopped at her door before glancing back. "Thanks for the conversation. Forgot what it was like to speak with a mature adult."

After she disappeared into her room, he slipped into his.

Slowly, he crept into bed. He propped his bum leg up on a pillow, hoping to stop the throbbing. In the morning, he'd take some aspirin even though it was never strong enough to manage the pain, but he refused to use the prescription meds the doctors offered. Too many of his fellow officers had become addicted to pain meds. He had enough problems and didn't need to add addiction to it.

Closing his eyes, he prayed for the nightmares to stay away. Just for a few hours.

Long enough for him to get some sleep.

Chapter Five

When he rolled onto his side, a sharp pain shot up Mitch's leg, waking him instantly. Sitting up in bed, with one hand rubbing his eyes free of the night's sleep and the other rubbing his knee, he fought to focus. He was in Marly's house. The room was brighter than it should be for early morning. Studying his watch, he cursed. It was eleven o'clock. He'd slept for almost seven hours. He had just gotten more sleep tonight than he had during the last six months.

Slowly he stood, waiting for his leg to revolt against movement. Once the initial throbbing passed, he continued to move. He threw on his T-shirt and pants. Opening the door, he found his duffle bag on the threshold. How considerate of Marly to bring it up from the garage. Limping to the bathroom with his toothbrush, he freshened up.

Before heading downstairs, he made sure to grab his cane, although he really wanted to do without it. His nose picked up the wonderful smell of fresh coffee and cooked bacon, but he took his time going down the stairs.

"Hey there, sleepy head," Marly greeted him, pouring a cup of coffee and placing it on the table. "Sit. I've got breakfast ready."

"You didn't have to go to any trouble," Mitch explained but was so grateful.

"Are you kidding?" Marly dismissed him. "Jeremy eats like a horse. Weekends are the only days I can make a big breakfast. It being Saturday, you luck out. I enjoy cooking and with you here it allows me to go a little overboard."

In the microwave, she warmed a dish piled high with French toast, scrambled eggs, sausage patties, bacon, and hash browns. She placed it in front of him with a fork, knife, and napkin. He breathed deeply, closed his eyes, and imagined waking up to this every day. Indulging in his little fantasy longer would only cause his food to get cold and he couldn't have that.

"I guess I did luck out. This smells delicious, Marly." He forked food into his mouth and was in heaven. The breakfast was hot and tasty, a bonus in his world. "I'm sorry I overslept. You should've woke me. I don't like to sleep late. Besides, I wanted to get a better look at my truck. Maybe I can fix it myself."

Marly sat across from him with a cup of coffee. Her blond hair was pulled back into a ponytail again and her bright blue eyes shimmered. "After last night, or should I say at three this morning, you looked more than exhausted. You needed your sleep. Thought about waking you, though, until I peaked into your room. You were sleeping so soundly that I couldn't bear to disturb you."

He wasn't sure how he felt about her watching him as he slept. His senses must be off because he never heard her enter, which unnerved him. He was better trained than to let someone sneak up on him. "Thanks for bringing up my bag. If I got my truck going, I could get out of your way."

She stood to refill both of their cups. "Don't go putting words in my mouth. I don't recall complaining about you being here. If you get in my way, I'll let you know. So we can debate this some more and let your food get cold, or you can enjoy a hot breakfast." She turned to him, hand on her hip. "Which will it be, Mitch?"

Mitch only raised a forkful of food and grinned.

"Smart man. Now if you'll excuse me, I have to get in the shower. Saturdays are also my errand days so you'll have to forgive me. I have to step out for a few hours, but you're welcome to watch TV or rest some more. I'll be making meatloaf with baked potatoes for dinner tonight. Hope you like meatloaf."

"Like I said yesterday, I'll eat whatever you put in front of me. But maybe I can find a mechanic to look at my truck today instead of waiting until Monday."

"What's the rush?"

"I really should get going," he stated, rising to clean his empty plate at the sink.

She picked up a laundry basket full of folded clothes and rested it on her hip as he turned to face her, drying his hands on a towel. She looked him in the eye, studying his face. "Oh, that's right. You're in a rush to get going nowhere."

"Excuse me?"

"You said you weren't headed to any particular place, so I don't see what the rush is all about. You won't get the town mechanic to look at your truck before Monday. I guess you're out of luck."

"Shit!" he muttered under his breath.

"Don't worry. You're welcome to stay as long as you need…or want to. Wouldn't want to keep you somewhere you didn't like." Her words dripped with sarcasm.

"There's nothing not to like about your home. Just don't like hanging in one place too long. That's all."

"I see." She studied him. "As long as storm troopers aren't going to bust down my door looking for you, then you can stay. Maybe I can put you to good use when I get home."

He raised his brows, very interested in that proposition.

Her laugh came as a surprise with her easy-going nature. "Get your mind out of the gutter, Mitch Allen. I'm not into one-night stands. Nor am I into one-weekend stands, as tempting as it may be."

He grinned wickedly. "Now you're putting words in my mouth, darling."

Her eyes danced with mischief. "No. Just because I think you're nice to look at doesn't mean I'm going to jump your bones."

"Wouldn't be hard considering I'm disabled and all."

She laughed louder and slapped at his shoulder, the basket still on her hip. "My ass
you're disabled."

Your cute little ass is gorgeous. It would fit perfectly in his hands as he held her while she wrapped those slender legs around his waist. "I promise to put up a little fight if that'll make you feel better," he whispered, grasping her hand, holding it gently.

The flash of heat was intense. He hadn't expected so much from a simple touch. It was apparent she felt something too given the way she looked at him, like she was frozen in place.

Their gaze connected, held.

"Mom!" Jeremy ran into the house agitated, bouncing up and down, fist clenched. Marly quickly removed her hand from Mitch's as he discreetly moved away from her.

She turned to Jeremy who had the dog in tow. "What is it, honey?"

The boy had grease on his hands and shirt. "My chain came off my bike again and I can't get it back on. I think I bent it. Will you fix it again?"

"Oh, Jeremy, I'm sorry but it'll have to wait until I get back from town. I have some errands to run and then I promise to look at it."

"That'll be too long. The whole day will be wasted. Can I call Granddad and see if he can come by to fix it?" His little face was flushed with temper.

Marly rolled her eyes. "No. You can't expect Granddad to close up the gas station every time you need something fixed."

The boy continued to protest, but Marly raised her hand silencing him. "It'll wait until I get home. Now if you can't find something to do, I'm sure your room can use some cleaning."

Jeremy gave in. "Nah. It's fine. I'm gonna get something to drink then take Jack to see the horses."

Mitch was finishing the last of his coffee, quietly taking in the mother and son duo.

"Remember my rule. You don't ride the horses unless I'm there," Marly said.

"Mom, I know how to ride, you know."

"Jeremy." There was no missing the stern tone.

"I know. I know. We're just gonna look at them."

"Maybe you can show me the horses?" Mitch asked, taking a big gulp of his coffee and watching the kid over the rim.

Jeremy looked at him. "Have you ever seen one?"

Marly slowly walked from the room, hauling the laundry basket.

Mitch grinned. "Of course. I'm not from Mars. As a kid, I rode horses at summer camp. Maybe I'll look at your bike too. Once Mom leaves. Don't want her to think I'm trying to do her job."

Jeremy's eyes lit up. "Will you? Awesome!" Then he studied Mitch's leg. "Wait. How you gonna fix my bike with a broken leg?"

Mitch looked at his leg then back to Jeremy. "Leg ain't broken. I can manage just fine. But if you piss me off any, then I won't help. Deal?"

Jeremy considered. "Deal. And don't you piss me off or I won't show you the horses."

Mitch laughed and extended his hand. They shook on it. "Deal. Except I've got to warn you that I'm exceptional at pissing people off."

"Yeah, me too. Come on, we'll go see the horses now. Come on, Jack. Come on, boy." Jeremy was half way out the door with Jack.

"Wait a minute. I've got to change. Give me two minutes." Mitch headed for the stairs.

"Oh, brother. It's gonna take you an hour to get up and down the stairs." Jeremy sank into the overstuffed chair in the living room.

"Keep up that attitude and I'll take longer," Mitch

yelled down. No way would he give the kid a reason to bust his balls about taking too long, so Mitch made it back downstairs in record time.

"Come on, Jack. Let's go. Mom, we're going out to see the horses."

Marly came to the top of the stairs dressed in the old ratty robe, her golden hair now hanging wildly around her. Why the sight of her like that ignited a fire in his belly, Mitch couldn't tell. It was best for him to get out of there fast before he didn't want to leave.

"Jeremy, no riding," Marly yelled the reminder then saw Mitch. Color pinkened her cheeks.

"I won't let him. Enjoy your shower."

She looked at his leg and he read her thoughts.

He raised his cane to show he had it with him. "I'll be careful."

"Mitch! Come on," Jeremy yelled from outside.

Marly smiled wide, softening her delicate features. "You're being summoned. You better go. He can be pretty persistent."

"I see that. I'm beginning to wonder what I've gotten myself into."

"Don't let him wear you out. He has boundless energy," she warned.

"Yeah. Wish I had half his energy. Thanks for the breakfast. See ya." He gave her a quick wink and walked out the door.

****

Marly crept down the stairs and watched Mitch and Jeremy walk through the field toward the horses. She wanted to kick herself for practically begging him to stay. What was wrong with her? She'd never behaved that way in her life, getting upset with Mitch for wanting to get back on the road. Of course he wanted to leave. Why would he want to stay in a small town like Courtsville any longer than he needed to? He was used to loud cities with their bright lights and drama.

She watched Mitch's tall, lean body walk while Jeremy ran ahead. It was such an unusual scene, a man walking over her land who wasn't her father or brother. She couldn't help but stare. Did Mitch know that the muscles in his arms and chest flexed under his tight T-shirts, driving her wild with the need to touch him? Now that she had been close enough to him a few times, she clearly identified the small scars on his jawbone and cheek. No doubt the results of a serious fight or two.

His freshly shaved face looked baby soft and the need to smooth her fingertips over his skin was overwhelming. Staring out the window, she imagined it was her taking a lazy stroll through her green fields with Mitch, allowing the sun to soak their skin, breathing the wildflowers in deeply.

With a long sigh for silly fantasies, she turned from the window and headed up to take the shower she should have when she woke up. But breakfast needed to be cooked and then she got busy with other chores. No surprise that things she needed for herself were forced to wait.

As she started up the stairs the phone rang. She answered it, immediately recognizing the number.

"Having company, Marly?" Howie's gravelly voice teased.

"Go to hell. I told you to stop calling me. I have nothing to say to you. My brother is my attorney, call him."

"Your brother is an asshole. I don't talk to assholes. I'd much rather talk to a slut and, seeing that your male company stayed the night, I'd say you're playing the part well."

Marly refused to let him get to her. With a shaking finger, she disconnected the call. She had too many things to do today to be bothered with a man whose only ambition in life was to rattle her whenever possible. She was grateful Jeremy wasn't here to witness the call.

She slowly walked up the stairs and entered the bathroom. A nice hot shower was exactly what she needed to relax and get on with her busy day.

****

The sun was bright and warm as Mitch walked across the field behind Jeremy. A faint breeze rustled through the tall pine and maple trees. Mitch appreciated the breathtaking scenery. All different colors mixed together mingling with the scents of flowers, wet earth, and grass. It was a far cry from Boston's cement pavements and dense neighborhoods.

For a single, working mom, Marly sure did take care of the place. The grass was mowed and the hedges around the house were neatly trimmed. Mulch in the front yard was landscaped superbly around the rocks and the flowerbeds, which held an assortment of orange and yellow marigolds, white petunias, and red impatiens. Where did she ever find the time to tend to such a large yard?

Mitch struggled to keep up with Jeremy's pace. The kid was full of energy. Mitch remembered when he used to have energy. He used to run for a solid hour, play street hockey, do some light boxing. But now he was lucky to walk without his knee caving in under him. At least Jack felt bad enough that he hung back, walking on the side of the cane. Every few minutes, Jack would bark and Jeremy would stop, look back and wave to Mitch and the dog. Actually, the wave was more like a hurry-up hand signal than anything else.

When Mitch finally caught up to Jeremy, the kid was standing on the bottom rung of the white wooden fence surrounding the horse pen. The horses were stunning. Well cared for and healthy. Atop the fence, Jeremy pointed them out to Mitch.

"That one there—the dark brown one—is mine. His name is Thunder."

"Is that so?" Mitch listened carefully, appreciating the fence as he leaned against it.

"Yeah, because he sounds like thunder when he runs fast. And that one—the white one—is my mom's. It's not as fast as mine but good enough for her to ride. You know, without her getting hurt or something. Her name is Sally."

Mitch noticed Jeremy didn't identify the third horse—a large, black, muscular breed. Now even though he didn't know squat about horses, Mitch could tell that one was a champion or at least once was since it did seem pretty old.

"What about that one?" Mitch pointed the cane in the direction of the beast.

"Storm. That's his name. He was my dad's. Only my dad knew how to ride him. He never lets anyone else ride him. Guess he misses my dad too much."

Mitch didn't respond. He was never good at emotional issues. Time to change the subject. "Maybe when your mom gets home, I can talk her into letting you ride. You know, to show me what the horses can do."

Like he had discovered a long lost ally, Jeremy cheered. "Come over here, Mitch. Open that latch and we can go into the pen. Then you can pet the horses. But not Storm. He won't let you."

"Okay. I'll follow you."

The horses smelled funny, a strong pungent smell like wet dirt, but Mitch took it all in stride especially since Jeremy was having so much fun showing him around. The barn was neat and stocked with hay and grain. Jeremy pointed out the tools used to groom the horses and explained how to muck out the stalls, which was utterly disgusting but Mitch understood the need for upkeep for the horses. Where in the world did Marly find the time to take care of the horses, too? Mitch could tell she was a remarkable woman, but he was discovering just how remarkable.

Jeremy spent the next hour teaching Mitch how to properly brush a horse, clean their hooves, remove their saddles, replace their saddles, and how to feed them.

"You sure know a lot about horses, kid," Mitch said, taking a break against the fence.

The afternoon sun warmed the earth nicely. The horses galloped around the pen, happy and content. Their bushy tails swayed side to side.

"My granddad taught me everything. And Uncle Seth, too. Mom knows a lot, but she's too girlie when it comes to certain things. You know like the cleaning and the feeding."

"Is that so?"

"Yup. That's what Uncle Seth says but then Granddad yells at him and says that when a man's around, he should take the burden from the woman of caring for farm pets since it isn't always a nice smelling job."

"That's very considerate of your granddad."

"Yeah, but when Mom has to do it, she never complains. Maybe about it smelling bad. But doesn't complain about having to do it."

Why would she complain? There was no other adult around to listen. Suddenly and unexpectedly, Mitch found himself caring for Marly in a way that wouldn't make it easy for him to leave. His chest tightened painfully. Too much fresh air in one day. That was all.

Storm approached Mitch with a slow, curious gait. Mitch kept his gaze on the beast and remained leaning on the fence. "What's he up to, Jeremy?"

"Don't know," the kid replied, wide-eyed. "Here…offer him a carrot." He took the vegetable from his pant's pocket and handed it to Mitch.

"Good boy, Storm," Mitch said, offering the carrot. His heart raced. He was in no condition to run if the beast acted up. When the horse took the food, Mitch breathed a sigh of relief.

"Pet him. I think he wants you to," Jeremy said.

Mitch frowned. "And what if he doesn't?"

The boy laughed. "Just scratch his nose. I think

he likes you."

Mitch scratched Storm's nose.

"Wait until I tell Mom. She'll never believe Storm trusted a total stranger. I bet it's because you're wounded. Horses are very caring creatures."

Caring or not, Mitch didn't want to push his luck. "What do you say, kid? Shall we head back?" He didn't want to show he was tiring.

"Okay." Jeremy ran to the fence and opened it wide and locked it behind them. "Come on, you can fix my bike now."

"Wait a minute, sport. I can only go so fast. And I said I would try to fix it. No guarantee."

"If you can't, my mom will," he teased.

A shot to his male pride had Mitch swinging back. "Didn't want you to cry if I couldn't fix it. Don't worry, I'll fix it."

They walked back more quickly than Mitch wanted to, but he hoped to keep his pride intact. The kid was shredding it.

Jeremy laughed. "Yeah, right. I don't cry."

"If you say so."

"Come on, Jack. We'll race back and give Mark time to catch up."

"It's Mitch."

"Whatever. Just don't take your sweet time walking back. I want to ride my bike before sunset." Jeremy and Jack bolted away before Mitch could reply.

"Smart ass just like his mother," Mitch said, for his own benefit. He sped up and walked as fast as his screaming knee would allow. He'd fix the kid's bike. Then kick his ass in the video game the kid bragged about.

Ten minutes later, Mitch was cursing and sweating as he walked across the field. With jaw clenched, he looked ahead to see how much farther it was to the house. He shouldn't be keeping pace with the boy, but his stubbornness ruled this decision instead of his brain.

Once back in front of the house, Mitch sat on the top step and rubbed his leg. He was so out of shape it was pathetic. What he wouldn't give to run again, take a morning jog, run off the frustrations of the job. He laughed. What job? God, it was so hard to remember that he was no longer on duty, no longer a cop, no longer in a daily routine. He could do what he wanted, when he wanted, and however the hell he wanted. Now he just had to find out what that was.

The screen door slammed behind him. Jeremy and Jack plopped down beside him. Mitch studied the boy who was obviously ticked off. "What's with the long face, kid?"

Jeremy kept his head hanging low. "Mom says we all got to go into town with her to do stupid errands."

Mitch smirked. "Wow. Road trip. Jack, too?" he teased, elbowing the boy's arm gently.

"No, he's the lucky one. He doesn't have to go on stupid errands. Now you can't fix my bike and I'll never get to ride today. What a sucky day!"

"Maybe the errands won't last all day. When we return, I'll look at your bike. But not if you're gonna swear."

Jeremy faced him and feigned shock. "What swears?"

69

Mitch cocked his head. "Come on, kid. Do I look dumb to you? Sucky?"

"Aw, man. That's not a swear word."

"No?" Mitch leaned back on his elbow on the porch and glared. "Then what is it?"

"An expression. Mom says it's important to express yourself."

Mitch laughed. "I don't think your mom wants you expressing yourself in that manner. Swearing isn't cool."

"Then why's it in all the movies?"

Damn kid had an answer for everything. "Don't know. But I'd keep that little bit of info to yourself because I don't think your mom will let you watch movies with cursing."

"No."

Marly appeared behind them. "There you are. Here." She handed them both a glass of lemonade and kept one for herself.

"Thanks," Mitch said, and waited for Jeremy to repeat it. When he didn't, Mitch elbowed him.

"Thanks," Jeremy mumbled.

"Has my son announced that we're going into town for an hour to do some errands?"

"An hour?" Mitch drank deeply from his lemonade. "Kid here said it'd take days."

She laughed and sipped her drink. "Oh, yes. It usually feels like that to him. But he has to go to the library for a book. That report is due next Friday."

"I told you to pick one out for me, Mom. I don't have to go."

"Yes, you most certainly do. It's your report not mine so you'll pick the book, you'll read it, and you'll write the report."

"Mom!"

"And if you choose not to then I will take the video games and give them to charity."

Mitch had to interrupt. "Hey, kid. You better do what you're told since I'll be here a few days and want to play video games."

"That's right," Marly confirmed. "Of course, Mitch, you're welcome to stay here if you'd rather, but I thought you might like to see some of the town. It'll beat hanging around here all day. But it's up to you."

"Sounds like a plan. And hanging here isn't so bad." Mitch stood up. "Ready when you are, Marly. Aren't we, Jeremy?"

"Yeah."

Chapter Six

They piled into Marly's car. Jeremy sulked in the backseat. Mitch wasn't used to sitting in the passenger seat, but he dealt with it.

It only took about ten minutes of driving long winding roads to get into town. Courtsville may have been a small town tucked inside the Smoky Mountains, but it was lively. For a bright Saturday afternoon, there were a lot of people walking around. One main road went through the center of town, with many side streets hosting small shops.

"See that building there, Mitch," Marly said, pointing to a small white building with a stone foundation and gray steps leading to a wrap-around porch. "That's Town Hall. And the police station is that blue building beside it."

"Your dad was disappointed I wouldn't run for sheriff," Mitch said, remembering the old man's comment.

"Why would you? We already have a sheriff. He's running unopposed in a few months." Marly shrugged but her voice had held concern. Mitch didn't understand how a simple statement could make her tense so quickly.

"If I were staying then it may be fun to challenge

the sheriff for his job, especially since your father made it sound like the guy wasn't fit for the job. Yeah. Always wanted to be my own boss."

"Around here, Mitch, things run much different than in the big city. The sheriff's job is better suited for fat, old men who want no excitement in their lives."

Mitch had had more than his share of excitement to last a lifetime.

Marly continued her tour guide service. "Over there is the best little bakery in the state. Jeremy loves their triple chocolate cookies. Don't you, sweetie?"

"Yeah. They're the size of Jack's head," Jeremy added with enthusiasm from the backseat. "Mom, can we stop and get some? Please?"

"Look who's talking to me now. Let's see how well you do at the library and I'll think about it."

Marly leaned over to Mitch and kept her voice low. "My favorite is the mocha cheesecake. It's to die for."

Mitch leaned toward her and talked low as well. "I take it we'll be stopping at the bakery after the library."

"Oh, yeah, we are," she said, and laughed.

Mitch's gut tightened. Her voice was soft and warm, tickling his ears with a sweet southern accent, excitement spoken in every word.

Marly parked in front of the library. Before Marly and Mitch could get out of the car, Jeremy was out the door and up the stairs, disappearing inside the library.

"Wow. Kid must like writing book reports," Mitch said, shutting his door and joining Marly on the sidewalk. His knee throbbed, but he did his best to ignore it.

"Hardly. He just wants to get the cookies and go home. He mentioned you would fix his bike."

"I offered to look at it. I'm not good with my hands, mechanically speaking that is." He appreciated the blush that slowly crossed her cheeks. "But I might rise to the challenge of a broken bike chain."

They walked side by side up the stairs to the library. "Please don't feel like you have to. Jeremy can be pretty persistent when he wants something. I just can't be in ten places at once and he has a hard time understanding that sometimes."

"It must be hard being both mom and dad for him."

She glanced up and hesitated before speaking. "Sometimes. But I do the best I can." Her voice filled with worry.

"You do more than enough from what I've seen." He opened the library's front door. "Let me help with this one thing, Marly. Shit, it'll give me something to do other than get in your way."

"Did I say you were in my way?"

He grinned. "No."

"Believe me, if I didn't want you around, you wouldn't be."

They stopped talking as they entered the quiet zone. It didn't look like a Boston library with big corridors and antique art and books. No this library was cozy. There were shiny wooden tables and chairs scattered throughout the first floor. Teenagers, doing more talking than reading or studying, occupied some. The air was stale since no windows were open. On both sides of the room, spiral staircases led to the second floor, to the adult section. The first floor was dedicated to children and young adults. Parents mulled about carrying babies or helping toddlers discover books. The fifty-something librarian behind the front desk shushed the group of teenagers who then snickered.

Jeremy ran up to Marly and Mitch. "Got it, Mom. Let's go."

"Hold on," she said, taking the book from him. "Go find something else. You're not doing a book report on trains."

"Why not?"

"Because you've already done one on trains. This report has to be on a person. A real person who has made a difference in the world. Now go find a book on a person." He walked away defeated. "I swear that he just likes to push my buttons sometimes."

"Boys are good at it. I can vouch for that."

"Oh? Do you have any kids, Mitch?" she asked, leaning against the wall while waiting for Jeremy to return.

"Me?" He laughed quietly. "Not that I know of. Not married either. Came close once, but I worked too much and she found other ways, actually other men, to occupy her time."

"That's awful."

"Yeah, it was. But I was glad to find out what she was like before we walked down the aisle. How about you? Any boyfriends that I'll piss off by staying at your house for the weekend?"

Her eyes widened in shock. "What? Oh no. That's one thing you don't have to worry about. It's just Jeremy and me. Hard for a single mom to date around here."

Jeremy jogged to them with another book in hand and wasn't alone. A tall, lanky blond kid stood beside him. Mitch couldn't help notice their shit-eating grins.

"Hi, Danny," Marly said to the boy. "Are you here for your report as well?"

"Yeah. Got my book." He held it up as proof.

Jeremy practically jumped up and down. "Me too, Mom. Can I go over Danny's house? Please."

Marly looked at Jeremy's book choice and nodded in approval.

"My dad said Jeremy could come over and we'll drive him home before supper," Danny said.

"Okay."

"See ya," Jeremy said. Both kids ran off.

"No running," the librarian scolded.

"I guess that frees us up for lunch. Hungry?" Marly turned to Mitch.

"Always. I'll follow you."

They walked two blocks to a small diner smartly called *The Last Stop Sandwich Shop*. Mitch commented on the name.

"Yeah, it's an odd one. Food's not that great, but it's cheap and service is fast. Just don't piss Millie off," Marly warned and entered the diner with Mitch.

"Who the hell is Millie?"

"I am," confirmed a short, round woman holding two menus in her hand. "What's it to you, hot stuff?"

Mitch raised his hands, one with the cane. "Nothing, ma'am. Just didn't expect such a lovely woman to be working in a diner."

Millie studied him for a minute before hollering with laughter. "You're a hot shit! I like you. Come on.

I'll give you my best booth. Hey there, Marly."

They followed obediently behind Millie. Marly turned back to Mitch. "Good answer. I don't ever remember seeing her laugh."

"Well, us hot shits are known to do that to people," he offered, grinning. The other customers were very interested in him, watching as he moved through the room.

"George, you move your ass up to the counter. No need of your scrawny ass taking up a booth," Millie ordered.

"Jesus in heaven, Millie. Can't a man get a little peace to enjoy his coffee?"

"Ha! If you wanted peace you should've married my sister," Millie quipped while placing menus, forks, knives, and napkins on the table. "She's dead," she whispered to Mitch and laughed. "I'll leave you folks to look over the menu although I have to say today's special is a steal."

"What's that?" Mitch asked, flashing his best smile.

"Stuffed chicken breast sandwich." She leaned closer. "For you, I'll even throw on some of that fancy mozzarella cheese, darlin'."

"Sold." He handed her back the menu.

"I'll have the chef salad, please," Marly said.

"Girl, that salad stuff won't put meat on your bones." She turned her attention to Mitch. "A man likes to have some meat on the bones he's loving." With another hoot of laughter, Millie strutted to the kitchen.

Marly stared at Mitch. "Looks like someone made a friend. That was pretty sly to compliment her so nicely."

"She scares me. What was I supposed to do?"

Marly giggled.

"Is it me or are we the center of attention?" Mitch wondered, looking around to see a dozen pairs of eyes on them.

She sat back amused. "Of course. Small town widow with a handsome, sexy stranger. Oh, yeah, we definitely have the tongues wagging."

Mitch leaned closer, resting his arms on the table. "Sexy, huh?"

Soft blue eyes studied him. "Yeah. Just don't let it go to your head. I don't have room in my car for swelled egos."

"I won't take up a lot of room. Promise."

After their order was served and they began to eat, two older women approached their table with very curious gazes solely fixed on Mitch. "Hello, Marly. It's nice to see you. How's your son?"

"He's at a friend's house for the afternoon. Ladies, this is Mitch Allen. Mitch, this is Lula and Lilly Stonewall."

"Hello," Mitch nodded.

Curiosity oozed out of their pores. "We're sisters. Our family has been in these parts for generations," Lilly confirmed, studying Mitch. "Haven't seen you around these mountains before."

"Can't say you have, ma'am."

"Will you be settling in town then, Mitch?" Lula asked.

"Well—" he began, but didn't have a chance to continue.

"Because if so then Marly had better keep her

grip on you. The women in this town will go stir crazy over such a handsome lad as yourself," Lilly explained.

Marly answered for him. "He's just passing through. But I am enjoying his company while he's here. Not every day a girl finds such a hot lover. Right, ladies?" Marly asked mockingly before sipping her iced tea through the straw.

Mitch almost choked as Marly continued.

"He's awfully sexy too, don't you think?" Marly asked. "And he's excellent in bed. You now have first-hand knowledge to spread like wild fire amongst your peers. Looking around here, it appears you'll have a group of interested souls wanting to know what this handsome gentleman is doing in my life." Marly looked ready to laugh when one of the women turned as red as a lobster.

"We'd better let you get back to eating." Lula quickly grabbed Lilly's arm and pulled her away. They stopped a number of times as they walked back through the restaurant to the exit, stopping to talk to inquiring fellow gossipers.

"What?" Marly asked when Mitch stared at her. "They're going to spread their wild gossip anyway. I've just deflated their balloons. Now they can't speculate because they heard it from my mouth and that makes for boring gossip. Much more interesting to dream up scenarios."

"I agree. And as your hot lover, I'm thinking of a few scenarios right now."

"Really?" Marly eyed him cautiously over a forkful of salad. "Who says I'm interested?"

Oh, there was no way in hell she wasn't. "Aren't

you?"

Marly thought for a moment. "No beating around the bush with you, is there?"

"I'm a man. A man who, right now, is having a wonderful lunch with a beautiful, witty woman. And yes, I'm excellent in bed. In case you really were wondering."

"I speak the truth, Mitch. I wasn't wondering. I already knew."

"Really? How so?" Mitch had devoured most of his sandwich and half his iced tea.

"Your eyes. They cloud over sometimes when we talk. Like you're happy, content, comfortable. Then when the conversation turns sexual, your eyes become almost animalistic. Like you're on the hunt. Hungry. Very hungry."

"That's how I feel right now. Very hungry. And I don't mean for food." As if in agreement, his cock stiffened painfully in his pants.

Her blond hair was fixed prettily in a ponytail. "I know. Believe me, I know, Mitch. It took me over two hours to fall asleep last night knowing you were in the house. I may not have much of a sex life, but I know when a man wants me."

"I've tried to be discreet. I can't help my attraction to you, but I know better than to pursue it. You've made that quite clear. And I'm doing my damnedest to honor your wishes."

"Trust me, if I didn't have Jeremy to consider, we wouldn't be eating lunch in this stupid diner. We'd be making love all day. I've imagined caressing every muscle on your body first with my hands then with my mouth."

A growl escaped his throat. "Darling, I'm warning you this one time. Talk to me like that again and your wishes will come true."

Her peel of laughter only tightened his gut further, leaving no room for the last bites of his sandwich.

****

"Like I was saying, Mitch. When you're a parent, and I happen to be both for Jeremy, I have to think of him first."

"You're a great mom, Marly. I mean it." He kissed her palm, and slowly pulled his hand from hers.

The simple gesture cracked the ice around her heart. Here she was telling him that she was lying awake at night dreaming of a roll in the hay with him and he didn't take the opportunity to pressure her or seduce her. And he didn't assume it was an open invitation for sex.

She stared into his eyes. Did he know how much they told about him? There was pain, great sadness, remorse, but deep in those golden brown depths was a little spark, a spark of hope. A spark of the life still left in this crushed man. She wished he were staying in town longer.

No. That wasn't a good idea. No matter how great the sex would be, the broken heart that was sure to follow wasn't worth it. She had suffered through the unbearable once before. No way would she set herself up to fall in love with this tender, sexy-as-all-hell man, just to have him move on to another town and leave her life in shambles.

81

And she did have to think of Jeremy. He was her life and had been for eleven years. He was the only thing that mattered.

In her daydreaming, Mitch had received the check and paid, leaving a sizeable tip for Millie that left her swooning over him even more. He totally ignored Marly's pleas to split the check.

When they stood to leave, a large burly man blocked Marly's way. "Well, well, well. Look who's steppin' out on a date."

"Get out of my way, Howie," Marly growled.

Howie Singleton, at over six feet, towered over Marly. His body was massive—wide shoulders, thick legs, and massive hands. The sneer he used as a greeting showed a cracked front tooth. He smelled of tobacco and whiskey, but he wasn't terribly drunk. His black eyes were as dark as coal and mean. His greasy thick hair hung close to his shoulders.

"Why don't you get out of my way, Marly?"

"Seems like you're the one blocking her passage. Now why not be a gentleman and step aside so the lady can pass?" Mitch asked, coolly.

"Wasn't talking to you, asshole," Howie growled and turned his attention back to Marly. "You'll be hearing from my lawyer any day now, sweets. That land you're sitting your pretty little ass on will be mine again. As it rightfully should be."

"Piss off, Howie. If you have something to say to me, say it to my lawyer. You know where to find him."

"Yeah, I do. He's probably still attached to your mama's tit, the whiny ass brat. Thinks he's a hell of a lawyer and he can't even wipe his own ass without your mama's help." He laughed low and deep.

"You son of a bitch—" she began but was cut off by Mitch who placed his body between her and Howie.

"Don't believe anyone taught you any manners," Mitch said, his teeth bared. "Where I come from a real man doesn't talk to a woman like that. But then again," he continued, stopping long enough to give a disgusted perusal of Howie. "You don't look like a real man to me, coming in here harassing a woman."

"Who the fuck are you?" Howie bellowed, getting all the other customers' attention.

"Doesn't matter. Stay away from the lady. You heard her. You need something, see her lawyer."

"Or else what?" Howie challenged as Mitch took Marly's hand and pulled her past him.

Mitch slowly faced Howie. He spoke very calmly but very seriously. "Or else you'll deal with me. And you won't like that because I can be very convincing. If you think I'm bluffing, you'd be the fool to find out."

"You threatening me, boy?"

"No, asshole, I'm not." Mitch walked to the door and turned back. "I'm promising you." There was hushed talk amongst the crowded diner. People whispered, stared, watched.

Once outside, Marly grasped Mitch's arm. "I'm sorry about that. Howie Singleton is the biggest jerk in town." She couldn't describe the giddiness at having a strong man like Mitch stand up for her like she was special.

"Seems to have a problem with you."

"He thinks his grandfather falsely sold my

grandfather my land years and years ago. Something about his grandfather being on his deathbed and only selling the land to my grandfather to spite his family who he hated or something. Anyhow, Howie claims that the sale should be voided and the land reverted back to him."

"Seems to be pretty pissed off about it."

"Yeah. He's threatened to sue me a thousand times, plus him and my brother go at it. My brother is my lawyer. I wish he would sue me then the courts could decide once and for all, and I could get on living on my land without putting up with his shit."

"Well, I don't think standing up for you will shut him up. He's the type that doesn't back down unless forced to in one way or another."

"You're right about that. But I'm not going to let his ranting ruin the day."

"As you wish," Mitch conceded.

Marly stood in front of him for a moment just studying him. He was so calm, so in control. She wished she could always be like that.

"Mitch," she said softly. "Thank you for understanding and not forcing the issue of intimacy between us."

His hand cupped the back of her head. Before she could protest, he pulled her close and touched his lips to hers. The kiss lasted for three seconds, because she counted every long stroke of time, but it was enough to steal her breath. Her lungs felt like a wrung-out dishtowel.

As quickly as he kissed her, he just as quickly released her.

"You're welcome. But, remember, talk sexy to

me again and I won't be responsible for forgetting my manners." The wicked grin he shot her affirmed his words before he walked back toward the car.

She stood speechless for a moment, an unusual thrill swirling through her body at his declaration. Could she really drive him so wild that he'd take her hard and fast without a second thought? Oh God, her pussy ached so badly. Since touching herself wasn't an option, she collected her thoughts, caught up to him, and walked silently until they were at the car.

"Any more errands?" Mitch asked.

For a brief second, very brief, Marly wanted to stop at the drug store for condoms, unable to remember if she had some in her nightstand. But her reasonable inner voice took control.

"Just the bakery and some groceries, then I think we're done. My parents are coming over for dinner tonight so I better get that started." Maybe keeping busy will keep my mind off you so I'm not thinking of having you for dessert.

Chapter Seven

Marly slowly drove home after the grocery store, concentrating on the road. Her thoughts were consumed by Mitch, his body, his eyes, his scent, everything. There was some kind of force swirling around him, sucking her into his world. The more she fought it, the deeper she fell. It must be due to the lack of male companionship in her life. Plus, he was totally hot.

Suddenly, out of nowhere, a car whizzed by her on the narrow road.

"Watch out! Here comes another one. Quick! Pull over," Mitch demanded, reaching for the steering wheel.

Marly had no choice but to do just that as the second car passed within inches. She slammed the brakes on with a cloud of dust enveloping them.

"Shit!" she yelled. "Asshole kids! Got nothing better to do than joy ride."

"That wasn't a joy ride. The second car was chasing the first. Mind if I drive?"

"Yes, I do. I can drive. A couple of idiots on the road don't unnerve me."

"Then get this thing moving. They were headed toward your place. Let's make sure they don't crash into your house."

"Sons of bitches," Marly said as she peeled rubber out of the spot.

"Like mother like son," Mitch murmured.

"What?"

"Nothing. You get pretty mouthy when your temper is up, huh?"

"Sorry if it's a big turn off, but yeah, I know how to swear."

"Didn't say it was a turn off. In fact, just the opposite. I like a smart mouth on a woman. Shows she's got guts. And when she's got guts, there'll never be a boring day."

When they reached her house in record time, she jumped out and ran inside, making sure everything was as she left it. And it was.

"I should've gotten the plates so you could report it to the police. I was more worried about you and didn't pay attention. No sense calling the police," Mitch complained.

"No sense is right, seeing as we have no police here. Just a fat, lazy sheriff and his useless deputies. Come on inside. I've got to start dinner."

Mitch hesitated and surveyed the area before he followed Marly inside.

****

Dinner was uneventful. Marly was still full from lunch, but Mitch cleaned his plate without a problem. Her father kept Mitch occupied, talking about politics, cars, and trains. Her dad loved his trains.

"If you ladies don't mind, I'm going to take

Mitch outside to enjoy a nice cigar."

Marly and her mom, Bethany, shook their heads as they poured themselves a glass of wine. Jeremy and Jack had already disappeared upstairs to play video games.

"You know, Marly. I don't want to pry, but you don't seem yourself tonight. Everything alright?" Bethany asked, holding her wine but keeping her gaze on her daughter.

"I guess I am tired, Mom."

"And you should be. What with all you do? Working full time, raising a son, taking care of a house and horses. I tell your father all the time, I don't know how you do it. You're amazing."

"I'm not talking about that kind of tired." Marly felt the sting of tears in the back of her eyes and fought to keep them from spilling over. "I'm tired of being alone. I'm tired of turning over in bed and not having someone there to snuggle to. I'm tired of not having someone to hold me."

Bethany patted Marly's hand as they sat at the kitchen table. "Oh, dear. I know. You deserve to have all that."

"One time I did have it. You know, sometimes I forget what Rick looked like, it's been so long," Marly confided. "Isn't that horrible of me?"

"Nonsense. That's your brain's way of dealing with the grief. It's also your brain's way of telling you to get on with your life. Marly, Rick would've wanted that, would've wanted you to have a full life," Bethany said, her voice soothing.

Marly stared at her wineglass. "I know. It's hard with Jeremy. I don't want him to ever think I'm trying to replace his father."

Bethany sighed. "Give the boy some credit. Of course he wouldn't think that. But he deserves a man in his life as much as you do." She glanced outside through the screen door. "Sometimes things happen for no reason at all. I'd say that young man, Mitch, has eyes only for you."

"Oh, Mom, it's so much more complicated than that. He's not interested in staying in a small town."

"Did he say that?"

"Well, no, but he was only passing through when his truck broke down."

"On his way to nowhere in particular from what I hear," Bethany said, her soft eyes offering understanding.

"Yeah." And back on the road as soon as he could get there.

"Why can't Courtsville be his no-where-in-particular-place?" Bethany asked with her usual enthusiasm.

Marly shrugged, knowing better than to get her hopes up. "I don't know. He's an ex-cop used to the sights and sounds of a big city. He'd be bored to death around these parts."

"Maybe you should let him be the judge of that. If he's smitten with you, he won't go far. You have to learn to trust your heart again. Not your brain. Hell, if I used my brain instead of my heart, I wouldn't have married your father when all he had was dreams. But he built those dreams into reality, bought his real estate and his business, and gave us a fine life. My brain still can't believe it."

Marly laughed. "Oh, Mama. I do love you. You

always know what to say."

"You can't mess with perfection."

Both men came in to find both women laughing hysterically.

"What'd we miss?" Joe asked.

"Girl talk," Bethany said, standing to hug and kiss her daughter then Mitch. "Now, Joe, let's go say goodnight to our grandson and tuck him in. Then these two can relax with this wine. They've had a long day."

"Got to listen to the boss," Joe announced to Mitch, extending his hand to shake.

"Absolutely. Any smart man would," Mitch agreed, then smiled and winked at Marly.

"Marly, excellent dinner as usual. Mitch, keep watch over my angel here."

"Daddy, I don't need any watching over. Stop it." She hugged him hard.

"I know, but it's something a dad likes to say." He faced Mitch and spoke so only he could hear. "She's as stubborn as her mother. She's a handful."

"Yes, sir."

****

"I am not a handful," Marly confirmed, as her parents drove off and her and Mitch settled in the living room with the wine.

"You have ears like your mom, too, it seems," Mitch said, smiling, from his seat next to Marly on the couch.

"Oh, my God! What the hell is that?" Marly asked at the sound of pounding beyond the living room windows and bolted to the door.

Mitch followed her.

"Oh, no! Storm!" Marly screamed and ran to the horse. "Storm!"

Mitch swore at the pain in his leg but ran after her into the blackness of the night.

Marly grabbed for the horse's tether but was knocked to the ground twice before Mitch reached her. To save Marly from getting trampled, he seized the reins and used every ounce of energy he had to hoist himself up onto the horse. Pain shot up his leg, but he blocked it out. Sweat beaded on his forehead, but he held on for Marly's sake.

"Mitch! Grab my hand! Grab my hand!"

Mitch caught Marly's hand and, with a grunt, hauled her up in front of him. She quickly shimmied into position and got control of the beast.

No time for celebration. She rode the horse right to the stable. Mitch kept one hand on hers tangled in the reins and one on her waist. He didn't know who was shaking more, him or her, or the horse.

"Damnit! The gate is wide open," Marly yelled, her normally cool composure gone. "No wonder Storm went for a midnight stroll."

Mitch thought it was best to keep his mouth shut. So he did.

Marly got Storm into the pen and barked orders at Mitch. "Listen, I'm sure your knee is killing you right now, but we don't have time for pain. I need you to jump down and get that fence shut. I don't know how long Storm will listen to me."

Mitch complied, worried that Jeremy and he had left it open earlier, but it was clear that the lock had been kicked in. He did his best at a temporary fix, jamming a splintered piece of wood into the gate to keep it from opening. Daylight would allow him to fix it properly.

"All set," he yelled to Marly who dismounted quickly.

Marly was out of breath as she walked to where Mitch stood near the fence. "Been kicked open, from the outside. Wasn't one of the horses," he said.

"Goddammit!" Marly studied the damage.

"I can fix it in the morning, but can you tie up the horses overnight?"

"I can lock them in the barn. Wait here."

She returned a few minutes later and they walked back to the house. Her pace was too fast for his knee to keep up. Doing the best he could, he fell behind five or six paces.

"Anything like this happen before?" he asked, his investigative instincts kicking in.

"Not really. There's stupid kids who play jokes, but this was different. I'm pissed."

"No shit," he replied, totally exhausted from the unexpected physical activity.

She stopped, faced him, grabbed him by the back of the neck, and kissed him hard, fast, deeply. She tasted faintly of wine, but all he concentrated on was the heat radiating from her, a fiery passion stirring his cock to a painful erection. Too soon she pulled away.

"There, now we can stop pussyfooting around each other for that kiss." She walked away.

"Hey, wait just a damn minute. Marly!"

Ignoring him, she never stopped. "I need to check on Jeremy." Starting to run, she took the front steps in two big leaps.

Mitch struggled, ignoring the fire in his leg. Oh, yeah. He'd regret this in the morning.

By the time he made it inside, Marly was coming back down the stairs. "Jeremy is sleeping. He's okay."

She collapsed onto the sofa and covered her face with her hands. His heart broke for this woman who was pulled in ten different directions at once. Discussion about that kiss would have to wait. She needed sleep.

"It's over, Marly. The horses are safe. Jeremy's safe. I'll fix the gate in the morning. You should get some sleep. Come on," he said, pulling her arm.

She didn't resist when he walked her upstairs. With a whispered goodnight, she disappeared into her room.

Mitch walked to his room and shut the door. He stood in the darkness, staring at the dark grounds around the house. Searching for anything out of the ordinary. Whoever was messing with Marly pissed him off. But exhaustion slowly won as he climbed under the covers and prayed to the heavens to distinguish the fire in his leg.

At least give him a decent night's sleep.

Chapter Eight

Sunday morning brought a bright sunrise and clear skies. Birds chirped loudly in the warm temperature. Mitch showered before heading down to the kitchen where he found Jeremy digging into a huge bowl of cereal.

"Hey, kid."

"Hey."

Mitch started coffee and prepared breakfast for his grumbling stomach.

"Want breakfast, kid?" Mitch asked, as Jeremy shoveled cereal into his mouth.

Mitch took the shrug of shoulders Jeremy offered as a yes. Soon, he had scrambled eggs, bacon, sausage, and toast on the table.

"Can I have pancakes," Jeremy asked.

Mitch stared at him. Did he not just bust his ass for half an hour making all this food? Now the kid wanted pancakes? "Sure, if you make them. Eat what's on the table or cook something yourself."

Jeremy heaped food onto his plate. Mitch prepared a plate for Marly and placed it in the microwave just like she had done for him.

Thinking about the escaped horse last night consumed Mitch's mind. "What's your plans for today, kid?"

"Not much. Sunday's are boring. Probably video games."

"I have to fix the fence to the horse pen. Thought maybe you could give me a riding lesson, if I can convince your mom to let you ride with me, that is."

"Okay. But what about your leg?"

"Hurts like hell. Might as well have some fun if it's going to hurt anyway."

"How much have you ridden before?"

Last night was the first time since he was a kid, and he had needed Marly's help. "Not much lately. So I hope you're a good teacher. I could use a re-fresher."

Jeremy chugged orange juice before speaking again. "I am. I ride really good. But Mom won't let me do any jumps."

"Mom's right on that. Take it from someone who knows, being injured is no fun." Mitch took bites of food between conversing.

"What happened to your leg?"

Mitch didn't want to talk about it. Especially to someone as young as Jeremy. He'd never understand. "Got hurt on my job."

"How?"

Mitch glanced up into innocent eyes full of intrigue. "Someone was in a bad mood and took it out on my leg. Now finish eating so we can ask your mom about riding."

Changing the subject worked. The kid dropped his inquiry and disappeared upstairs to get dressed.

Mitch felt edgy and needed to move around. Walking outside, he found Jeremy's bike and sat on the bottom step to work on it. It was barely past seven and he didn't want to wake Marly so he was quiet.

The bike chain was slightly bent, but Mitch worked out the kink. His fingers turned black from the grease, but he re-attached the chain and spun the back wheel to confirm his success. He was in the middle of some other minor adjustments as Jeremy and Jack ran out of the house, practically falling over Mitch where he sat on the stairs with the bike.

"Hey, kid. Trying to knock me on my ass."

Jeremy just laughed. "Nah. You're already on your ass."

Mitch smirked. "You like cursing, don't you?"

"Sometimes. But Mom doesn't like me to."

"Don't get in the habit of doing it around me. I'm no tattletale, so I'd just have to make you my slave or tell your mom the truth."

"Hey," Jeremy plopped down beside Mitch. His eyes went wide. "You fixed my bike! Thanks."

Jeremy jumped on the bike for a ride, but Mitch stopped him. "Not so fast, buddy. I'm not done cleaning it up."

"It's a bike. It doesn't need to be cleaned."

"It needs to be cared for if you want it to work properly. Sit down. I'll give you some tips and it'll be up to you to use them."

****

Mitch sat with Jeremy on the front porch explaining the ins and outs of bike mechanics. It didn't sound really technical, but Mitch had Jeremy's full attention as Marly watched from the screen door. It was like the man and boy had known each other forever. She wondered if this is how it would've been if Rick had lived.

Jeremy needed a dad. He deserved one. It really stunk how he got cheated out of a life with his dad. Did Mitch know how good he was with kids? What could've happened in Boston that made him run?

Marly wasn't about to wait for the townspeople to tell her some tall tale they spun from gossip. Once she cooked breakfast, she'd go to her room and scan the Internet. Her dad mentioned he had been a police officer and injured on the job. She'd find out who Mitch Allen really was. Then she'd decide if she wanted to pursue him.

"Good morning, gentlemen," she said, stepping onto the porch in jeans and a T-shirt. "Anyone up for breakfast?"

"Sure," Mitch said, rising and holding the door open for her with his elbow, his hands greasy.

Jeremy jumped on his bike and rode away with Jack chasing him, barking.

A car pulled up. Marly and Mitch waited on the porch to see who it was.

"It's the town constable," she announced with a dry tone.

"Morning, ma'am. Got a letter for you. Sign here please," the elderly man asked, pointing to a line on a yellow paper.

"Thank you," Marly said, accepting the official looking envelope then watching as the man walked back to his car.

"It's pretty early for a constable. Does he know it's Sunday? Open it up," Mitch prodded, leaning against the stairs.

"It's some kind of legal document. Looks like Howie is finally putting his money where his mouth is and suing me. Good," she exclaimed, shoving the papers back into the envelope. "I'll give it to my brother. He can handle it. No sense getting all worked up over something that's been going on for years and will probably continue to go on for years."

"Good idea. How about breakfast now?" Mitch held the porch door for her and followed her into the living room.

She placed the envelope on the small desk near the phone and walked into the kitchen. "Wow, something smells great."

"It's called breakfast and your plate is in the microwave," Mitch said, stopping at the sink to scrub his hands.

"Oh, that looks so good." She pressed the keypad and the microwave hummed to life. "I can't remember the last time someone made me breakfast."

When she faced Mitch, he had already poured her a cup of coffee and pressed it into her hands while pulling out a chair. "Sit. Enjoy your breakfast."

"What's the occasion?"

"I woke up early. And I'm not a bad cook, either."

"You should've woken me up. I would've helped you."

"Can't let anyone do anything for you, can you?" Mitch asked, placing her steaming food in front of her along with the salt and peppershakers, a napkin, and utensils.

She looked up and caught the stern glare. "No. It's not that. I'm just used to doing it all on my own."

"And that's your comfort zone."

"Excuse me?"

"You feel safest when you're in control, right?"

"I have to be in control. If you haven't noticed, it's just me here." What was his problem?

"Jeremy's here. He's got arms and legs and can help you. Your parents are always willing to help from what I saw at dinner last night."

"Who are you to give me parenting advice?" Her first bite of food was divine.

He laughed. "No authority on the subject whatsoever. But I do know that if you keep up this pace you'll be no good to yourself, Jeremy, or anyone else. Reach out to those around you, Marly. You're not a failure if someone helps you do the dishes, clean the house, or make breakfast."

She let his comments sink in as she continued eating. Hadn't she told herself that for years?

Food tasted so much better when someone else cooked it. "You're right. Thank you for breakfast. It was delicious." She stood, placed her dish in the sink and faced him again. "I'm going to take a shower. You and Jeremy can take care of the dishes."

He smiled at her slowly, her belly feeling like a swarm of butterflies were trapped in there. Her heart thudded against her chest as she willed herself to remain in control, don't look like a starry-eyed schoolgirl for Christ's sakes.

"Now see. Not so hard, was it? Letting go of the reigns a little," Mitch said, moving closer until he pinned her against the sink.

"Just don't break any dishes." Hoping he didn't hear the slight tremble in her voice, she swallowed hard.

It was bad enough that just his presence could light her insides on fire. She wouldn't make a fool out of herself by shaking and quivering because his strong body brushed against hers.

"You don't mind if Jeremy comes down to the stables with me to fix the gate, do you?"

Her son. That was good. Change the subject to her son. She could talk about Jeremy while restoring her mushy brain to its useful state.

"No." She cleared her throat. "I'm sure he'd like to learn how to do that kind of stuff. He'll probably glue himself to your hip."

Mitch dipped his head low to her ear. He smelled of soap, leathery aftershave, and everything male. Raw desire swarmed through her, threatening to shatter her last bit of control and leave her a needy mess melting into his arms.

His voice was a mere whisper. "That's okay. I could use his help." His breath tickled her ear with every word. "He's going to teach me how to ride after. We'll be careful. That okay?"

She nodded her head, more to get the blood flowing back into it than to approve. She spoke as carefully as she could, hoping to conceal the effect he had on her. "Be very careful. He's not allowed to jump or do any acrobatics. He'll try to talk you into it. Don't let him."

He leaned back, putting distance between them. Marly wanted to haul him against her. God, how she wanted that.

"Agreed," he said simply and walked away.

He left her there not knowing how close he'd

come to having his bones jumped. She had images in her head of him naked, sweaty, and begging her for mercy. Or was that her begging for mercy? Either way, she would never look at Mitch Allen again without imagining his naked muscles covering her slim body and taking complete control of her needs.

He had said she always needed to be in control. Well, this was one time she'd be willing to give up control. And she was sure Mitch knew how to work a woman's body.

She slowly walked upstairs. God help her she prayed. He was leaving town soon and that was for the best. She didn't need a man like Mitch around who jumbled her brains without any effort and sent her body pulsing in areas she had forgotten years ago.

****

Mitch found a small toolbox in the shed and had Jeremy carry it to the horse pen. The two of them removed the hinges, fixed the wood with nails, and refastened the hinges. When they were done, the fence looked almost brand new.

"There. Now it looks tight. Want to let the horses out of the barn, Jeremy?"

The boy did so in record time and had his horse saddled by the time Mitch put the tools away.

"Easy, Thunder," Jeremy instructed. "Watch me, Mitch. You'll learn how to ride by watching first, then we'll saddle up Sally and you can try it."

For twenty minutes, Mitch did just that. He leaned against the fence, watching the boy handle the horse the same way he handled his dog, playful yet commanding. Mitch was thankful for the brief rest. His knee throbbed, but he was proud to ignore the pain and do things instead of lying around.

"Ready to try?" Jeremy asked, stopping his horse in front of Mitch.

Mitch looked at the size of the horse and couldn't help having reservations about climbing onto a beast that could send him flying to the ground with the flick of his back. But if the kid could do it, then he sure the hell could.

Mitch watched attentively as Jeremy saddled Sally with such ease. "You know, you're really good at this, buddy."

"Been doing it since I could walk. Now put your foot in there, use it to push your body over the top so you can sit. Leave the cane against the fence."

How Mitch had managed to do this last night in the dark with little experience was probably due purely to the adrenaline rush he had been under.

Once Mitch was situated on top of the horse, Jeremy showed him how to properly hold the reigns. They walked the horses around the pen. Jeremy stayed beside Mitch until he was comfortable with the horse. The bumpy ride reminded him of the dirt bike he had as a kid. For the next hour, they trotted around the pen until Mitch could no longer sit in the saddle.

"Sorry, buddy. That's it for me," Mitch announced, stopping alongside Jeremy. "I don't know what hurts more, my ass or my knee."

Jeremy burst out laughing, which had Mitch cracking a smile.

"Okay, come over here. I'll show you how to dismount."

That sounded easier than it was. Mitch's knee locked and a streak of fire tore up his leg. When he was done rattling off a string of curses, he bent over to catch his breath. Pulling himself together, he'd forgotten Jeremy was there. Oh, well, the boy must've heard those words before. Besides, Mitch couldn't help the knee-jerk reaction to the pain.

"Want to see me do a jump?" Jeremy asked.

Even in severe pain, Mitch knew when he was being played. "No way. Your mom already gave strict orders—no jumping."

"Just one. She won't know."

"You break your neck and she'll know. Now hurry up and get off your horse. I need to get back and take some medicine." Yeah, he'd definitely take pain meds. He wasn't only saying uncle. He was screaming it.

To his surprise and gratitude, Jeremy did as asked and soon they were walking back to the house.

"Thanks for teaching me how to ride. It's been so long since I did. I had a great time. You really know your stuff when it comes to horses." Mitch prayed simple conversation would distract him from the pain.

The boy shrugged and kicked rocks and grass as they walked. "I guess."

"Tell you what, buddy. As my way of showing you I'm thankful for today's lesson, I'll talk to your mom, see if she'll let you do any jumps."

The boy's face lit up instantly. "Really? Awesome!"

"Easy now. I said I'd ask. There's no guarantee she'll agree. She was pretty adamant this morning. But I'll put in a good word that I think you can handle the horse."

"She'll listen to you. I hope."

Mitch swung his arm over Jeremy's shoulders without realizing it and they walked home.

"But you have to promise that if she allows you to do a jump, you'll never do it by yourself."

"Promise."

"Good. Let's go get something cold to drink." But he'd take something for the pain too.

The day had warmed up to an enjoyable eighty degrees. A slight breeze tickled his skin, filling the air with scents of flowers and grass. Birds flew around all the massive trees in the area. Butterflies circled the grass.

Jack was outside on the porch, sleeping in the sunshine. When Jeremy saw him, he started off into a run, yelling at the dog who jumped up and ran to meet the boy halfway. Mitch smiled as he watched the two interact.

With each step, Mitch's leg screamed for mercy. Thank God he was almost at the house. Out of the corner of his police-trained eye, he noticed a lump on the ground. Squinting to see what it was, it definitely looked out of place in the field and trees.

He continued to the house but stopped when the policeman in him couldn't go on. He walked over to the lump. Getting closer, it looked like a pile of someone's laundry.

Then Mitch stilled.

Chapter Nine

The body was of a man who'd had his head blown off. The smell of death, one Mitch would never forget, choked his senses.

"Mitch," Jeremy called from not far away at the edge of the house.

"Shit! Stay there, kid. I'm coming."

The body looked fresh, like it hadn't been there long. Of course, Mitch wasn't about to move it to see anything else. Dead is dead. He'd call the local authorities and let them take over.

Mitch walked as quickly as he could to Jeremy's side. "Jeremy, look there's been a change of plans. I need to use the phone. I want you to come inside."

"No. I want to ride my bike now that it's fixed."

Mitch grabbed his shoulder. "You need to come in. I need to make an important phone call with you inside."

"Why?"

"Because I said so. Look, I need to call the police. Can you help me do that? Then I'll explain." Mitch didn't want Jeremy seeing the body.

He shrugged, not really interested, but led the way into the house. Marly had left a note on the table that she ran out and would be right back.

105

"Great," Mitch complained, picking up the phone.

Mitch called the authorities, wishing Marly would hurry up and get home. She should be here to talk to the sheriff.

"Yes, I'd like to report a murder," Mitch explained to a woman who answered the phone at the Sheriff's Office.

"A murder? Oh, dear, hold please."

Hold? Since when does 911 put someone on hold?

"Sheriff Ridgeley. Is this a prank?" a man bellowed from the other end.

"No, it isn't. A man's been murdered outside in the field at Marly Hampton's house. I don't know the address here."

"So a man's been murdered?" he asked, doubt filling his tone.

Mitch rolled his eyes. "That's what I said."

"I heard what you said, but I can't believe it's a murder."

"Believe me, it's murder. The guy couldn't have done this to himself." Mitch didn't want to talk too loud and risk Jeremy overhearing.

"You said Marly Hampton's place, right?"

"That's right."

"You the stranger staying there?"

What's that got to do with anything? "That'd be me. Now are you going to send someone out here, or did you not hear that there's a dead body outside?" Mitch's temper boiled. This sheriff was a dickhead.

"Now hold on a minute. Before you get yourself any more worked up, how do you know the person is dead? I mean, men around here are known to put back one too many beers and pass out. Could that be the case?"

Worked up? Count to ten. "Stop acting like I don't know what a dead body looks like, Sheriff. Most intoxicated men who pass out don't have a hole in their fucking forehead." Complete silence came from the other end. "I take it you believe me now and will send someone."

"Hang tight. We'll be there."

The receiver went dead. What an asshole!

Mitch waited for the sheriff. After fifteen minutes passed, he thought the man would never show. Maybe he was just used to city time, that's all. He needed patience. Small towns sure moved slower.

The sheriff finally showed up twenty-five minutes after Mitch's call.

"Let's see what you got out here," Sheriff Ridgeley announced, pulling himself out of his cruiser and putting on his gray cowboy hat in a weak attempt to cover a comb-over.

"The body's over that way about thirty yards. I'm not making the trek again with this leg, so you're on your own," Mitch told him, gripping his cane.

Mitch watched the heavyset man of about fifty waddle away. His double chins sagged to conceal his neck, if it even existed. The cigar hanging out of his mouth hadn't been lit and was either for show or an attempt to break a bad habit. By the way the sheriff gnawed at it, you'd think he hadn't eaten in a week. From the size of him, though, Mitch would bet any amount of money that Sheriff Lard Ass didn't miss any meals.

The sheriff returned about five minutes later. He

waddled back to his cruiser and spoke into the radio then returned to Mitch.

"You're not from around these parts," Sheriff Ridgeley said, wiping sweat from his brow onto a hankie that he pulled from his shirt pocket.

Mitch stood in front of the man. "I could've told you that."

"I happen to know every citizen in my town."

Mitch nodded his head toward the field. "Is he one of yours?"

"Yup," he confirmed, out of breath and red-faced. "Can't say he'll be missed much, considering he's the biggest asshole around here."

"Now he's the biggest dead asshole," Mitch conceded.

"That's for sure. Give me your name, son." He took out a small notepad and scribbled.

"Mitch Allen. Call me Mitch." He didn't care for the son notation.

"Where you from?"

"Boston."

The sheriff removed his sunglasses to peer at him. "You're pretty far away from home, aren't you?"

Mitch kept eye contact. "It's not my home any more."

"Really? Got a new one?"

"No, sir. I'm staying here for a few nights 'til I get my truck fixed, then I'll be on my way."

"Where to?"

"Don't know. Why? Do you want me to send you a postcard when I get there?"

Sheriff Ridgeley narrowed his eyes. "You city folk think you're so smart. So I guess you could be called a drifter."

"No, I can be called Mitch," he said, standing with arms folded and refusing to be intimidated by the man.

"This here's the first murder we've had in this town in over forty years."

There was something about the way the sheriff sneered his words. Mitch didn't like him and sure the hell didn't trust him. So he didn't respond.

"Seems like a big coincidence that a stranger shows up in my town and then a well-known citizen gets murdered. *And,* that stranger happens to find the body."

"If I did it, why the hell would I call you? I could've been long gone before anyone found him," Mitch countered, his aggravation increasing.

"Just seems like a big coincidence is all I'm saying. The medical examiner is on the way to get the body."

Great. Around here that'll probably take days.

Marly drove up in a cloud of dust as she sped to a stop. "Jeremy! What's wrong, Mitch?" she screamed, running toward them.

"Jeremy's fine, Marly," Mitch said.

"Seems your guest has stumbled upon Howard Singleton's body over in your field. Been shot dead."

Marly didn't gasp like Mitch knew other women would have. Instead, she looked pissed off. "Where's Jeremy?"

"Inside," Mitch said. "He's practicing the video game so we can have a match later. It was the only way to keep him inside."

"Thank you. Does he know? Oh, God, did he

see…"

"No. He ran ahead of me. I found the body. Made sure Jeremy didn't see or know anything. I figured that's up to you to tell him."

"Sheriff, do you know who could've done this?" Marly asked, hands on her hips.

The man shot a glance at Mitch, but Marly stepped in before Mitch could respond.

"Oh, Sheriff Ridgeley, be real. Mitch wouldn't do that. Why would he when more than half the town wanted that man dead, including his own family?"

The sheriff replaced his sunglasses. "I agree. Strange, though, how the man ends up dead on your property when you have…company."

"How long's he been dead, Sheriff?" Marly ignored his comments.

"I'd guess a day or so."

"More like twelve hours. He still had some color to his skin. Indicates time of death no more than twelve hours ago," Mitch said.

"Oh? So now you're a forensic scientist? I get it. You're one of those fellas that likes to watch all those cop shows on television."

"Hardly. I'm an ex-homicide detective from Boston, Sheriff. No more than twelve hours. Bet that's what the ME says, too. I need to rest my knee. I've been on it too long as it is." He climbed the stairs to go inside.

"Mitch?" The sheriff continued once Mitch had faced him again. "I'll be needing you to stick around until my investigation is complete."

Mitch squashed the urge to curse. "And how long will that be?"

"Well, us small towns move at a slower pace than you big city folk, so I'm guessing a couple of weeks."

"Sorry, Sheriff, but I'm not hanging around that long."

"You will if I lock your ass up," the sheriff countered.

Mitch's temper wanted to lash out. It was all he could do to restrain it. "On what grounds?"

"Suspicion of murder. Maybe accessory to murder," he aimed his words at Marly.

"What? Now, you think I killed him?" Marly asked, shocked.

"You two were involved in a land dispute."

"I'd have to stand in line in this town to get my shot at him and you know it, Sheriff," Marly proclaimed.

"I believe you're innocent, Marly, as the evidence hasn't told me otherwise. However, Allen, you stay put or you'll find yourself locked up. I can do just that if I even have a little bit of suspicion."

"Fuck that! That's lame and you know it. Besides, you have to charge me within forty-eight hours or let me go."

The sheriff stepped closer and smirked before speaking. "Maybe that's how things work in Boston, but they don't work that way here. You see, the Town of Courtsville gives the sheriff the authority to hold a person if he suspects that person may have committed a crime. It also says I can hold that person as long as needed." He pointed to his badge. "This here badge says I'm the sheriff, so what I say goes."

"Sheriff Ridgeley," Marly interrupted. "Mitch will be staying here. You can reach him here until your investigation is over. I expect you'll do your best to move it along seeing as I have a young boy and all. I don't want some killer roaming my land."

He looked at Mitch. "You ought to be careful who you open your door to then."

Marly ignored his comment. "Now, if you don't mind, Mitch really should get off that knee."

"Don't mind at all. I'll be in touch." He tipped his hat at Marly and glared at Mitch who gave it right back to him.

"I'll make some tea then you can fill me in," Marly said sternly, walking past Mitch to the kitchen.

He followed slowly. His knee was on fire. "Not much to fill in," he began before gulping some aspirin and water. "We went to ride the horses. Jeremy raced back to the house to ride his bike. He and the dog were in front of the house when I saw what I thought was a heap of clothes. Went over to investigate, and the guy was dead. Came back and called the sheriff, who is a real dickhead by the way."

"I couldn't agree more." She smiled, a wondrous highlight to her lovely face.

Mitch sat at the table, his knee relieved. "He's an asshole. Doesn't know the first thing about crime scene investigations. Christ, every deputy the sheriff has is trampling through any damn evidence. How the hell did he manage to become sheriff? Did he draw the longest straw or something?"

"Something like that," Marly acknowledged.

"He thinks I did it."

Marly stared at him. "We both know you didn't. You wouldn't have gotten out of this house without me knowing."

"Yeah, three o'clock tea. I remember."

From the other room, Jeremy yelled, "Mom? What's going on? The sheriff and some guy have a white stretcher in our yard."

Marly talked to Jeremy from the kitchen door. "Howie Singleton was found dead in our field. They're here to take him away. Now I don't want you to be frightened—"

"Wow! This is so cool. Wait until I tell Danny!" Jeremy said and rushed back to the window to watch.

"Well, not exactly what I expected, but I'd rather him think it's cool than be scared in his own house."

"How about his mom? How are you holding up?" Mitch asked, watching her rush about making the tea.

"Been through worse. I'll be just fine. Here. You can help me get dinner started. You can peel potatoes, can't you?" She placed a bag of potatoes on the table in front of him.

"Not really. Cops eat take out. Always been willing to learn though. Just show me what to do."

She did. Quickly. It didn't seem too complicated. He'd never peeled potatoes in his life. That seemed amusing considering he'd just found a dead man on his walk and was supposed to have left this kind of lifestyle. The investigating, the findings. The unknown.

And here he was preparing dinner with a woman he'd barely known but a few days. Just the mere sight of her, or the sound of her voice, was enough to get his blood pumping and his mind conjuring up erotic images of them naked together. Sweaty.

And not to forget, now he was the prime suspect in a murder case with a sheriff on his ass just for being an outsider from a big city. Being an ex-cop only seemed to piss off the sheriff more.

"So tell me why you left the force." Marly sat down next to him with a bag of green beans and began stripping them of their ends and cracking them in half. Her question came out of left field and struck him in the gut like a foul pitch.

"No."

She looked at him with raised brows. "Why not?"

"That's the past. Don't need to bring it up now."

"Well, even though we are a small town, we do have access to the Internet in these parts. I can guarantee that the sheriff is either on the phone to Boston finding out about you, or on the Internet searching for your dirty secrets, or both. By tomorrow, you'll be the talk of the town, and I'd like to know what to expect to hear from people."

"Then you won't like what you hear. I can't help that."

She never missed a beat. She kept at the green beans, her fingers moving swiftly, while he clumsily raked the peeler over the potato, removing one strip at a time. Thank God for take-out or he'd have starved by now if he'd had to feed himself all these years. The best he ever did was grill a steak or chicken.

"I've thought a lot about what it would be like to have sex with you." She said it so matter-of-factly that he stopped peeling to stare at her.

"Ditto," was all his fuzzy brain managed.

"There's something sexy about the mystery surrounding you. If you don't give me some insight, I may just have to use my womanly powers to drag it out of you." Her lips curved into a feline grin, like a cat watching a mouse.

He smirked. "I can play that game."

"Oh, it won't be a game, Mitch. Or should I call you Detective Allen?"

"I'm no longer in a uniform so Mitch will do. And while we're on the subject of prying into personal lives," Mitch looked behind his shoulder and lowered his voice. "Do you want to talk about why no other man has shared your bed since your husband died?"

By the way her face paled and her eyes grew wide as saucers, he guessed he'd discovered why she was still alone. Hadn't let go of the husband yet. Sore subject was written all over her face.

"You son of a bitch," Marly seemed to vibrate with anger as she jumped up from her chair.

Mitch stood on his wobbly leg. "Exactly! My past is as touchy for me as your husband's death is for you. So if you don't mind, I'd rather not talk about it."

"Fine!"

Marly stood by the sink and stared out the window. The sun would soon set in the sky and dusk would settle over the land.

Mitch felt like an ass. He had no right to talk to her like that. He was a guest in her house, and she'd just had a corpse removed from her backyard. And she was clearly, admittedly, sexually frustrated. But he wouldn't be pressed on his past. It hurt just as much as hers hurt her.

"Marly, I'm sorry. That was inexcusable and I'm sorry."

"No. You pretty much summed it up." She sighed and faced him, folding her arms. Her eyes appeared a little misty, tugging at Mitch's heart. "After Rick died,

I concentrated on raising our son, the only child I would ever have with him. He never even got to see Jeremy. Damn it!" Her fist clenched. "Only saw the pictures I sent. And I can't even be sure that he got the pictures before he died since military mail is slower than a snail. Internet access back then wasn't as reliable like now and they had no computers where he was stationed."

"You don't have to talk about this unless you want."

She looked at him. "If I didn't want to talk, I wouldn't. But you're right. I haven't had a relationship with another man since Rick. Don't get me wrong, I want that companionship again. I don't do one-night stands because they didn't work for me. I didn't want to get close to another man, so I thought I could at least satisfy my needs with a few simple, no-strings affairs, but I felt dirty afterward. Cheap."

"You're not cheap. No way in hell could you be considered a cheap woman. You have more honor than most men I know. You've built a life here. You've raised a very decent son by yourself. Your husband would be proud of you. And of Jeremy."

"I want you, Mitch. I just don't know how to have you and then let you go. You fit in here too easily and that scares the hell out of me because you won't be here long."

"Let's just enjoy one day at a time, Marly. I think we're both a little too exhausted for much more." Because tears welled in her eyes, he changed the subject quickly. He was not a man who knew how to handle a crying woman. "Speaking of your son, let's get this dinner ready. I've got to kick his ass in the video game."

She quickly swiped at her eyes and settled at the counter to mix the meatloaf. "I'd tread carefully in those waters, Mitch. He's awfully good."

"We'll see about that. I didn't have much else to do while recuperating, so I discovered video games and just about became a pro at all of them."

"If you say so. Just don't let him con you into a wager. You'll lose." Placing the meatloaf in the oven, she set the timer.

Mitch snorted. "I don't like to lose so I make it a rule not to."

She laughed. "So does Jeremy."

"Why don't you take a few minutes for yourself? And I don't mean go clean something. Lay down. Read a book. Take a bath. Do something for you," Mitch commanded.

"My…look who's getting bossy."

"Sorry. I get like that when I'm comfortable. Now go."

Mitch shooed her away and turned his attentions to Jeremy and the TV.

****

Marly took a few minutes for herself upstairs in her room. What she really wanted to do was cry her eyes out. She was so damn confused and now she was scared, too. Howie Singleton's dead body had been in her field for how long? What if Jeremy had found him instead of Mitch? Why would someone kill him here or dump him here? Was someone trying to scare her off her land? Well, if they thought she'd scare easily, they better think again.

She rubbed her aching forehead. Right now, she needed to concentrate on what to do with Mitch. Oh, she knew what she wanted to do with him. Yeah, she'd thought of a lot of different ways they could do it, too, but she needed to be careful. He wasn't here to stay, even if he was attracted to her. No. He had too much of a troubled past to settle down in this small, no-thrills town. A man like Mitch Allen needed excitement in his life to keep him waking up every day. And the only excitement she had to offer him was some spectacular sex.

Oh, yes, the sex would be spectacular. She leaned back against her pillow and closed her eyes. She'd allow herself a few minutes to dream of the sexy Mitch Allen, then have dinner, then bed the man who had consumed her thoughts since he showed up in her living room looking more broken than she had ever been.

Chapter Ten

Marly entered the living room after cleaning up dinner. "Okay, Jeremy, time for a bath and bed. And you shouldn't take advantage of our guest the way you did."

Mitch stood from the couch. "Nope. He won fair and square. Now go do as your mom says so we can play tomorrow."

Without a word, Jeremy flew up the stairs and Marly could hear the water going. She turned to Mitch in amazement.

"What?" Mitch appeared stumped.

"He's never gone to take a bath without a fight. You're good."

"No, he is. He just wants to beat me again tomorrow." He stretched that long, lean body. "Oh, to be eleven again and have no cares in the world other than video games, huh?"

Keeping her mind off his sexy body proved difficult. "Tell me about it. Can I get you anything?"

Mitch thought about it. "Yeah. I could go for a little adult company."

She stiffened. "I've got to get Jeremy ready for bed and…"

"Jeremy's a big boy. I'm sure he can tuck himself

in while his mom takes a load off her feet and fills me in on this town and its history. You wouldn't want to be rude to your guest, would you?" He pulled her down to sit on the couch next to him.

"Okay. Where you do want me to start?" she asked, knowing she wanted the adult company just as much.

"With you. If you don't mind me saying so, Marly, you didn't seem too upset that a dead body was found on your property. Most women would be hysterical."

Marly's brain was in a fog. Was it because of the day's events or because Mitch was sitting so close to her? His sandy brown hair was unruly and the puffy circles under his eyes showed his exhaustion. But the sight of him had her mouth watering and made her insides tighten.

She had to focus on the conversation at hand. It was never a good thing to allow thoughts to wander. She didn't have time for idle fantasies no matter how yummy the lead character looked.

"Sorry. There's no love lost there. Howie was a bully and a jerk. As far as I'm concerned, he got what he deserved. It's really no surprise."

"Every town has one of those I guess."

"Yeah, well, Howie was the worst. He wanted to rob me of my land."

Mitch frowned and stared at her. "So you've said. But you didn't go into much detail."

She blew out a long breath. "It's a long, complicated story."

"Well, according to the sheriff, he's going to drag his sweet ass on this investigation so I have a lot of time on my hands. I'm all ears."

She grinned. "Howie owns the land to the west of mine. He's never been a very good neighbor. My parents gave Rick and me this house and the land as a wedding present."

"That got you two off to a good start."

"It did. Rick and I were high school sweethearts. Rick joined the Army to earn money for college and I studied four years at the community college to get my degree in business administration. We married after he returned from a long deployment, and I discovered I was pregnant soon after."

"You don't say."

A warm blush spread across her cheeks. "Yeah. We had been away from each other six long months, so when he came home we didn't leave our bedroom for four days after the wedding."

Mitch laughed then smiled. "I don't blame your husband. If I had a sexy wife like you waiting for me at home, I'd spend my days making love to her."

His words floated through her ears to her brain. Just hearing him say "making love" had her arms loosening and her knees shaking.

Look at her. Sitting there like a schoolgirl waiting to be felt up. Not only waiting, but hoping.

Mitch had remained silent, focusing his gaze on her, watching her, studying her. He didn't pry. Didn't ask questions. Just waited for her to continue.

"Our time together flew by. He only had a little time off and then the Gulf War happened. He was immediately deployed for Dessert Storm and sent to the Gulf Region."

"And you were left here to worry."

"Uh huh. But I didn't worry much. I had faith in Rick. He was well trained and had a good head on his shoulders. When I sent word I was pregnant, Rick was elated. He couldn't wait to come home to us. Me and the baby. He knew he wouldn't make it home in time to see Jeremy born, but he was happy anyway."

"And he never returned."

"Nope." She took a long, slow breath. The pain of those days still just as real almost twelve years later. "So I was a twenty-three-year-old widow with a new baby and great parents. Rick's family was great, too. They live in the next county over."

"Where's Howie come into all of this?"

"He decided to knock down the trees on my land abutting his on the west. Normally, I wouldn't have given a damn. I was in tough shape back then. I cried whenever the baby slept and was exhausted. But Rick had told him not to touch the trees because we weren't going to merge the lands like Howie wanted so he could build some casino."

"A casino? Here?"

"Yes. Howie figured he could build himself a casino and make a ton of money while sitting on his ass. But Rick was against any such business so close to his family. He didn't want us exposed to lowlifes, the crime, or the late-night crowds. And that type of business would definitely change the character of the area we had fallen in love with. It was ours. Howie had no right to cut down my damn trees. I wish one had fallen on his head. It would've saved us a lot of headaches now."

She stood and paced the room before cringing. "No. I don't mean that."

"Can't blame you if you did."

"No, because then that would make me like him. I love life and so did Rick. We were planning to make a very good one for ourselves here with our new baby and the other kids we'd have."

"I think you've made a very good life for yourself here. You should be proud of that. And if Howie met his end by messing with the wrong person, then that's his problem. Once the sheriff finishes his investigation, you can continue on with your life knowing that you won't have to deal with the likes of this Howie guy anymore."

Marly sighed, her shoulders heavy. "There's more. I reported to the sheriff that Howie had been following me. Of course, Howie denied it and I couldn't prove otherwise, but I wouldn't make it up. Then a few months back the vandalism started."

"Vandalism?"

"Yeah. One of my fences in the horse area was damaged and cost me a fortune to repair, but at least the horses didn't get loose that time."

Mitch sat up straight. "You didn't mention that the other night when Storm got out."

She shrugged her shoulders. "Guess I forgot because it was much different. The other night I thought Jeremy and you had left it unlocked."

"What else?"

"Then the barn windows were all busted out. The sheriff suggested Jeremy did it and was too ashamed to tell me."

Mitch shook his head. "He's not afraid to tell you anything."

"Right. If it were my son, he would've only

123

broken one window and that by accident. He would've told me. But they were all broken. Had to pay another small fortune to repair those."

"Sounds like Howie was hitting you where it hurts—in the pocketbook."

She laughed without the humor. "Well, that's pretty much empty now. I just got two new tires for my car and...oh, my God! How could I be so stupid?"

Mitch frowned. "What?"

"My car. Damnit! Three weeks ago, I went into town on errands and got a nail in my tire. I had to have it towed and buy two new tires since one would have put the thing off balance or so says the mechanic."

"You think Howie got your tire?"

"Makes sense. Maybe that's what he was doing here. To try it again or do something else. I'm sorry, Mitch."

"Why are you sorry?"

"Because now you're stuck here longer than you wanted. You should be on the road tomorrow." How did her life get so complicated?

"I'm not worried unless you've conspired with that asshole sheriff to keep me here, sexually frustrated by your beauty and charm."

She laughed. "I'm caught. My master plan to kidnap you and keep you in my tower."

The smile he offered relaxed her. "If it was Howie to fuck with your car, that would explain him being here. But doesn't explain who killed him. Maybe someone saw him and wanted to protect you."

"No. Around here, they would've just called the sheriff. If they had to do things on their own, they would've stayed to take responsibility."

"Well, someone had it out for him and finally got him."

"Can't say I'm not glad. That's horrible, but he deserved it for the way he lived his life."

Marly heard no noise from upstairs. "If you don't mind, I'm going to check on Jeremy for a minute. If he's quiet, then that means he's up to something."

"I'll be here."

Within a few minutes, Marly returned to the living room in shock. "I think I may have to kidnap you after all."

"Why's that?" Mitch asked, half stretched out on the couch.

"Jeremy is in bed, with the lights out, and he took a bath. You have some kind of magical powers, Mitch Allen. You deserve some chocolate cake for your reward."

Mitch stood quickly, but shakily, and reached her before she could turn away. "I know one way you can thank me."

His mouth landed on hers so fast it caught her off guard. Her hands automatically rested on his chest. Her mouth gave in to the pleasures of his as the hardness of his lips crushed onto hers, sending sparks of pleasure throughout her body to places she'd long forgotten.

She remembered this kind of need. The hunger deep within her to be wanted, needed, taken. It was too powerful for her. Marly didn't know if it was the kiss taking her breath away or the need to have more.

Mitch stopped the kiss. Her lips tingled and her cheeks warmed where the day's old growth on his face had scraped. She rubbed at it absent mindedly while

125

staring at him.

His fingers caressed her jaw. "Sorry about the stubble. Didn't plan on kissing anyone, so I hadn't bothered to shave."

"I'm not sure we should do this as much as I want to. My life is way too complicated for intimacy." She walked quickly to the kitchen.

He followed her, staying on her heels. It unnerved her to have him so close. She could clear the counter and have him take her right there. Good God, where are these thoughts coming from?

"It was just a kiss. And you kissed me first yesterday, so you started this."

"That was yesterday and I only kissed you out of anger. I was pissed off."

He cocked an eyebrow. "That's the only reason?"

"This is too complicated." She rubbed her fingertips against her temples, hoping to allow blood to flow back into her foggy brain. Nerves got the best of her, even when she had spent the evening fantasizing about being alone with Mitch.

"What the hell is so complicated about a kiss?" he asked, holding his arms open, palms up.

"It was not just a kiss and you know it. That was an awesome kiss. And an invitation for more."

He smiled wickedly.

"Oh, knock it off. You can't take all the credit. I can take half."

"True. But I wouldn't say it was awesome."

Her mouth dropped open. "Really? What would you call it? I may not be a fancy city girl, but I know how to kiss damn good, and that was a damn good kiss."

"But I can take half the credit."

"My half was damn good!"

"Agreed. And you didn't give me a chance to say that it was not just awesome, it was exceptional. You stirred me in ways I haven't felt in months."

This close, she smelled his light, woodsy cologne, the scent teasing her more than the kiss. "That's why it's complicated. We're both starved for intimacy and, of course, we have a spark here. Any blind person could see the sparks between us. But what do we do? Huh? Have a few nights of passion and then, when you get the go ahead from the sheriff and your truck's fixed, you leave? No. Sorry."

He stepped back. "I guess it was more than a kiss when you put it like that."

"That's because men never think with their heads just their…well, you know what they think with."

"I'm doing a lot of thinking right now," he said, grinning wickedly, staring down at the noticeable bulge in his pants.

She wanted to scream. "Then I guess it's a good thing one of us is thinking clearly. I don't take men into my house to have an affair."

"Do you want me to leave?"

Her eyes caught his, the sensitivity surprising. "What? No. Yes. No. You can't. The sheriff wants you to stay."

"The sheriff said I only have to stay in town. He didn't place me under house arrest here. If my being here makes you that uncomfortable, then say the word and I'll leave," he offered, calmly.

She hesitated. "No. I promised you that you can stay, and I don't break promises."

"I'll be on my best behavior then. No more kisses." He ran his hand along her cheek. "Unless you say differently."

The pang that hit her in the chest stunned her. She wanted more. But how could she have more without getting hurt? It would surely be a mistake. Why did his truck have to break down near her house?

"Thank you. I never meant to tease you or string you along. That's not me." Why couldn't she just accept the intimacy she craved and he offered?

"You didn't do anything. The sparks did, remember?"

His smile melted her heart. His touch scalded her skin. Marly backed away before she couldn't. "Want tea?"

"No, thanks. I need a very cold shower."

"Oh. Okay. Good night." He turned to walk away and she shouted after him. "Make sure you leave me some cold water."

****

That smile stayed on his face up the stairs and until the cold water hit his skin. He'd managed to stir her juices just as badly as she'd done to his. Good.

No more kisses my ass. Marly didn't know it yet, but Mitch was a very patient man. She'd soon understand that they couldn't ignore the sparks between them.

But for now, the cold shower would be his new best friend until Marly said differently.

Chapter Eleven

Monday morning came with a slew of activity in the Hampton household.

"Jeremy, get your backpack," Marly yelled up the stairs.

Mitch came in wiping his hands on an old rag. "Okay, the tow truck just picked up my truck. I fixed your windshield washer and checked your fluids. You're due for an oil change and need some brake fluid."

"Okay. I'll get some next time I stop for gas. Thanks. Come on, Jeremy. I'm leaving."

"Okay. Okay," Jeremy said as he bounced down the stairs. "Hey, Mitch, you can use my video game to practice today."

"Smart ass. I don't need to practice. You just got lucky." He rubbed the boy's head.

Jeremy squirmed away from his reach. "Yeah, right. You'd better practice if you ever want to beat me. Or if you ever want to get past the sixth board."

"Get in the truck. You're going to be late for school. And I hope they give you a lot of homework," Mitch said, gently shoving Jeremy past him to the door.

On the ride to town, Jeremy filled in Mitch about his classmates and what he was studying. "Math and science are cool because we get to build projects. I hate English because it's boring. And there's no need for me to take history since I don't live back then and don't care what the cavemen or the Romans did."

By the time Marly and Mitch were alone in the truck, Mitch needed an aspirin. "Wow. Is he always that talkative first thing in the morning?"

"Never. Especially not on a Monday morning. You two have hit it off pretty good."

"Nah," Mitch said, waving his hand and ignoring the little tug in his heart. "That's just male bonding bullshit. It's natural."

"Still, I see you two have a lot in common, and I see how Jeremy looks up to you."

Mitch sensed something with the way she spoke in that preachy, lecturing tone. "Spill it. What are you trying to say?" From the passenger seat, Mitch's gaze bounced back between the road and her.

She took a deep breath before speaking. "I just don't want to see Jeremy get hurt when you leave. So don't feel like you have to be nice to him to make me happy."

She could've slapped him across the face and not hurt him more than she just did. "Is that what you think I'm doing? Using Jeremy to get in your pants?"

"What? No! No, of course not. I didn't mean it that way, Mitch. I'm just saying—"

He cut off her words. "I know what you're saying. Your son's off limits. I get it."

His gut tightened but not like it usually did when Marly was involved. It tightened like he'd just been kicked in the gut, hard and viciously. Had he given her any reason to think that way? Hadn't he been respectful toward her? He hung with the kid because he wanted to. Not to use him as a pawn for his mother's affection.

A gray building called Maddy's Automotive was on his right. Marly pulled her truck into the driveway and drove around to the front of the building. As soon as the truck came to a stop, Mitch grabbed his cane and, without a word, opened the door and got out as quickly as his leg would allow.

"Mitch," Marly called after him.

He refused to answer her. What he wanted to say was simply not nice. So it was best to keep his mouth shut before saying something he'd ultimately regret.

But she jumped out and followed him to the back of the truck, blocking his way. If he didn't have the damn cane, he could have easily picked her up and moved her out of his way.

"Mitch, I would never think that so don't you dare put words in my mouth."

"I didn't have to. Your words were very clear to me."

Marly's hands fisted on her hips. Damn, she was adorable. "If I did think that, I would never have allowed you to get to first base."

"Allowed? Oh, that's right. I forgot about your control issues. You go ahead and keep letting yourself believe you *allowed* the kiss."

"I may have control issues, but that's better than running away from my problems."

He wasn't going to be sucked into this argument. This was about her, not him. "Move out of my way, please," he said without looking at her.

"I'll move when I'm good and ready." She placed

her palm flat on his chest. "I have no choice but to constantly be in control of everything in my life because I have no one else to depend on. I had that once with my husband and, if I found someone again, then sharing wouldn't be an issue. But until then, I have no choice. You, however, had a choice. And you chose to leave your life behind to go God knows where. So don't you dare chastise me for trying to keep my life together the best I know how."

Well, didn't he feel like a heel. The wounded look in her eyes tore at his heart until he thought the pain would make him cringe. He had to give her credit. She certainly was a fighter. Tough and hard as nails on the outside. But did she realize how close she teetered on the edge, holding her life together on her own, allowing her pride to keep her from leaning on others?

"All I'm saying is that Jeremy's gotten used to having you around. He's never had that. Never had a man living with us that he could be friends with and have the male chats that you two easily have. Damnit! This is why I stay away from men and relationships. They just don't work for me."

Mitch struggled to follow her to the front of her truck and caught her door before she could slam it shut once she slipped inside. "Now wait just a damn minute."

"No! You wait. Maybe you don't realize that a boy his age could easily get used to male company after being stuck with just me all these years." The tears spilled from her eyes. "Christ! I hate crying."

"Of course you do. Then you'd have to admit you're human." He leaned in the door, his body hovering over hers. "Marly, I promise you I won't hurt your son. I've never given him any reason to believe that I would stay long term and I've never tried to pretend to be his father."

"I know that. He's just enjoying your company so much and that's something I can't give him."

"So what? You give him everything else. The kid's not going to break because he doesn't have a father or a father figure in his life. And from what I can see, it's bothering you more than it is Jeremy. He hasn't complained about not having another male around. You're trying to protect him too much. At some point, he's going to get hurt in life and you can't play Super Mom forever. So let us enjoy hanging out and you enjoy the fact that he'll go to bed on time, take a bath without a fight, and eat his veggies for as long as I'm here."

She smiled and wiped her eyes but kept her head down. "I don't want to get used to having you around. You've blended into our lives too easily and too fast."

"Hey," he pushed her chin up so their eyes could meet. "Let's take care of one day at a time. I haven't been good for much else for a long time now. One day at a time is about all I can handle."

She sniffled. "Okay. I'm sorry if I insulted you. I didn't mean to imply you had any bad intentions. I can see you genuinely like Jeremy and it warms my heart."

Mitch smiled, relieved at the end of the tears. "I do like the kid. I'm not going to lie, I never intended to get involved with the everyday life of the Hampton household. But you guys are like magnets, you drew me in."

"Having a dead body show up in my fields forced

you stay longer than expected."

"Yeah. But I'm not complaining. I wasn't headed to any particular place. Now that I'm here, I might as well deal with it."

"Go get your truck fixed. My dad will be in shortly to give you a lift back to the house. I'm late for work."

He rolled down her window before shutting the door. Then he leaned in and softly kissed her lips. "For the record, that kiss was because you are a beautiful, sexy woman with a heart of gold. And because I wanted to."

Mitch stood back to give her room to drive off. Slowly, he walked to the shop to check on his truck. Right now, he needed his brain to concentrate on something other than Marly, at least until he had sense enough to think clearly about his life over the past few days. Maybe then, the strange tightening in his gut would subside as well.

The two-bay garage was typical for a repair shop, Mitch noted as he entered. It had the usual stuff—car lifts, air tools, vehicle fluids, old tires, new tires, used car parts. The air smelled of oil and stale tobacco. But, considering it was a repair shop on the outskirts of a small mountain town, it was surprisingly clean. No. It was friggin' spotless.

Mitch's truck was already up on one of the lifts. Country music blared from a small beat-up radio on a shelf. It wasn't today's country music. At least that Mitch could've handled. But this was the country music from the 50s and 60s. The slow, poor-me-I-break my-ass-for-what-music.

"Can I help ya?" a tall, thin man about sixty

asked as he came from the front of the truck.

"Yes. Truck's mine."

"Oh, yeah? Mitch was it?"

"Yes, sir."

"Maddy Olson." They shook hands. "Got a good truck here."

"She's been good to me. Great on gas. This is the first time I've had to put her in the shop since I got a brake job six months ago." Mitch leaned against the wall for support. Fatigue finally hitting him.

"Yeah. Can tell you've taken good care of her. One thing I can't stand is seeing simple vehicle maintenance ignored cuz the owner is plain lazy. If you're lucky to buy a nice vehicle, then take care of it. It'll last longer and you'll get your money's worth."

"Ol' Joe said I cracked my radiator. How soon 'til it can be fixed?"

"Ol' Joe was right, as usual. Radiator needs replacing as well as the serpentine belt. I'm fair on my prices. You won't get cheated out of your hard earned money here, Mitch."

Mitch nodded. "No, sir. I know that. You come highly recommended."

The man let out a loud laugh then coughed. "Of course I do. I'm the only mechanic for fifteen miles."

"Ol' Joe was picking me up. Should I tell him not to? Can you fix it today?"

"Today? Sorry, not today. If I had the radiator, I could. But I don't. Have to order it from an automotive store in the next county over."

"Really?" Mitch couldn't hide his disappointment. He really wanted his own wheels back. "I guess I have no choice but to wait."

"Probably have it fixed by Wednesday. I'll call you."

Mitch shrugged, not letting the news get him down. "Okay. That's fair."

"Since Ol' Joe ain't here yet to pick you up and you have time on your hands, I can talk while I work. Did you kill Howie Singleton?"

Mitch was caught off guard. "No, sir, I didn't. And no, I don't know who did."

"If you ask me, the jerk deserved what he got. Has had it coming for a long time."

"That's what I'm hearing," Mitch said, moving over to lean against a counter.

"I'm glad the bum is dead. Just sorry Ms. Marly had to have it happen on her land. Poor girl's been through enough."

"Yeah. Tough break."

"Howie had it out for that poor girl, and there wasn't much her lawyer brother or her daddy could do."

"Some people just live to make others miserable," Mitch agreed. "I don't know much about this Howie guy."

"Would you like some coffee?"

Mitch accepted and let the man talk.

"Howie had made an enemy of everyone in town, me included. He thought because of his size that he could bully his way around, and he did just that. Hell, his own family hated him."

"That's what Marly said."

"Howie was brutal to Marly. He'd come into town telling anyone who'd listen that she couldn't take care of her son and maintain such a huge amount of land."

Mitch felt sick to his stomach, getting a small insight into Marly's life that he didn't want. He remembered the diner and wished he had gone with his emotions and punched the bastard in the face instead of trying to end the altercation peacefully. But that was how he'd been trained. He'd learned all those years back in the police academy how to handle his short fuse of a temper, including verbal intervention skills.

"One time, I remember, about a year ago, Marly and a friend were out celebrating Marly's birthday at the Millis Tavern and Howie taunted her in front of everyone. When Marly decided to leave instead of listen to him, he followed her out to her car. Her girlfriend said Howie threatened to do vile things to Marly if she didn't agree to hand over her land."

"Why wasn't Howie in jail for such threats?" Mitch's temper rose, thinking of Howie picking on a single mom doing her best.

Maddy sipped from his mug of coffee. "Because his cousin is the sheriff and Marly wouldn't press charges. Guess she wanted it all to be in the past."

Mitch's jaw dropped. "Sheriff Ridgeley is Howie's cousin?"

"Sure as the sun is yellow."

"Wonder why that fat shit conveniently left out that important piece of information from our conversation."

"Probably because Howie was more of a liability than an asset. And Howie and Ridgeley weren't exactly on friendly terms."

"Funny, but I can see the family resemblance in their similar, miserable personalities."

Maddy grunted and swigged some coffee then lit a cigarette.

"Now tell me, Maddy, just how does a lazy slug like Ridgeley become sheriff when it's painfully clear he's not cut out for the job? He knows nothing about the law, whether it's state or federal. And his professionalism is questionable."

Maddy just shrugged. "Small towns have to use what they have. And Ridgeley's daddy was sheriff before him, so it became a right-of-passage almost that his son would take over when he retired."

Shock consumed Mitch. "What? Since when is the local law enforcement agency a family business to be handed down?"

"Small towns."

"Yeah. Small towns. Pretty fucked up if you asked me."

Maddy moved around the garage as he talked. "I heard you were a big city policeman. Got the sheriff's back up on that."

"Homicide detective and special ops. I'm retired."

Maddy looked him over from his head to his toes, without being discreet. He stamped out his cigarette in an ashtray before he spoke. "Seem too young to be retired. That because of that bum leg."

"Yeah. Pretty much."

"Leg looks fine to me."

Mitch scowled. "Yeah, well, my knee says differently."

"Not meaning anything by it. Just that when a man can still walk on his own two legs, then he shouldn't let life pass him by. If you can't do a big city cop job anymore, and seeing how you're now in a small town, then maybe you ought to consider working in law enforcement around these parts. I think you'd make a great sheriff."

Mitch had to admit the idea of working again interested him. Could he lift a gun again? "I couldn't do any worse than what you already have. But guess it's too bad that position is already filled and I don't seem to be family."

"Small towns. We run differently than big cities. Sheriff can be voted out of office if a good candidate arrived. Think about it."

"If I were staying, I'd give it some thought. Since I'm only passing through, you're stuck with Ridgeley for however long he decides."

Marly's father pulled up and parked on the side of the building before getting out and heading toward them. After shaking hands with Maddy, he turned to Mitch and offered him a handshake as well. "Marly will have my head, Mitch, if I don't give you a ride back to her house. Seeing how your truck is in the air, I guess you need it."

"Yes, sir, if you don't mind." Mitch faced Maddy and shook his hand. "I'll wait for your call. Appreciate you fixing her for me."

"Gives me a paycheck. Just remember, Mitch, we take care of our own here. Not everyone is like Howie and Ridgeley."

Ol' Joe climbed into the driver's seat while Mitch sat in the passenger seat.

"Appreciate the lift home, Ol' Joe." Home? It wasn't his home. Where did that come from? "I mean, back to Marly's house," Mitch corrected.

"Not a problem. Listen, I have an old car at my

139

house just sitting around collecting dust. You're welcome to borrow it until Maddy gets your truck fixed."

"Really? That'd be great so I don't have to burden Marly for rides."

"It's no prize, but it'll get you where you got to go."

Mitch rolled down his window. "I'm in no position to be picky. If it has four wheels and runs, I'm happy. And grateful. Thank you."

Joe's eyes offered a warning. "Not much I can do about my wife force feeding you breakfast. So be a smart man and just eat."

Mitch laughed. "Okay. Will do."

Ol' Joe drove with a steady pace along the winding roads. "Marly wouldn't let me come over to the house yesterday after you found Howie's body. She said everything was under control."

Control. There it was again. Marly and control.

"Considering the sheriff and the ME took their sweet time removing the body, it was pretty much under control. Nothing anyone could really do."

"How's she holding up?" Joe asked, his paternal concern written all over his face.

"She's herself. Didn't take me long to figure out that Marly likes to do everything on her own. I'm sure it bothers her, but she's strong for Jeremy's sake."

"Her mom and I believe she does everything on her own as a defense mechanism. If she doesn't depend on anyone, then she can't get hurt if they disappear for whatever reason. She wanted to prove to herself that she could be a good mom. Then she had to prove to herself that she could fill Rick's shoes. Now she has to prove to herself that she can juggle work, horses, house, and Jeremy because she believes she will always be alone."

Mitch shrugged. "She's a beautiful woman, if you don't mind me saying so. She could easily meet someone. She doesn't have to be alone."

"And you don't have to be on the run from your past, but sometimes we do things just because we do them."

Mitch stared at him. His private life had never been so open for everyone to comment on. Now strangers knew more about his life than close friends back home did.

"Don't look at me like I have three heads, boy. News travels fast in these parts and if you think I wouldn't do some background checks with you staying at my little girl's house then you're crazy."

Mitch smirked. "You're the one who approved of me staying there."

"Exactly. And only because my gut said you were a good person. Any good father would do some checking." Joe laughed. "And as a good father, I have to ask you one question."

Mitch knew where this was headed. It just didn't pay to discover dead bodies. "I'm listening."

"Did you kill Howie? Now before you answer, this is between you and me. I'd just like to know so I could shake your hand for getting that bastard off my daughter's back."

Mitch smirked. Small towns and their way of dealing with things. "After realizing how much of a scumbag this Howie guy was to Marly, I really wish I could say that I put an end to it for her. But I wasn't.

Even though I'm no longer an officer, I still respect the law."

Joe only shrugged. "Had to ask. At least you being here gives her mom and I a little peace of mind. But don't tell Marly that or she'll be throwing you out the door thinking I set up a babysitter for her."

How true that was. "I can definitely see her doing that."

Ol' Joe turned into his driveway. "Remember, I warned you."

As promised, Bethany fed Mitch a breakfast of pancakes, bacon, grits, and a bottomless cup of coffee.

"Doc Peterson has an office in town. Very nice man," Bethany said. "Now that you have a set of wheels, Mitch, make an appointment to get that leg checked."

"I'm fine, Bethany. But thanks for the info. My doctors said I just had to keep up with my physical therapy."

"Now, I didn't ask if you'd be fine. You can call and make an appointment, or I will for you," she said simply, removing dishes from the table and setting them in the sink.

"She will, too," Joe confirmed.

Bethany's eyes narrowed, earning a squirm from Mitch. "I'm a mother, and a mother knows when a person needs to see a doctor. That limp is not good, Mitch. Doc Peterson will help you. If you don't call and I find out, you will definitely need a doctor, understand?"

"Yes, ma'am. I promise I'll call," Mitch conceded, seeing a part of Marly in the older woman. "I enjoyed breakfast. Thank you." Because it seemed like the thing to do, he kissed her cheek. "And thank you, Joe, for the use of the car. Appreciate it."

He left with a full belly and a well-chewed ear. From his shirt pocket, he took out the small piece of paper that Bethany wrote Doc Peterson's number on. He laughed. Now he understood where Marly got her backbone. He carefully made a mental note not to forget that phone call.

Returning to Marly's house, Mitch stopped on the porch.

"Shit." He realized that he had no keys to the house. "Small towns. No, she wouldn't. Would she?" Mitch walked to the door to check if it was unlocked.

"She did. Hey, Jack," Mitch said as the dog greeted him.

Son of a bitch! Marly left the door unlocked with only her friendly dog to watch the house. Mitch contemplated speaking to her about that safety concern. Maybe now that a dead man had been found on her property, he could convince her to be a little more careful.

"Come on, Jack. I need to piss like a racehorse after all that coffee Bethany gave me."

****

The school bus had broken down and Marly had to pick Jeremy up from school. It was one more chore to add to her busy schedule. She didn't mind since it was a treat to see her son right after school. Working full time didn't allow her a lot of opportunity for that.

Jeremy talked a mile a minute about his day. There was his science project he received an A on.

And the homerun he made at recess during a game of kickball. Then one of the frogs in his homeroom escaped the aquarium and all the kids laughed so hard they took forever to catch him.

At the house, Mitch was waiting. What a strange feeling to come home to a man.

"Hey, Mitch," Jeremy exclaimed, running to him.

"Hey, buddy. Marly."

She just smiled.

Jeremy stood in front of Mitch, talking quickly. "The bus broke down and Mom had to drive me. I got an A on my science report, you know the one you helped me with. I got a homerun at kickball and Danny was so mad because he wasn't on my team and my homerun made us win. We came inside from recess and Gilbert, he's our classroom frog, kinda like a mascot, well, he got loose and it took six tries to catch him."

Marly watched as Mitch gave Jeremy his complete attention. He didn't feign interest but was truly intrigued with Jeremy's tale. Marly's heart melted as the two shared the highlights of her son's day. Mitch laughed when Jeremy illustrated the frog's adventure.

Marly brought her hand to her lips. She moved to the kitchen doorway to enjoy the interaction from afar, offering them privacy for man talk. After watching for a few minutes, she prepared a snack for Jeremy, pouring a glass of milk and one for Mitch. She placed the glasses on the table with some cookies. On cue, Jeremy and Mitch strolled into the kitchen and, without being told, sat and enjoyed the snack, forgetting she was there while they switched their conversation to fishing.

"Mom, can I take Mitch down to the pond to fish? Please?"

Marly shot a glance to Mitch. "That's entirely up to him, honey. He's a big boy and can make up his mind if he'd like to go fishing."

"Yeah, but can I go?"

"Oh. Is that what you're asking?"

Mitch smirked and whispered to Jeremy. "Told you nothing would get by her."

"Mom," Jeremy begged.

"Okay. I'll make a deal with you. Both of you."

Mitch raised a brow and looked her way. "What'd I do?"

"Nothing. Yet." She turned her attention to her son. "No swimming. I don't care how warm you think it is. It's still too cool for swimming."

"Got it."

"And," she continued, Jeremy rolling his eyes. "You come home and get that room of yours clean. There's probably a small family of aliens living under that clutter. And do all your homework."

"Okay," Jeremy groaned the words.

"And, Mitch? Don't overdo that leg. Call it quits if it bothers you. I'm sure Jeremy would understand." For assurance, she sent a look at her son that said he'd better understand.

"Got it," Mitch said, mimicking Jeremy's words. "So we can go fishing?"

"Sure. Have fun and be back by five o'clock for dinner."

****

Mitch and Jeremy walked slowly to the pond, which would have only been about a five-minute brisk walk, but with Mitch's leg it took about fifteen.

"You know you have a pretty cool mom to let you go fishing before you clean your room or do your homework."

Jeremy climbed onto a rock and settled his tackle box. He got to work wrapping shiny bait on the line. Mitch hadn't fished in years, probably not since he was Jeremy's age. But he got the hang of it quick enough and soon they were sitting on the cold rock with their poles hanging over the water.

"What are we going to do if we catch something? Keep it or throw it back?" Mitch asked.

"Throw it back. Mom won't cook it."

"No." Mitch laughed. "I didn't think she would want to clean a fish and smell up her house to cook it."

"Are you in love with my mom?"

The question stunned Mitch. He stared at the kid, his mouth opened wide, but it took a while for the words to come out. "Now why would you think that? I've just met you guys. People don't fall in love that quickly."

"My best friend Danny has an older sister who met this boy on a Friday and the next day she was in love."

Mitch laughed. "And you thought that's what happens with adults, too?"

He shrugged his shoulders. "I guess."

"Well, it doesn't. I think your mom is a wonderful lady, very pretty as a matter of fact, but I'm not in love with her." His heart pounded for no apparent reason. Odd.

Jeremy didn't respond so Mitch waited him out. After a few minutes of silence, Mitch decided to keep the conversation going.

"You know, Jeremy, I'm sure that someday there will be a man who falls in love with your mother. How's that going to make you feel?"

"She should have someone to play with."

Mitch choked on a laugh. The kid certainly could choose his words.

"I have Danny and my dog, but Mom doesn't have anyone. And since you came, she's been smiling and, I don't know, different."

Mitch was prying, but his curiosity couldn't help him. "Different? Like how?"

"She's been taking a long time to get dressed. Now, she's putting on makeup and perfume. She messes with her hair and I hear her cursing it."

"She does smell pretty. And her hair always looks nice, so I don't know why she fuses with it," Mitch said, thrilled to have an inside scoop on the fascinating woman.

"I never knew my dad and never had a guy live in the house before. I know you're only staying for a little while. But I thought if you liked it then I should tell you, since Granddad always tells me I'm the man of the house, that if you were in love with Mom then that was okay with me."

Mitch's heart swelled, a feeling he'd never experienced before. "I'll tell you what, buddy. If my feelings for your mom change, I'll be sure to talk to you first, since you are indeed the man of the house, and see if we can come to an understanding. Deal?"

147

"Deal. Wow! Did you see that? I got one." Jeremy pointed to the water. From the pull on the line, it was a big one.

"Reel it in, kid. Pull back," Mitch shouted commands as Jeremy struggled.

"What…do…you…think…I'm…doing?" Jeremy panted.

Mitch so badly wanted to take the pole to help, but this was Jeremy's catch and he either had to bring it in himself or lose it.

"Pull straight up," Mitch commanded.

"I am. But it's not working. Mitch, help me! I don't want to lose it."

That's all he needed to hear. Mitch stood behind Jeremy and, without taking the pole, placed his hands over Jeremy's and guided him to pull, twist, reel. After what seemed like forever, the fish was out of the water and Jeremy screamed with pride. Mitch sat again.

"We did it, Mitch! We did it!"

Mitch's heart melted. He could deny it to himself and everyone around, but his heart wouldn't lie. This kid and his mom were sucking Mitch quickly into their lives. If he wasn't careful, he'd have to admit that not only was he falling in love with Marly but with her son, too. "Great job. He's a big one."

Jeremy beamed with pride as he struggled to hold on to the wiggling fish. "Biggest I ever caught."

"Me too."

"Guess I better throw him back so he'll live." Jeremy's small fingers quickly released the hook from the bass' mouth and set him in the water to float away. "You're my witness. You'll have to tell Mom and Danny that I caught a big one."

"You tell them. I'll back you up." He tasseled his hair. "Don't know about you kid but my ass is stiff from sitting on this rock. Wanna head back?"

"Yeah, my ass is stiff, too."

Mitch glared at him. "Get your tackle box and come on. You know, you're going to get me in trouble with your mom if you keep talking like that. Then I'll never get to second base."

"Second base? You're going to play baseball with Mom?"

Mitch winced. "Um. Something like that."

"Then I want to play, too."

Once he was steady on his feet, Mitch stared at him. "Boy can I put my foot in my mouth. Look, kid, it was a figure of speech. It's not really playing baseball."

Jeremy stared at Mitch like he had three heads.

"Aw, shit. Come on. Let's walk. I'll explain on the way home, but this is man talk. Women, like your mom, really shouldn't know how men talk about women."

"Why not?"

Mitch grinned. "Because it's more fun when they're trying to figure us out."

"I don't get it," Jeremy said, innocently.

"Neither do I, but I know it's like a law in the female's world that they have to figure out men. You see…it's like this."

They walked slowly and, this time, Jeremy didn't complain that they walked slower than a snail. He hung on every word Mitch said, with some giggles and eewws and yuks thrown in.

Jack trailed behind them slowly.

149

Chapter Twelve

Hostage situation ends in tragedy.

The headline flashed across the computer screen. For the last hour, Marly had scanned old articles from the online Massachusetts newspapers. Reading the article dated six months earlier, she was stunned at the revelations.

Detective Mitch Allen, a highly decorated officer in the Boston Police Department, has been upgraded from serious to stable condition after being wounded when his tactical team attempted to defuse a hostage situation. A gunman holed up in a liquor store after a botched robbery held two female customers at gunpoint.

After five hours, negotiations broke down. The tactical team, led by Allen, rushed the store and was greeted by a hail of bullets. Three officers, including Allen, were shot but all are expected to recover. One hostage survived her wounds. The other, a seventeen-year-old girl, was pronounced dead at the scene.

What was a seventeen-year-old doing in a liquor store to begin with?

An independent review by the Attorney General's Office and Internal Affairs found the officers followed procedure and no disciplinary action was taken.

A picture of Mitch with four fellow officers was above the article. He looked different, younger. He still had the same build, but his hair had grown and his face was no longer clean-shaven as it was in the year-old picture.

Such a transformation for a man in less than a year's time. Then again, what a tragedy to experience first-hand. He had tried to save lives and almost lost his in exchange.

Now that she understood his ghosts, maybe she could help him lose them.

Reading the articles reminded her of the stories that ran in the local papers for months after Rick had been killed. Being the only serviceman from this area to die in combat gave Rick an after death famous reputation. His story headlined for so long that Marly stopped reading the newspapers or watching the news. It was probably a good thing Mitch wouldn't stay in town. There was no way Marly could ever have another man in her life with a dangerous job, where death chased him daily. And then caught up.

Jack barked outside in the distance. Marly strolled to her window and spotted the dog racing back and forth from the house to the field. Mitch walked with his hand loosely across Jeremy's shoulders. The sight of the man and her little boy warmed her heart. They looked like best buddies, out wasting away the lazy hours of a day. How she wished Jeremy could've had that with his own dad. Her eyes threatened to water with painful memories. Doing the final preparations for dinner would keep her mind off of the past.

Mitch and Jeremy sauntered through the front

door as Marly entered the living room. Neither man nor boy sported any visible injuries, a good sign that Jeremy hadn't had a boyhood mishap.

"Mom, I caught the biggest fish. You should have seen it. It was this big." Jeremy illustrated using his stretched out arms. "Ask Mitch. He had to help reel it in."

"Is that so? Then you both must've worked up an appetite. Go wash up, guys. Dinner's ready. I made something simple tonight. Hope you guys don't mind."

"Not at all. Food is food. Right, buddy?" Mitch asked, eyeing Jeremy.

"Right."

They disappeared upstairs with Jack right behind them.

Marly had cooked grilled cheese sandwiches with slices of tomatoes. Since Jeremy was so adamant about not eating veggies, she used any opportunity to get them into his diet. All she could hope is that he was famished enough to chow down the sandwich before discovering the hidden tomato.

Mitch and Jeremy returned, debating something about football and which team would go to the championship this year.

"You're outta your mind, kid, if you think your team has a chance at winning against mine. We've been hot for years while your team has fizzled."

"No way. We got the first round draft pick and we were in second place last season."

They took their seats, so immersed in their conversation that they forgot Marly was there. When she placed sandwiches in front of them, she gave them credit for continuing the debate while scooping up the grilled cheese and eating.

"Hah! What's a first round pick going to do if the quarterback can't find the receiver in the end zone? And they were in second place by the hair on their chin. Besides, second place is still a loser either way you look at it," Mitch debated.

Mitch was the first to realize Marly was watching them. Jeremy followed his stare. "Something wrong?" Mitch asked.

"No. Just trying to follow along with this football stuff. Jeremy's been teaching me, but it just doesn't make sense."

"Yeah, she still calls the quarterback the pitcher." He giggled and clutched his stomach in a dramatic fashion.

Marly's chin dropped as they laughed at her. "It's not nice to make fun of your mom, you know. I might forget to make someone's favorite dessert tonight."

"Brownies? Yes!" Jeremy was half way through his sandwich when he discovered the tomatoes. "Mom! Geez. Why'd you have to put these things in here? They're nasty."

Marly braced herself for an argument but, before she could respond, Mitch simply shut Jeremy's sandwich before he removed the dreaded tomato.

"Stop your whining and eat. They're not that bad."

"Says you."

"Yup." Mitch shoved the last bit of sandwich in his mouth.

When Jeremy finished the entire sandwich, tomatoes and all, Marly was in awe.

"Kid, why don't you go tackle your homework

and your room like you promised? I want to talk to your mom."

"Okay." Jeremy brought his plate to the sink and kissed his mom's cheek when she sat at the table. To Mitch he spoke softly. "Are you going to play baseball with her?"

Mitch laughed. "Get out of here." Jeremy ran out with Jack.

"Play baseball? With your bum leg? Is he out of his mind?"

Mitch cleared his throat. "Oh. Yeah. That. Well, you see, um." He dragged a hand through his hair. "Me and Jeremy kind of had a talk on the way back. Man to man."

"Oh? And what did this conversation entail?" His woodsy cologne teased her, creating a vision of her nibbling from his neck to his jaw.

"Not much that you haven't already covered with him, you know, birds and bees stuff."

Alarm bells rang inside her head. "What kind of man talk did you add to that, Mitch?"

"I just explained first base, second base, you know, that stuff."

"How much of that stuff?"

"To the homerun part."

She glared at him, debating whether to strangle him or kick him.

"What was I to do, Marly? The kid had questions he didn't feel comfortable asking his mom. Look. Sometimes guys needs to talk to guys about certain things."

"He knows he can ask his grandfather or his uncle."

"Please. A kid Jeremy's age hardly feels comfortable talking to a man my age let alone to a man your father's age. No offense to your father."

She stood. "I should talk to him. Make sure he doesn't have any more questions."

Mitch stood and grasped her arm to keep her in front of him. "Oh, yeah, that's a great plan. You'll mortally embarrass the kid and scar him for life if he knows you know what we talked about. It's a guy thing. Just leave it at that."

"I'm his mother. I should be the one to talk to him."

"And you have. But you can't be both a mother and a father, as much as you want to, and Jeremy knows that. I thought it was best to be honest with him when he started asking questions. I know you don't lie to him, so I didn't want to either."

"But—"

Holding her arms, he shook his head. "Jesus, Marly. This is what I mean about control. I was put on the spot when he asked questions and wanted to do the right thing and answer him truthfully. Stop trying to handle every detail of your life and his on your own. Please, don't make a big deal of it. Just accept that I had a talk with him and he's good with it."

She hesitated, thought it over. "Okay. I'll let it go. And you can let me go, too."

He kept her in front of him, only slightly easing his grip. His hands rubbed her arms as he stared into her eyes. She wanted to tell him to stop but, more than that, she wanted to tell him to continue rubbing those strong hands over her entire body. The slight touch of his skin on hers gave her goose bumps. The ones that

155

drove her crazy with desire and need. She didn't want the thrilling sensation to stop.

"I don't want to let go. I want to go to first base."

"We've already done that. Remember the kisses?"

"Couldn't forget them if I wanted to. But they were hardly long kisses." He grinned wickedly. "I want to go to first base again then second base. Maybe we'll aim for third."

As tempting as it would be to have his hungry hands roam her body, Jeremy could walk in any minute.

"Don't worry. He complained about having a ton of no-good homework."

Without any further hesitation, Mitch bent down and took her mouth, hard. She melted into his arms, leaning her weight into his. He pulled away, staring into her eyes, and grinned. His hand came up to the back of her neck and fisted in her hair, pulling her mouth back up to his. Pure animal need raced through her, blinding her, erasing her thoughts. Only Mitch filled her head. His hand, tough and strong, brushed along the side of her sweater, tugging it until it came free from her pants. Without a moment's hesitation, his hand found her breast and cupped it hard and eagerly.

She moaned. God, she wanted this. Hadn't she wanted it the moment she set eyes on him, standing in her living room looking so lost and out of place? But she couldn't have it now. No. It had to wait. She couldn't risk Jeremy walking in and didn't want any interruptions. "Mitch." Her tone was heavy and deep. He kept his hand under her shirt, his thumb flicking over the nipple. The strain in her voice showed how undone she had become. It didn't sound like her voice.

"Please don't say no. I want you. God, I want to hit a homerun with you, Marly."

His gaze captured hers and held. She thoroughly enjoyed the baseball lingo. It was unique, something that was theirs.

"I'm not saying no. But we can't do this. Not in my kitchen. Not with Jeremy here."

"I understand." Without hesitation, he removed his hand and fixed her sweater.

Pulling her close once more, he devoured her mouth, his tongue whipping inside, stealing her breath as she braced for more. The hardness of his lips on hers only added to her pleasure. That searing, hot kiss proved his desire for her but ended way too quickly.

With a step backward, he increased the space between them. "When I make love to you, Marly, we won't be getting much sleep that night." He retreated to the front door.

"Mitch?" He faced her, one hand on the screen door and the other grasping his cane. "When we make love, I guarantee you'll hit a grand slam."

His smile flashed to light up his whole face. "I like a woman who knows her baseball."

The screen door slammed behind him. Marly rubbed her flushed cheeks and poured a glass of water, even if it wouldn't distinguish the fire in her belly and everywhere else.

"And I like a man who can last nine innings, Mitch Allen." She watched him from the window, letting the evening breeze blow over his face. The air wouldn't be cool enough to cool him off.

Mitch Allen was good for her. And for her son. But would that be enough for him stick around longer than the sheriff needed?

Only time would tell. Marly would make the best of that time. She grinned wickedly, sexy images floating in her mind as she baked brownies.

Chapter Thirteen

Mitch made a doctor's appointment since Bethany had insisted he should be under medical care. When Mitch called, Doc Peterson was very understanding and even had an early morning cancellation.

Mitch arrived ahead of time for his appointment and completed the required forms that Doc Peterson's secretary handed him. The small waiting area had a television, magazines and a massive fish tank. It didn't smell of antiseptic like the hospital had during his recovery. God, how he hated that medicinal smell.

"Good morning, Mr. Allen. Sorry to keep you waiting. I'm Doc Peterson. Follow me, please," the fifty-ish year-old tall, lean man said before disappearing into a hallway.

Mitch did as instructed and entered an exam room.

"Why don't you have a seat on the table? Be careful now."

Mitch sat facing the man. God, how he hated these appointments.

Doc Peterson took a few minutes to review the medical records had Mitch brought with him. "Got to say, it's not every day a patient comes in with their medical records in tow. Pretty extensive injuries you suffered, Mr. Allen."

"Mitch. Please just call me Mitch."

"Very well. Remove your shirt. I'll take a look at the shoulder injury first." Mitch disrobed quickly. "Says you were shot. From the looks of this scar, I'd say that's about right."

"Yeah."

"Any residual pain?"

"Not in the shoulder. Just the knee."

"We'll get to that in a minute. This scar may fade a little with time, but I'm afraid that you'll have it for life. Looks like you have normal mobility. Now the knee."

Doc Peterson stared at Mitch who was really confused as to why. "What, Doc?"

"Use your head, boy. I can't very well check your knee through your jeans. So get them off."

Mitch grimaced, hating this part. He wasn't shy about taking off his clothes. Hell, hundreds of nurses and medical staff saw his naked body those weeks they tended him. It was the searing pain that came from the prodding the doctor would do. Mitch sat, naked except for his boxers and socks, as nervous as a schoolboy getting his balls checked for the first time.

Doc Peterson studied both knees without touching them. He scribbled notes in Mitch's new file.

"Lift this one up," he said pointing to the good leg. "Lift it straight up as far as it will go."

Mitch complied.

"Good. Now the other one."

Mitch hesitated, but did so. He could only lift it inches before pain seared up his leg like wild fire. He gritted his teeth.

"I bet that hurts."

"No. It friggin' tickles," Mitch growled, dropping his leg back down before remembering his manners. "Sorry, Doc. Pain gets so bad, I lose my mind sometimes."

"I'd expect no less from a man suffering like you are. How long have you had this pain?" "Since my injury six months ago."

"At any point did it get worse?"

"Yeah. When I started physical therapy, but the therapist told me I had to work through the pain."

"Idiots," Doc said, his fingers pressing above the swollen knee. "See this. I'll be gentle."

When he pushed down, the skin turned yellowish and the indent remained for a long time after he released the pressure.

"What about it? That's done that since the injury."

"No, it hasn't," Doc said, sternly.

Mitch crossed his brows. "What? Now you want to tell me how my knee has been all along? Before you knew me? This appointment is over."

When Mitch started to slide off of the table, the doctor placed his hand on his good shoulder and issued orders. "You'll stay put. I'll say when this appointment is over. Now pay attention. Your knee is badly infected. That's why you're in so much pain. Some pain is expected right after surgery but, as you get stronger, the pain should subside. Don't get me wrong. You'll probably always have some pain, worse some days than others. But it shouldn't be like this."

"An infection? How in the world would I have

gotten an infection?"

"They're very common after surgery," the doctor stated, writing on a prescription pad. "Here's a prescription for a very strong antibiotic. Get it filled at Macy's Prescription across the street right away."

"Thanks. If this cures my pain, I'll be forever indebted to you," Mitch said, standing up to put his pants back on. And to Bethany.

"Don't get dressed yet. We're not done."

All Mitch could think was that this guy was slipping on some latex gloves, lubing one and telling him to bend over. Mitch wasn't in the mood to have the boys checked out.

"I think we are. I only needed the knee checked, nothing else."

The doctor laughed. "Men are big babies when it comes to a simple prostate test. But that's not scheduled for you today."

Mitch breathed a sigh of relief.

"Although what I have to do to that knee will make a finger test look really good."

The blood drained from Mitch's face. "What do you have to do?"

"Drain some of that fluid from the knee. That way the antibiotic shot I give you, and the prescription, will have a fighting chance."

"Shot? I need a shot, too?"

"Let me guess. You're afraid of needles, too? Men." The stern man lambasted.

Mitch stuck his jaw out. "I didn't say that. Just didn't know that was part of the plan." So what if he hated needles. Who could blame him after everything he'd been through?

"Lay down while I set things up. It'll take me less than five minutes to drain the fluid. I'll send it off to the lab to identify the infection so we can be sure I'm treating it with the correct antibiotic. Then I'll give you the shot and you'll be on your way. My guess is that by tonight you'll feel much better and improve each day after."

Wouldn't that be nice? Diminished pain. He'd take that. He lay down and waited for the doctor to start.

With unbelievable tenderness, Doc Peterson numbed the area around his knee, scrubbed it with disinfectant, and inserted a thin needle attached to a large tube. Mitch only felt a faint pinch. In keeping with his word, the procedure was done in less than five minutes.

"Now for the hardest part. Need you to stand up, Mitch, be very careful on the bad knee since it's numb. Then bend over."

Damn! He had a feeling he would hear those words out of the doc's mouth. But at least it was only for a shot.

Doc Peterson tugged his boxers down, wiped the skin with alcohol, and landed the needle deep in the muscle. Mitch's ass was on fire. He fisted his hands to deal with the pain and keep from yelling out.

"What the hell kind of shot is that, Doc. Acid? That kills."

"All done. Fill your prescription immediately and start it as soon as you can. This shot will at least introduce the medicine to your bloodstream quickly and start fighting the infection. The injection site may be sore for a few days."

"No shit," Mitch complained, getting dressed.

"I want to see you back here in a week. Don't forget. And, of course, call me if it gets worse. But I think you'll be pleased by tonight."

"Thank you, Doc. I think." Mitch winced.

When they walked out to the reception area, Sheriff Ridgeley was waiting for them.

"Morning, Doc Peterson," the sheriff said.

"Sheriff. What brings you here? Are you ill?"

In the head maybe, Mitch thought, and ignored the sheriff who blocked his exit.

"Nope. Heard this guy was getting a checkup."

"Is that a crime?" Mitch snarled.

"No, but murder is. Tell me, does an officer with your background and experience know the difference between a homicide and an accidental shooting?"

"If you're referring to the Singleton shooting—that was not accidental. That was murder."

"Exactly."

"Cut the shit, Sheriff. Why are you riding my ass like I'm your enemy? I don't recall giving you cause to bust my balls."

"Depends on how you see it."

"Whatever happened to professional courtesy? Thought you southern boys were taught manners down here?" Mitch said between clenched teeth.

"We're also taught to take care of our own. Which you're not." The snide remark only reminded Mitch that he didn't call Courtsville home, even if Marly had welcomed him more than anywhere else he'd ever been.

"Okay. So you don't like me. I can live with that. But unless you came here to talk to me specifically

about something, then this conversation is over."
Mitch picked up his cane to leave.

"I wouldn't seek you out otherwise. I'm a busy
man and not into making social calls on work time.
The ME got back to me with the autopsy results," the
sheriff said, keeping his fat body in front of Mitch.

"Let me guess. The guy died of a gunshot to the
head. That was pretty fucking obvious."

"Look, Allen, you're testing my patience."

"And you mine, Sheriff." Mitch stood still. "Get
to the point."

"The point is Howard was killed by a small
caliber weapon."

"Didn't look that way to me. Looked like a
magnum, or around that size."

"We found the weapon near the body."

Mitch paused, thinking back. "Funny. I don't
recall seeing a gun. A man with my experience
would've noticed that immediately. But go ahead, I'm
listening."

"Guess you didn't look close enough. Or maybe
you're losing your touch. Ran the necessary tests to be
sure the bullet matched the gun and it did. And the gun
was registered."

Mitch was losing patience with the sheriff.
"Good. Then the owner probably took out your victim
and was stupid enough to leave behind the evidence.
Sounds like you have an airtight case."

The sheriff's grin was pure evil. "I thought you'd
think that. What would you say if I told you the gun
was owned and registered to Marly?"

Mitch froze. No way was this true. There had to
be another reason. "Come on, Sheriff. I've only been

165

here a few days and can already tell that Marly wouldn't kill that man."

"Maybe she had a good reason."

"Then she would've called you once she could."

"Just because she owned the gun, doesn't mean she shot it. Could've been someone else," Ridgeley theorized.

"What are you getting at, Sheriff?" Mitch had played these head games with suspects before.

"Mitch Allen, you're under arrest for the murder of Howie Singleton."

"Are you serious? That's fucking ridiculous and you know it."

"Turn around and put your hands behind your back. If you resist, you'll make it worse for yourself."

"Sheriff," Doc Peterson interrupted. "This man is a patient of mine and just had a procedure done. You need to see to it that his knee is not further injured."

"Then he'll follow my instructions, won't you, Allen?"

Mitch glared at him. He handed his cane to Peterson and slowly turned around, with his hands behind his back. This was a first for him. He was used to putting the cuffs on, not wearing them. Ridgeley lost no time cuffing him. Mitch winced when he over-tightened the links, but he refused to give him the satisfaction of knowing he hurt him.

After he was read his rights, rights he'd recited to people hundreds of times, he was escorted out to the sheriff's car. Immediately, the spectacle was of interest to the townspeople. Mitch ignored their glares and finger pointing.

The ride was a short one to the station a few

blocks up the street. But Mitch's ass, knee, and wrists hurt so the ride felt like forever.

"Would you be willing to take a gun residue test, Allen?"

Mitch's jaw clenched. "Tell me the time and the place. While you're at it, why don't you do the same for Marly? I'm sure she'd pass as well," he demanded from the backseat.

"Right this way then," the sheriff announced, opening the back door. "Way ahead of you. Marly's already here. That's how I knew where to find you."

Mitch followed the sheriff into a back room where Marly sat pale faced.

"Mitch! They think I shot Howie. Can you believe that? Why are you cuffed?"

"Don't worry. Sheriff was nice enough to arrest me for murder. Their fancy tests will tell them otherwise and then we'll be allowed to leave. It's procedure," Mitch said, deliberately throwing the sheriff's words back at him.

Marly stood up. "What? Why would you? You didn't even know Howie."

"Go with Deputy Johnston, Allen. He'll do the test. By the way, Marly you passed. I won't be arresting you. You're free to go."

"I'll be waiting for Mitch," she said, hands on her hips, chin out.

"You'll be waiting a while seeing as he's under arrest and will need to post bond. I've already spoken with the judge. Probably doesn't have that kind of money in his pocket." Arrogance flowed from the fat sheriff.

Mitch smiled at Marly. "I'll be okay. Don't

worry. You know I'm innocent."

Another deputy pulled him to the back and they disappeared.

"You know, Marly, you shouldn't be so free to open your door to men you don't know," Sheriff Ridgeley lectured.

"Gee, Sheriff, that's very nice of you to be concerned for my safety considering you've never been in the past. Never once did you take seriously any of the reports I filed about being stalked by Howie."

"Now come on, dear. The man pissed off everyone. Can't bring him in for being in the same places as you."

"I wasn't born yesterday. I know Howie was your cousin. I understand all about family ties, no matter how disturbing, and what that means around here. So I believe you had a sense of duty to Howie more than to me and allowed him to continue harassing me. Tell me, Sheriff, where's the justice there?"

"Are you accusing me of not doing my job?"

"I'm telling you that you didn't do your job. Not when it came to my complaints or a hundred others. In the end, someone finally got pissed off enough and took the law into their own hands. I'll tell you another thing, it wasn't my houseguest or me. Do your job and find out who trespassed on my land. You owe me that much."

"And I'm giving you that. This man is being charged so my job is done." He thumbed toward Mitch as he walked back into the room witnessing the heated words.

"Sheriff, you've got the wrong man," Marly complained. "I reported that gun stolen months ago.

Mitch wasn't even here then so how would he have it to use on Howie?"

"Maybe you filed a false police report. There are laws against that. I may have to open up a separate investigation," the sheriff warned.

"Intimidating a lady doesn't suit you, Ridgeley. You're bordering on pathetic," Mitch said.

"And you're facing life in prison, maybe even death row, so you should be more worried about yourself, Allen."

"The way I see it, you have a hell of a case to prove against me. Meanwhile, the real killer roams Courtsville. You know how small town gossip works. By the end of the day, you'll have mass panic on your hands and be out of a job."

The sheriff laughed. "No one will be worried since your sorry ass will be locked up. You can't make bail so you won't kill again."

"Who says I can't make bail?"

Marly interrupted. "Mitch, I'm posting your bail. Just tell me an amount, Sheriff, and don't even think about making it outrageous."

Mitch stared. She didn't have the money for this. But the offer swelled his heart.

The fat bastard's evil grin split across his face. "The deed to your property would be sufficient."

"No way, Marly," Mitch said, shock consuming him.

"Mitch, shut up," she said with no heat. "Show me where to sign and take those foolish cuffs off him. He's not a threat to anyone."

Marly signed the bail form while a deputy roughly removed the cuffs.

"There. Let's go home, Mitch. You better have sufficient evidence, Sheriff, or I promise you…by the time Mitch's contacts in the FBI finish tearing apart your office, you'll be in the unemployment line and I'll have Mitch sitting in your office."

That was twice he'd been considered a contender for the sheriff's job.

The sheriff's pudgy face reddened. "Go. But I'm warning both of you, don't leave town. Not even for an hour or I'll have every uniform in these parts scouring the roads for you. Don't forget you have a son to take care of."

Mitch's voice was raw, edged with danger. "You keep Jeremy out of this or I promise to make your life a living hell."

"Are you threatening an officer?" the sheriff asked, pushing his big belly at Mitch.

"No, sir. I'm making a promise to an asshole. Just try me, Sheriff. My lawyer will be in touch to discuss your evidence against me…or lack thereof."

Mitch grasped Marly's elbow and led her out of the office.

"I'll drive you back to Doc Peterson's for your car," Marly said, her temper dissipating. "I can just forget the rest of the workday. I can't believe he charged you with murder and that my stolen gun was used. Sounds too damn easy."

Mitch shrugged. "Of course it is. I'm an easy target as an outsider. He pegs the murder on a stranger and then he doesn't have to do an actual investigation. There's no evidence so it'll be cleared up soon. But why lose a day's pay or interrupt your schedule for that jerk? I can't believe you told me to shut up." He smiled.

She sighed hard. "I'm sorry. My temper had been pushed too far."

"You were damn good back there. Would it be a bad thing to admit it turned me on?"

She laughed. "You're crazy, you know that?"

"Been told that a few times. So I have scary FBI friends?"

Marly laughed again. "Sounded good to me. Give him something to think about before messing with you anymore. Hey, how come he didn't drop the charges after the residue test like he did for me?"

They parked next to where he left his car. "Um, because they found residue. Means I shot a gun recently."

Her eyes widened and stared. "But how? You didn't shoot him."

"I'm an ex-cop. I went to target practice the week before I arrived here just to keep in shape. Residue sticks around for a while. Unfortunately, it doesn't prove I didn't use the gun in the murder."

"So now what?"

"I've got to get myself a lawyer since the sheriff won't drop the charges." Mitch grimaced.

"I'll talk to my brother. He's got some contacts," Marly offered, her eyes showing her exhaustion.

"I'm being set up. My guess is the sheriff will run me out of town in exchange for dropping the charges."

Her pretty eyes blinked twice. "He can't do that. You should be able to leave when you decide to."

His hand covered hers, his thumb rubbing her knuckles. "I know. Thank you for bailing me out. I'm not leaving until this murder is solved and you can get on with your life." And he wasn't leaving until he figured out what he'd do with his life.

"I just don't want the sheriff to put an innocent man in jail."

"You made sure he didn't by bailing me out. I won't put your property in jeopardy. With my experience, I'll shadow this investigation until I solve it."

"That's more than what Ridgeley will do. I don't trust him, Mitch. I don't want him to pull anything on you."

"Too late. He's framed me quite nicely for his cousin's murder."

"We'll get through this. Just tell me what you need me to do. By the way, how did the doctor's appointment go?"

Mitch shivered. "Like hell. There is an infection in my leg causing the pain. Remind me to thank your mom."

"Mom's do know best."

"That's for sure. Doc drained my knee, gave me a shot in the ass, and a prescription for antibiotics."

"Doc Peterson is the best. I'm glad you saw him."

"He said there was a pharmacy around here," Mitch said, glancing around.

"Sure is. Right across the street." Her slender finger pointed to a small white building.

"I'll fill it before heading back to the house. Have to take it right away."

"Good boy," Marly said, leaning over to lay a quick kiss on his lips.

"Does Jeremy come right home from school?" Mitch asked.

"He's supposed to. Then he gets ten minutes for a snack and then he better do his homework."

"Okay. Considering everything that's happened, I'll make sure I'm there when he gets home."

"Thanks, Mitch. That's a big relief to me."

He leaned over to the driver's seat and stole a longer kiss. "Just don't let the kid know or he'll think I'm treating him like a baby or something. Then he'll give me a ration of shit."

"I'm sure he'll find something else to give you crap about."

Mitch laughed. "How true."

Chapter Fourteen

While waiting for Jeremy to get home, Mitch repaired the barn door and tossed Jack the ball about a hundred times. Something about Howie's murder gnawed at his gut. He walked to where he'd found the body. The tall grass in the area would've been a better place for someone to hide the body if they really didn't want it to be found. But as Mitch surveyed the land, he realized someone wanted this body to be discovered. He could only be grateful that Jeremy hadn't stumbled upon it. Once the picture of death was in your head, you could never shake it. Hide it maybe. But never shake it.

He surveyed the scene like he would've back in Boston. There was nothing out of the ordinary. Nothing but grass and a tree with large branches full of leaves.

Mitch studied the land. It would have been easy to see someone in this area from the house in daylight but not in the dark. A gunshot probably wouldn't have been heard either.

He leaned against the tree, enjoying the tranquility of the land. It was huge and expansive but Marly had made it homey. What a great place to bring up a boy. All the adventure he needed within the safety of his own backyard. Well, until the homicide made it no longer safe. How sad was it that someone would take that security from a kid?

Jeremy would be home soon so he pushed back from the tree to head to the house. His hand scraped along a jagged piece of wood. He studied it closer and found a hole where a bullet had lodged. He took out his pocketknife and dug deep, retrieving the bullet, probably the one that missed Howie before the other shot got him.

Small caliber my ass. The shell belonged to a 45 magnum just like he suspected. He slipped the slug in the front pocket of his jeans and headed back to wait for Jeremy. He may be retired, but he was about to go call in some favors and find out where this bullet came from.

Not trusting the sheriff meant he'd come out of retirement just this once.

****

"I hate algebra. And why do I need a babysitter?" Jeremy complained when Mitch wouldn't let him ride his bike before doing his homework.

Mitch glared. "Let's get one thing straight. I ain't babysitting your ass and you need algebra because they say so."

"That's two things," Jeremy corrected, sitting at the kitchen table.

"No one likes a smart ass," Mitch said, leaning against the counter.

"Really? Then why does Mom like you?"

Mitch couldn't help but grin. "Because I'm

irresistible."

"Eeww."

"Get cracking on that algebra. I have to go into town and you're coming with me."

Rolling his eyes, Jeremy tapped his pencil on his notebook. "Why? Afraid you'll get lost?"

"Keep it up. You're going to show me to the post office. Your mom said you couldn't do anything until the homework is done so get going."

"How we getting to town? On my bike?"

Kid definitely had guts. "No, wise guy. Your granddad lent me his car."

Jeremy's eyes widened. "No way. That car sucks. Besides, you leave mail in our box outside and the postman takes it. Wrestling comes on at four and I'm watching it."

Mitch raised an eyebrow and offered a grin. "Gonna be pretty hard to do when you're in the car driving to the post office."

No way would he leave his precious evidence in an unprotected box. For all he knew, with this backward town, the postman was related to the sheriff and, poof, his evidence would mysteriously disappear.

"Awww man! Then you better not drive like a girl. I want to get back to watch wrestling."

Mitch pointed to the homework. "Why do you watch that crap? Isn't it all fake?"

"No. You can learn some good defense moves." Jeremy illustrated by standing and kicking his leg in the air.

Now Mitch had a bargaining tool. "Tell you what. You show me the post office and, when we get back, I'll show you moves that will crush your opponent."

Jeremy's face lit up. "Really?"

"Sure. If you think you can handle it."

"Bet your ass I can," the boy said, sinking back into his chair.

Mitch raised an eyebrow and spoke sternly. "Okay. Let's get one thing straight. No more swearing. It's not cool." Mitch's voice reminded him of his father's when he was scolded for the trillion times he got himself into trouble. It surprised Mitch that he even had fatherly qualities in him.

Jeremy shrugged. "Whatever."

Mitch stood his ground. "I'm serious, buddy. No more swearing or we won't hang out. Your mom wouldn't appreciate the swearing and I won't be an accomplice. Deal?"

He offered his hand and Jeremy shook it. "Deal."

"Okay. Now get that homework done so we can go. I want to surprise your mom with dinner so we have to get back in time."

"You cook?"

"Yeah. Pretty good to. Well, at least I can grill."

"If it turns out to be crap, I mean awful, then I'll feed it to Jack."

"Homework." Mitch ordered with a laugh.

Forty-five minutes later, Mitch was relieved when Jeremy finished the miserable homework so they could head to the post office before it closed.

Jeremy talked the whole ride there and back about anything and everything. Mitch didn't mind. With Jeremy talking, Mitch couldn't dwell on his past or contemplate his future. A future that was thrusting itself into his face daily. The kid turned out to be good company. He pointed out landmarks, shortcuts, and neighbors and their family history.

As luck would have it, they were home in time for wrestling. Mitch grilled steaks on the deck before joining Jeremy in the living room. Marly caught them cheering on the underdog.

"Hello, gentlemen," Marly said. "Homework done, Jeremy?"

"Yup, and the Strong Man just won the title from Aldo."

"What's that smell?" she asked, looking around the room.

"Dinner." Mitch responded while standing to stretch.

"You made dinner?"

"Yeah. Thought I should lend a hand and be useful."

"Did he really finish his homework?"

"Said he did." Mitch glanced at Jeremy. "He better not be pulling one over on me."

"Oh, yeah, how come?" Jeremy challenged and laughed.

"Cause I'm bigger than you and can make you my slave," Mitch teased, enjoying the banter between him and the kid.

"Ha! Not after the moves you taught me." For emphasis Jeremy kicked his leg and fisted his hands.

Marly glared at Mitch who raised his hands in defense. "Just taught him some self-defense moves. That's all."

"I don't condone fighting or solving problems with fists, Mitch."

Didn't she look adorable with her chin high and eyes narrowed, standing in a sexy beige business suit?

"Me either." He winked at Jeremy when Marly headed into the kitchen, her heels clacking on the floor.

"I saw that. And unless you want me to poke your eyes out, Mitch, don't do it again," Marly yelled, never turning around.

Mitch's mouth dropped as he stared at Jeremy.

"I told you she had eyes in the back of her head. She can see everything."

Mitch had heard of motherly instincts, but that was pretty cool. "I believe you, buddy. Why don't you go wash up for dinner?"

"Aw, man. After this round."

"Now." Mitch clicked the TV off and Jeremy scrambled up the stairs.

Mitch found Marly in the kitchen inspecting his dinner. He leaned against the counter and folded his arms. "Well, Inspector Hampton, does it meet your approval?"

"Smells wonderful. What's left for me to do?"

He slid over to her and took her hands in his. Gently, he scraped a kiss across her knuckles. "You can go upstairs to take a fifteen minute break while I get dinner on the table."

"But Jeremy—"

"Is upstairs getting washed up for dinner. Now his mom better listen, too."

She smiled and walked out of the kitchen. Enjoying the delightful sway of her ass, Mitch watched until she was out of sight.

Now to remember what was he supposed to be doing.

****

Marly was impressed with dinner. The steak was tender and flavorful. The baked potatoes were fluffy. And the crisp green salad was the perfect complement to it all.

When she began clearing the dishes from the table, Mitch stopped her. "I've got those."

"Nonsense. You cooked, so I'll clean the table."

"Can't let you do that." He took the plates from her and strolled to the sink.

"And why not?"

Facing her, he nodded to her son. "Because I lost the bet and the kid will never let me live it down if I don't own up to it. It's a man thing." He winked at Jeremy who smirked in return.

She propped her hands on her hips and looked at both the man and boy. "Okay, then. I'll make his lunch for tomorrow." She opened the fridge.

"I already made my lunch," Jeremy said.

Marly stared at him. "You did?"

"Yeah. Mitch said I had to have everything ready for school tomorrow before I could watch wrestling. I told him you did that stuff, but he said I should be doing it."

Marly glanced at Mitch then back to Jeremy. "I guess there's no reason you can't. But what did you pack for lunch. I bet all junk, right?"

"No. Mitch made me make a ham and cheese sandwich and pack carrots for snack. Yuk!"

Marly smiled.

"And what did we talk about you doing after dinner, kid?" Mitch asked, while adding a stream of liquid soap to the water in the sink.

"I know. I know. I'm going to take a bath." He dragged himself from the room.

Marly studied the man who had transformed her son. "Well, Mitch Allen. I'm impressed. You're either a miracle worker or I'm in the wrong house."

"He's a great kid. Maybe the carrots were pushing it a bit. I plan to give him cookies for snack. I'll sneak them into his bag when he goes to sleep."

Marly's heart melted. What a sincere gesture. "You'll be his hero for sure. And you're mine for today. Thank you. I needed a nice end to my crazy day."

"I've got a surprise for you." He let the dishes soak and opened the fridge to produce a bottle of wine. "A little birdie at the liquor store told me this was your favorite."

Thank God it was a small town and everyone knew everyone else's business. "It is. We can have it with dessert once Jeremy goes to bed."

His face dropped. "I didn't make any dessert. I'm sorry. I didn't think about it."

"I've got dessert under control." She leaned up and placed a kiss on his lips. "That is if you have an appetite."

His grin was wicked. "Depends. What is it?"

"Me."

The hard angles of his face softened with his smile. "In that case, I'm famished."

Pulling her against his chest, he devoured her lips just enough to spin her head. He took the bottle from her, placed it back in the fridge. "I bet Jeremy is out of the bath. It's time his mom slipped into a nice hot tub

181

and collected her energy. She's gonna need it."

Marly laughed, stunned at his thoughtful ideas. "I think I have plenty of energy in reserve. Been saving it for a long time. Consider yourself warned, Mitch Allen."

"I'm already getting hard," Mitch announced, cleaning the dishes at express speed. "I'm finally going to seduce you. There's no stopping me now."

She trailed a finger along his forearm. "I'll be back."

"I'll be here."

****

Marly smothered her skin with fragrant cream. She took extra time to style her hair so it would fall in soft curls down her back. With two fingers, she dabbed a few drops of her favorite perfume behind her ears, between her breasts, down her belly.

She chose her sexiest panties—red lace ones she called 'barely there.' Her best bra was also sheer lace but a snowy white. She dressed in a fresh pair of jeans and plain white T-shirt. Going barefoot would be sexier than wearing sneakers so she brushed her toenails with a light pink polish.

One more glance in the mirror confirmed that she'd done all the beauty prep possible. She'd thoroughly enjoyed the last hour. Primping herself had awakened her feminine side again, one she had long ago buried. Peeking into Jeremy's room, she was surprised to see him fast asleep.

Walking downstairs created a storm of butterflies in her stomach in anticipation of intimacy. Mitch sat in the living room, two glasses of wine beside him on the small table. He had lit a fire and was staring into it as she approached.

Noticing her, he handed her a wineglass and motioned for her to sit next to him on the couch. "Did you enjoy your bath?"

"Very much." She sipped the wine.

"You're so beautiful." His voice was low, almost a growl.

"I feel beautiful, like a queen, thanks to all you did around here today. Thank you. It really means a lot to me. And to Jeremy."

He sipped his wine, relaxed as she'd ever seen him. "Didn't do anything I didn't want to."

Her lips tingled in anticipation of his kisses. "I know. That's what made me feel so special."

"Enjoy your wine because, I promise you, tonight I'm going to make you feel a lotta something."

"I do hope so." Every private place ached and tingled with that promise.

"But before we have time to ourselves, I want to fill you in on something. You have to promise not to let it ruin the evening. Because I really need this evening with you." His eyes flashed heat, the sensation thrilling her.

She swallowed hard. "Not any more than I need it. Tell me so I can seduce you."

He cleared his throat. "Today I found a bullet hole in the tree where I found Howie's body."

"What's that mean? The shooter missed and hit the tree before hitting Howie's forehead?"

"Something like that. I retrieved the bullet from the hole."

She could listen to that Boston accent all night. "And that's significant why?"

"The shell wasn't from a small caliber weapon like your stolen gun as the sheriff claimed. It was a 45 magnum, popular gun mostly for law enforcement personnel."

"Which means the heat's still on you?" How was she not supposed to let this upset her?

"Yeah, but the sheriff doesn't know I found the bullet. I mailed it this afternoon to my contacts back in Boston. I'm hoping to identify who purchased those bullets."

She sat on the edge of her seat, wanting to jump up and cheer. "Really? That's great. Then they'll catch the real killer."

"Hopefully, but that killer will be pretty pissed if he discovers I found the bullet and having it analyzed. We just have to be careful and pay attention to what's going on around us until I get the results and contact the state police here."

"Do you think the sheriff knows who the murderer is?"

Mitch shrugged and rubbed his jaw. "Good possibility. Especially since he's lied about the type of weapon used."

Marly hissed. "That bastard had the nerve to arrest you." She sighed. "Can we let it go for tonight? I appreciate you telling me and all, but I don't want to ruin tonight." She stood and held out her hand to him. "I need you, Mitch. I want you. Now."

"Thought I was supposed to seduce you, but who am I not to oblige such a beautiful, sexy woman? Lead the way," he said as he stood.

She studied his leg. "Mitch. What about your leg?"

"What about it?"

"I don't want to hurt it or cause you any pain."

His laugh came from deep in his chest. "Honey, if you don't get me upstairs into bed, then the leg will be the least of my problems. I've had a bad ache for you since I arrived. And, darling, if I don't relieve that ache, the pain will be worse than my leg ever was." His voice deepened, filled with need and lust.

"I'm not the type of woman to turn her back on a man in need," she said, taking him by the hand and leading the way up the stairs.

"I promise this bum leg won't interfere with my performance."

"Good because I'd hate to have to do all the work."

The sound of male laughter echoed through the hall for the first time in years. "Smart ass."

"I know. And you love it," she teased, missing this banter between lovers.

"That I do."

They pushed through Marly's bedroom door, shutting it behind them. Mitch tugged her into his arms, the possession welcomed as her heart skipped a beat. His lips found hers in a flash of heat. She clawed at his shirt. All she wanted to feel was his flesh under her fingers. She had fantasized far too long about running her hands over his hard muscles. There was no way to control her desires now. When they broke their kiss long enough for her to pull his shirt over his head, she breathed deeply. His naked chest was as wonderful as she remembered from that early morning tea. With her fingertips, she traced his pecs and biceps.

"Sorry, my muscles aren't as defined as they once were," he whispered.

"I like them. They're perfect. Like here and here and here," she said softly, laying gentle kisses across his chest.

When her fingertips brushed over the scar on his shoulder, he tensed. He'd said before that he was constantly inundated with questions about his scars. She wasn't curious enough to be a mood killer.

"Fuck the scars. We all have some. Get over it and kiss me," she said, not willing to let him shut down when they were so close to being one.

Surprise covered his face as she kissed the entire scar slowly, carefully, then without any questions, continued up his neck until her lips found his. Her tongue outlined his lips before pushing inside the warmth of his mouth. His hands caressed her back in long, swift circles before lifting her shirt over her head and continuing the kiss. Without breaking away from her mouth, his fingers unclasped her bra and pushed it from her shoulders until it fell from her body, exposing her breasts. Oh, how she yearned to feel his hands all over her body, taking, possessing.

Her lungs begged for air, but she couldn't tear her lips from his. All Marly wanted was the taste of his hot mouth on hers. His cock flexed in his jeans against her belly. Her hips bucked against his until he tore his lips from hers.

"You're driving me insane, Marly," Mitch said through ragged breaths.

His hand dipped to the button on her jeans. With a quick snap of his wrist, he undid the metal clasp, lifted her around the waist with one arm, and dragged the jeans from her body with the other. Standing in her barely-there panties, she felt more alive than she had in years.

"You have the hottest body, baby," he said, while his eyes feasted on her lithe form from head to toe.

Capturing her mouth again, he deepened the kiss until she felt like she was flying. Her only thoughts were of getting him naked. When a ripping sound filled the room, she gasped, the noise swallowed by his kisses.

Taking his lips from hers, Mitch stared at the shredded lace in his hand. "Shit. Sorry about that. Should've let you remove the panties."

Taking deep breaths into her starved lungs, Marly shrugged. "I can always buy another pair. Since I can't lift you like you did me, bad boy, get those jeans off now."

"Yes, ma'am. I love it when you're demanding."

Wild and aching, she tore at the remainder of his clothes until they were scattered around the floor. They stood before each other, naked and aroused.

Mitch kissed her neck, his teeth scraping against her skin. His stubble was gone, replaced by soft skin and the scent of leather aftershave. Her head fell back giving him full access to her throat. She felt alive, sensual, desired.

Marly wanted Mitch and she was about to have him. This was different than any causal sex she had since Rick's death. There was a primal need for both of them tonight. For her to feel like a vibrant woman again and for Mitch to feel like a complete man again.

"Mitch, take me. Now." She claimed his mouth

again, her tongue pushing past his lips, entangling with his. Exploring the depths of his gorgeous mouth, she sank into the moment.

He trembled as her hand descended to his hard cock. She stroked the length of him, enjoying the low moan that rumbled from his throat. This is what she missed. The thrill of bringing a man to his knees with one touch.

"Now, Mitch. I want to feel you move inside me." Pulling him toward the bed, they fell onto the comforter.

With his hands on the sides of her head, Mitch held himself over her breasts and feasted. His tongue toyed with the nipples, licking and laving, until their firm peaks throbbed. A dull ache formed in her midsection, the foretelling of the pleasure to come. Oh, how she loved getting lost in the moment.

With Mitch struggling to hold his weight off of his bum leg, Marly changed her focus. "Better if I'm on top," she said without giving him a chance to argue and wiggled out from under him.

When he lay on his back, she leaned over him and opened her nightstand. She removed a condom and handed it to him with nervous hands. Once his erection was sheathed in the thin latex, Mitch pulled her up to straddle his hips.

"God, you are so friggin' sexy," he said, his chest rising and falling with sharp breaths.

Rising above him, she clasped her hands with his above his head. "I believe the same can be said about you. I'm loving your hard body."

Slowly, she raised her hips and lowered herself onto his cock. She arched back, taking him all the way into her throbbing pussy. He filled her so completely, so perfectly.

His hands grasped her waist, the slight pinch of his fingers a welcomed sensation on her fiery flesh. Had sex always been this glorious? The way her pussy stretched to accommodate his size contributed to her arousal, knowing that his cock was flexing deep inside her.

She controlled her hips, rocking slightly to allow the length of him to slide in and out of her pussy. She rode him, rubbing her clit against his flexing flesh. Under her, he kept up with her rhythm, matching her stroke for stroke.

Marly held onto the moment until urgency took the upper hand. "Mitch. Don't stop."

"Don't. Plan. To," he said, emphasizing each word.

Faster, she bucked her hips. Lying over his long body, she watched his golden brown eyes darken with lust, an animal on the prowl. It thrilled her completely and utterly.

The familiar rush of pleasure hit her so intensely, it threatened to undo her very soul. Her body shook, trembled, and succumbed to his thrusts. Within seconds, he followed her over the edge and into the clouds. Riding out their orgasm, they clung to each other.

"Marly!"

Her pussy convulsed with small spasms that ignited into exploding waves of pleasure that crashed through her womb. Over and over, delightful pulses of heat within her core stole her breath away. Her spasming pussy lips milked his cock, keeping the thick erection deep inside her until she collapsed on top of him, gasping for breath. The only regret was the need for a condom. How she wished she could feel his cum spurt deep inside her.

Only when his arms wrapped around her back, keeping her on his chest, holding her tighter than she ever thought possible, did the stray tear escape her eye. She willed herself not to bawl. She'd take what he offered now and deal with the aftermath once he left. Her heart would survive. Didn't she know better than anyone how to deal with a broken heart?

And leave he would. Courtsville offered a man like Mitch no job, no future. Even the silly notion that he could run for sheriff against Ridgeley would still keep them apart because she couldn't have another lover in a dangerous job, no matter if Courtsville was one of the safest places in the country. The job meant the same kind of risk that took her Rick away.

For the moment, though, Mitch was all hers. And she made him all hers for the next three hours, as they made love, exploring each other's bodies, fulfilling promises of pleasure.

She didn't remember dozing off, but was awakened when he slipped out of the bed.

"Where are you going?" she asked as he dressed.

"To my room. Probably wouldn't be good for Jeremy to catch me in his mom's room until we know how to explain it."

She sat up in bed and pulled her knees to her chest, the sheet falling around her. "You're right," she said, sleepily. "Mitch? Was it what you thought it would be?"

He stared at her for a moment. "No."

Her heart felt like a knife sliced through it. She shielded herself from the hurt. But then his words continued and the hurt disappeared.

"It was better than I could've ever imagined. You're a hard lady to keep up with. You're insatiable, darling. I like that. A lot. I hope I did you justice."

She laughed and bit down on her lip to scare away the tears of joy. "That you did. I'm sorry you have to go to your room. But you're right. It's for the best. For now."

He leaned down and gently kissed her lips. "For now." He walked to the door and turned back to her. "Don't get suspicious when you hear a noise downstairs. It's just me."

"Why are you going downstairs?"

"Got to go switch the carrots for the cookies." He hesitated a minute. "You raised a great boy, Marly. Your husband would be very proud of him. And you should be proud of yourself. You're a great mother. And lover."

"He's no longer my husband."

"But he'll always be Jeremy's dad and always be your first husband."

"Only husband. Getting married again just isn't in my future."

"Darling, I've become fond of the expression 'never say never'. You're too wonderful a woman to be alone. Night, baby." He mouthed her a kiss and was gone.

That did it. As soon as he shut the door behind him, the tears flowed. But, for the first time in eleven years, they were tears of joy instead of mourning.

Deep inside, Marly felt sexually attractive,

sexually alive for the first time since her husband had shared this bed with her. Rick would understand her moving on, finally putting their life together where it belonged, in her memory and not in the present. Making love to Mitch tonight was more than a man and a woman enjoying the pleasures of the flesh.

For tonight…Mitch Allen stole her heart. A heart she swore she'd never give to anyone again.

Chapter Fifteen

Mitch awoke early after surprisingly sleeping like a rock. Making love with Marly took the edge off his arousal, but he wasn't sated and still craved the beauty's touch.

Always mindful of his knee, he slowly rolled out of bed and was shocked when his knee didn't revolt with screaming pain. The swelling in his bad leg had decreased and the coloring looked better. So Doc Peterson was right. The antibiotics did work fast. His knee hadn't felt like this since before the injury.

Quietly, he walked to the bathroom for a shower. The room was already filled with steam and feminine scents of lavender and roses. He inhaled deeply, closing his eyes to picture Marly standing there a few minutes earlier, naked and wet. His body reacted to his wandering thoughts with a hard-on that wouldn't get relief any time soon.

So he set the water to cool and jumped in, suppressing the yell from the blast of cold water. He shaved to prevent scratching Marly's delicate skin with his stubble. And given the places he wanted to kiss, he aimed for pleasurable not scratchy.

After his shower, Mitch didn't interrupt Marly even though he wanted to barge into her room, sweep her off her feet, toss her on the bed, and make love to her all morning. Since that wasn't possible, he forced himself to walk back to his room. Needing coffee badly, he dressed, grabbed his cane, and headed to the kitchen.

Mitch was on his second cup of coffee when Jeremy came down the stairs, rubbing his eyes.

"Hey, buddy. Why the long face?"

"Can't see why I can't stay home for one day from stupid school. All my friends get to play hooky once in a while."

Jeremy filled a bowl with chocolate cereal. What he did next had Mitch staring in shock.

"Why the hell are you adding chocolate milk to your cereal?" Mitch asked.

"Why the hell not?" He caught Mitch's stare. "I mean, why not?"

"Because it's gross?"

Jeremy spooned in a mouthful and talked with a full mouth. "Why do you drink your coffee without cream? That's gross."

Mitch looked into the dark liquid in his cup. "How would you know? Have you ever had coffee?"

"Yup."

"You're lying. Your mom wouldn't allow it."

"I sipped hers once when she wasn't looking. Not bad."

Mitch hated how easily he got sucked into a silly debate with the kid. "I happen to like my coffee black, thank you."

"It's still gross. I add chocolate milk to the cereal because if you add white milk it will turn chocolate anyways so I just make it quicker."

And there it was. How the mind of an eleven-year-old worked.

"Try some," Jeremy demanded, pushing the cereal box in front of Mitch.

"Try what?" Marly asked, walking into the kitchen dressed in a pantsuit and looking refreshed. "And don't talk with your mouth full."

Mitch shot him a mocking glance. Jeremy responded with a snarl that had Mitch grinning. "Your son was introducing me to his famous chocolate milk cereal concoction."

"My son better hurry up and finish eating. Come on. You're not going to be late for school. And since you can't go in your pajamas, you'd better go get changed quickly."

Jeremy disappeared upstairs after choking down the rest of his cereal and complaining more about school.

Mitch cornered Marly at the counter. From behind, he kissed her neck. She moaned slightly. He buried his face on the side of her neck, breathing in deeply as the smell of lavender surrounded his senses.

She turned into his arms and kissed his lips. "Now, Mitch. We shouldn't start something we can't finish. Won't help either of us get through the day."

"Take a lunch break at home. I'll let you choose anything from the menu," he said, holding his arms open.

Her eyes filled with lazy clouds. "Sounds tempting. What's on the menu?"

"Me." He kissed her forehead. "Me." He kissed her nose. "And definitely me." He kissed her lips.

"Hmmm. A three-course lunch. As much as I'd

like that, I'm afraid I can't get away today. But there's always tonight."

Jeremy came down the stairs like a herd of elephants, giving Mitch and Marly time to step away from each other.

"Mitch, will you be here when I get home from school?"

"Sure will."

"Can you teach me some more karate moves?"

Mitch felt Marly's eyes burning into the back of his head and cringed. "If you get your homework done. And it's self-defense moves."

"Don't care what it's called. It's cool. Can't wait to show the kids at school."

At the sound of Marly sharply sucking in her breath, Mitch had only seconds for damage control. "Now wait a minute, kid. Those moves aren't for school. Hear me? I hear about you showing off in school, I won't show you any more. Understood?"

"Yeah."

"Okay. Now get going before you get me in any more trouble with your mom." Mitch offered Marly a smile that wasn't returned.

"Bye, Jack." Jeremy ran to the door. "Hey, Mitch. Thanks for the cookies for my lunch. I knew you were cool."

Mitch smiled.

"Don't let it go to your head because if he tries to be cool in school with those moves then you'll answer to me, Mitch Allen," Marly warned, sticking a finger in his chest.

"I do love how you say my name, darling. Especially when you're scolding me," he grinned wickedly.

"You've got issues," she said but laughed.

Jeremy beeped the horn.

"You better go." He quickly kissed her on the lips, wanting to linger for much longer.

"Yeah," she said reluctantly. "We know how much Jeremy likes to get to school."

She stopped at the door and turned to him. "I haven't told Jeremy about you being arrested. Thought we'd tell him tonight. He needs to know what's going on because it affects him, too."

"Absolutely," Mitch agreed, stepping to the door to watch her walk to the truck.

Did she realize that she'd just allowed herself to share control of something with him? That was a big step in her world. She was opening up to him finally. She was actually going to include him in an important conversation.

God, she was getting deeper into his heart every minute. As he watched them drive out of sight, he admitted that it was harder and harder to resist letting her into his stubborn heart.

****

Mitch was in the middle of his physical therapy exercises when his cell phone rang.

Recognizing the number, he answered like he had all those years on the force. "Allen."

"Well, well, well. If it ain't Mitch Allen. How the hell are you doing?" The gravelly voice on the other end was familiar. His retired captain, Ted Amory, sounded like his usual self—professional but stern.

"Hey, Captain. I'm hanging in there. Just taking one day at a time."

"Yeah, right. This is me you're talking to. You don't take anything one at a time. You always jump in head first."

Mitch paced the living room. "Yeah, not anymore. Can't jump with a bum leg."

"Hey, we all got our limps. Got your package this morning. You got yourself in some trouble where you're at?"

He ran a hand through his thick hair. Damn, he really needed a haircut. "You could say that. I was arrested for murder."

"Get the fuck out of here. Murder? You? Okay, who'd you piss off?"

Peeking out the window showed nothing but grass and forest. "Some backward, small town sheriff with a badge from a gumball machine. I stumbled upon the dead body of a man who wasn't very much liked in these parts. Someone put him out of his misery with a bullet between the eyes."

The captain coughed on the other end. "Is this the bullet you sent me? You want me to analyze this?"

"Yes. And as fast as possible."

"What? They don't have crime labs in Courtsville?" Captain Amory asked with a chuckle.

Mitch frowned. "Let's just say I'm a little suspicious of how the sheriff's handling of the case. Hell, his only two suspects are me and the lady I'm staying here with, who happens to be a widow with a young son, not a suspect in my eyes. He cleared her, but I'm out on bail."

Chuckles carried over the line again. "So you

finally have yourself a lady friend, Allen. 'Bout friggin' time. Thought you'd work yourself to death and never settle down."

"I tried the working myself to death bit," he said, looking down at his recovering leg. "Can't say I liked it much. And I'm hardly settling down. I'm only here because my truck broke down and now I can't leave until I beat this murder rap."

"I can make some calls for you. Get you out of there by day's end."

Mitch thought of his captain's offer. He could do it. Even in retirement, Captain Amory was one of the most respected law enforcement officers in the country with senators and congressmen as longtime friends. But Mitch wasn't ready to leave. Telling himself he just wanted to follow the case through to the end, he ignored the irritating voice in his head reminding him it wasn't his case. He had other reasons to stay, but it was best not to dwell on them.

"Thanks, Captain. But I'll stick it out for now. Don't have much else to do, so I might as well help Marly out."

"Sounds like you'll be helping yourself out as well, seeing as you're the one charged. I'm just a phone call away. If you change your mind or need anything at all."

"Yes, sir. There is something else I could use help with besides analyzing bullet. Can you see what you can find out about Howard "Howie" Singleton? He's the victim. Also, his cousin, who happens to be the sheriff, Jonas Ridgeley?"

"Absolutely. If they've been pinched for anything, even a parking ticket, I'll find out."

199

Mitch paced again. "Great. Appreciate it. I'm going to speak with some locals to see if any more names need to be checked out."

"Should have the results from this shell for you by tomorrow. I'll be in touch as soon as I get the info on these guys."

He hung up his cell phone just as Jack barked. Mitch looked at him for a second, realizing he'd never heard him bark before unless he was playing with Jeremy. Out of habit, he reached for his gun at his waist before he remembered that he didn't carry anymore.

When the doorbell chimed, he walked slowly to the window. He peered out the curtain to see a tall, husky man in a gray suit standing on the porch. He looked familiar, but Mitch couldn't place him.

Mitch opened the door and Jack bolted past him before he could pull him back.

"Shit!" Mitch complained. "Sorry. Jack!"

"Hi, Jack. No! Down," the man said as Jack recognized him. "Go play, Jack. Hi, I'm Seth McFadden." He extended his hand to Mitch. "I'm Marly's brother. I've heard you've been staying here."

"Come in." Mitch didn't wait for a reply, knowing the man would enter. "So, as her brother, you've come to check out the stranger that's bedding down at your sister's house?"

"You got it."

Mitch stood back, arms crossed, facing Seth. "Good. Glad to hear it. I'd do the same thing. What do you want to know about me?"

"Did you kill Howie?"

Pretty direct. Definitely fit the lawyerly

personality. "Nope."

Seth laughed, his posture relaxed. "I heard you weren't the conversational type."

Mitch raised an eyebrow. "Let me guess which part of my fan club said that. The sheriff."

Seth stood the same height as Mitch, which made eye contact easier. "Right, Ridgeley. As you know I'm an attorney. Handle mostly civil matters. Wills. Land sales. Inheritances. I've noticed a change in Marly the last few days. Guess that has to do with you."

"Sorry. You'll have to ask her about that."

With his hands in his trouser pockets, Seth eased back on his heels. "I did. She told me to mind my business."

Mitch laughed, shaking his head. "Lady knows how to take care of herself. Looks like she's been doing it for a while. And doing a damn fine job. But, God forbid, she let anyone step in to give her a hand."

Seth smiled, the resemblance to Marly unmistakable. "Agreed. But I still wouldn't feel right unless I did my brotherly duties and checked you out."

A smirk formed on Mitch's mouth. "She doesn't know you're here, does she?"

"No, and if she finds out she'll probably kick my ass."

Mitch opened his arms wide. "Nothing to hide, big brother. I was just passing through. Stayed here after my truck broke down. Found a dead body. Been arrested and bailed out by your sister. Not happy about that since she put her house on the line for bogus charges. But I wasn't talking her out of it even if I used every breath in my lungs."

"You seem to know her pretty well in a short

time," Seth said, with a shit-eating grin.

Mitch chose to ignore what he implied. He wasn't about to admit just how well he and Marly had gotten to know each other. "I've been warned not to leave town until Ridgeley says so. Been to Doc Peterson, at your mom's insistence, and got meds for an infection in my injured knee. Have butted heads with your sister and her incessant need to control everything around her and pretty much got put in my place for it. Anything else?"

"Hell. I already knew most of that. Small towns don't have secrets. At least not for long. And I totally believe that about Sis. She's never let anyone help and never will."

Mitch enjoyed a decent challenge every now and then. "While I'm here, I plan on helping out. She can wear out her little temper on me if she cares to, but I'm not sitting back while she busts her ass to be two people when I'm doing nothing waiting for the sheriff to pull his head out of his ass."

Seth rocked on his heels, arms crossed. "First, I wouldn't call Marly's temper little. Be careful. She gets herself fired up and it takes a lot to calm her down. Believe me, I'm her big brother, stronger and bigger than her, and even I'll walk away after a certain point."

"I'm not that smart I guess. I'm the type to stand my ground."

Seth studied him for a minute, making Mitch uncomfortable. "Heard you came from Boston and that injury there almost killed you," Seth said, effectively changing the subject.

Mitch's insides turned sour. He despised the

memories of that day. "Don't want to talk about it. That's in the past."

"But pasts have a funny way of resurfacing, especially in small towns. Seeing as my sister is fond of you, I just want you to know you have an ally in me. If I thought for one minute you were a murderer, believe me, no way in hell would you be staying here with my sister and my nephew. I may be a suit, but I have a temper when it comes to family."

Mitch appreciated the man's honesty. "Good to know. Thanks for the offer, but I don't need any allies to protect me for something I haven't done."

Pacing a few feet back and forth, Seth looked like he was in a courtroom discussing a case. "I know that. You know that. But the sheriff, who hasn't a clue how to investigate a murder, has to make himself look good. Plus, he fears you're out to steal his job."

Standing with his thumbs hitched in his pockets, Mitch huffed. "Then he's a bigger fool than I thought. I've never given any indication of being remotely interested in Ridgeley's job. Fuck him."

Seth laughed, calm and reserved. Damn lawyers. "You didn't have to. Town's full of people humming about the former cop stranded in town, who would be a welcome replacement for the lard ass sheriff who hardly knows the law and certainly doesn't enforce it half the time. Other than locking up drunks to let them sleep off the booze, the sheriff can't be bothered with anything physical like arresting criminals. Town's folk generally just take matters into their own hands rather than deal with the sheriff. Guess you can call it some playground justice—you bother me I'll bother you."

"Apparently that's true since Howie lies cold in

the county morgue."

Seth sighed. "If Ridgeley has his way, he'll pin this murder on you so he has to do the least amount of work necessary. Watch your back is all I'm saying. He's a weasel."

"That's an understatement."

"Here," he handed him two business cards, his and another lawyer's. "I've taken the liberty of speaking with this attorney. He's a remarkable criminal defense attorney and will fight to get the charges dropped. He owes me a few favors, so he'll give you a very decent deal. I don't want to hear any shit about you not needing an ally. I wouldn't offer help if I didn't believe in your innocence. Besides, my baby sister thinks you're a good guy."

Mitch accepted the cards and put them in his back pocket. "Thanks. I appreciate it. I'm not sitting back waiting for the sheriff to make his next move. I'm doing my own investigation to clear my name and give Marly some answers as to what happened on her property."

Seth raised an eyebrow. "You should receive a fair amount of cooperation from folks around here since the sheriff isn't well liked and we all know neither was Howie. Don't hesitate to contact me if I can be of any assistance. I mean it." He offered a handshake. "I've got to get going. Been nice meeting you."

"Same here."

By the time Seth left, it was eleven o'clock. Mitch had already pissed off his leg with exercises, talked to an old friend to pursue an investigation that wasn't his, and was sized up by Marly's brother. "And who said small towns were boring?" he said. "Jack, come inside."

He needed more coffee to think about his next step. If the sheriff wanted to play games then Mitch would be sure he was ready.

Chapter Sixteen

Mitch drove to town and quickly became the center of attention as soon as he strolled into *The Last Stop Sandwich Shop*. The smell of strong coffee and bacon permeated the air. He gripped his cane and walked to a stool at the u-shaped counter. He wasn't hungry, but the best way to find out the happenings in a small town was to meet the locals.

Millie greeted him instantly, placing a cup in front of him and filling it with coffee. "Hey, handsome. Good to see you again. What can I get you?"

"Coffee's good."

She glared, her face distorting to show off many wrinkles. "Ain't planning on taking up a good seat for a paying customer, are you?"

Mitch smirked. "No, ma'am. Why don't you give me whatever special you have? And keep the coffee coming, please."

"Don't think I caught your name the other day?" asked a young man from three stools over.

"You from around here?" Mitch asked, taking a sip of the strong coffee.

"Sure am."

Mitch glanced around the room before looking

back at the man. "Then you already know my name. Word travels quickly in this town."

The man moved over to the stool next to Mitch. "Amos. I work at the liquor store."

Mitch studied him. "Okay. Now I remember. You helped me buy the right kind of wine. Appreciate it."

Amos smiled, showcasing crooked teeth. "No problem. And don't mind people talking. Hell. Not much else to do around these parts."

"Yup, I've heard you haven't had a murder here until I arrived. Bet people are talking pretty loudly about that."

"That and, well, you and Marly."

"What about Marly?" Mitch's voice deepened.

"You're staying at her place. Bought her wine. Doesn't take a rocket scientist to figure out that you two are, shall we say, getting acquainted." Amos made a sound that Mitch took as a giggle.

Mitch bared his teeth. "Shall we say mind your damn business?"

Visibly shaken, Amos cleared his throat. "My apologies, sir. Just making conversation. Didn't mean anything by it. I'm fond of Marly. We went to school together. Then she went on to college while I stayed here and worked at the store. She's nice."

Mitch didn't respond.

Millie placed a plate of very greasy steak and eggs in front of him. Mitch felt fortunate that he only had to pay for it. Not eat it.

"Tell me something, Amos," Mitch said, slowly. "How's people in town know that I bought Marly wine if you didn't tell them?"

The man paled. "Well, I...I...guess...guess I may

have mentioned it in passing to someone. Didn't mean any harm."

"Amos, the next time I buy something, I expect you'll keep my purchases private. Pisses me off when people meddle in my business." Mitch glared at the nervous man.

"No, sir. I mean, yes, sir. I've got to be going now," Amos announced, sliding off the chair and scurrying out the door.

Maddy entered wearing greasy overalls and a baseball hat. "Hello, Mitch," he said, taking the seat beside him. "How's things?"

"Great for what it's worth. How's the truck coming?"

"I was going to call you after breakfast, so I'm glad I ran into you. They sent the wrong darn hose. I should have it today and be done by tonight. Apologize for the delay, but I'll call you when it's ready."

Mitch chose his words carefully, knowing all ears were listening. "Not a problem. Since I was arrested yesterday for Howie's murder, I can't leave town until that business is settled. Take your time. Ol' Joe lent me one of his vehicles."

"Looks like Millie's set you up with one of her heart attack specials. That should be considered murder on a plate," Maddy quipped, sipping the coffee that had been placed in front of him.

Mitch laughed and so did the other six men sitting around the counter. If he needed any confirmation that people watched his every move and listened to his every word, he just got it.

"It's no secret Marly posted her house for your

bail. That's ironic really," Maddy said in a low tone.

"How's it ironic?" Mitch asked.

"That Howie was after her land and now Marly posted it to bail out the man accused of killing him," Maddy said, as Millie placed his food before him without even taking his order.

When Mitch set down his cup, Millie automatically refilled it, her ears practically standing at attention to get every word of his conversation with Maddy. "I'm innocent. Don't expect anyone to believe me. Don't give a shit what people think either. But one thing is for certain, I won't let Marly lose her property. I'll remain in town until this is resolved."

"From what I hear, there's no evidence against you."

"Of course not because there is no evidence. The sheriff has it out for me because I'm new in town and I'm an ex-cop from the big city. Piss-poor reasons to falsely accuse a man."

"Maybe you make him nervous," a man from around the counter spoke up. "Name's Jerry Thacker. Own the convenience store up the street."

"How do I make him nervous?" Mitch asked.

Jerry glanced around the counter before answering. "Been a lot of talk around town that you were a great police detective back in Boston. I think the sheriff is jealous of your track record, considering he's never had to deal with anything more than a simple domestic argument or vandalism. No fancy court cases here and parents take care of their children who get in trouble."

Mitch only offered a shrug. "I'm not looking for pats on the back from anyone. I'm no longer a cop so my reputation shouldn't concern him."

"Your very presence threatens him," Maddy said.

Well, that was comforting. "Is that so? Then why not make me leave town? Why arrest me on a bogus charge when he has no evidence to support it, forcing me to stay?"

"Maybe he was counting on you sitting in jail for a while," Jerry said.

"Yeah. Where he can keep an eye on you," Maddy said.

"Didn't count on Ms. Marly bailing you out, did he? Betcha it never crossed his mind that she'd put up her land," Jerry said.

"Now he's backed himself into a corner. You can't leave because of the charges and he can't legitimately keep you locked up."

Interesting concept. "Then I guess it sucks to be him, doesn't it?" Mitch snorted. "I better stop in and say hello to the sheriff. You know. In case he thinks I've skipped town." He placed some money on the counter.

"Did you kill Howie?" Jerry asked.

Why did every one ask him that as if he'd openly admit to it if he did? "Nope."

"Of course, you didn't. Everyone knows that. Just had to ask," Jerry said. "Hell. Anyone at this counter would love to lay claim to the deed. Maybe someone did. But until the sheriff can prove it, then it'll remain a secret."

"Aw, come on, fellas, we know there's no secrets in small towns. Someone out there knows who killed the man," Mitch said. "And I'm not just talking about the killer." Scanning his audience, they all returned to looking at their plates, suddenly only interested in the food.

"Maybe so. The man had more enemies than a field has blades of grass. Word around town is that Marly's gun was found at the scene. What do you know about that?" Maddy asked.

Mitch didn't feel comfortable talking to these strangers about Marly, but he wanted to set the record straight. "Ridgeley says it was her gun, but I haven't seen it or any other evidence. Marly's gun was reported stolen months ago. So, again, could've been anyone."

Millie scooped up Mitch's money and placed it in the front of her apron without counting it. "Something wrong with the food?"

Maddy spoke up. "Guy's young, Millie. He wants to live longer than that heart attack waiting to happen."

She cursed him bitterly, earning a hoot of laughter from them all.

Mitch grabbed his cane and headed for the door.

"You know. Any time you feel like talking, you can come down here. Someone's always around," Jerry offered.

Mitch nodded. "I'll keep that in mind."

****

At the sheriff's office, Mitch wasn't surprised to see hardly any modern technology. The desks were old and a typewriter sat on one. There was a fax machine that looked like it was one of the first to come on the market. The smell of stale tobacco clung in the air, making Mitch nauseous. He had always hated the smell of tobacco. Mitch had barely stepped into the office when a deputy came from a back office.

"Can I help you?"

"Came to see the sheriff."

"Sorry, but he's busy right now. Something I can help you with?"

"Nope. I'll wait." Mitch said, studying the pictures on the wall. "Just let him know Mitch Allen is waiting."

"May be a while."

Mitch took a seat and stretched out. "It's all right. I've got nothing else to do. I'll wait."

The deputy disappeared into the back again and returned with the sheriff only moments later. Mitch remained seated.

"Allen. Didn't expect you. What's so important that I had to interrupt my busy day to assist you?"

"Sorry if your deputy got it wrong. I don't need your assistance. Just came by to visit."

Beady eyes narrowed. "If you don't mind, I have a lot of work to do. Not all men can travel the country doing nothing. I happen to be investigating a murder case. Oh, but since you're the prime suspect, you already know that, don't you?"

Mitch smirked, the man became more revolting with each encounter. "Thought the investigating was done since you arrested me. I wanted to ask you what evidence you had to charge me with murder. Word around town is you have none. That would be consistent with the fact that I'm innocent."

The sheriff gnawed on a wet cigar. "Enjoying small town talk, are you?"

Mitch smiled without humor. "Let's not mess

around, Sheriff. I'm asking a simple question. I know the law."

"I'm not under any obligation to answer your questions immediately, Allen. I'm a busy man. I also know the law and know what you're entitled to. Things just move slower around here. Don't think you can waltz your city ass in here with demands. This is my office. My town. Don't you forget that."

Narrowing his eyes, Mitch pinned Ridgeley with a hard stare. "Don't you forget there's a lady with a young son involved in this fiasco. You have an obligation to keep her updated on your progress. I suggest you do so."

"As a matter of fact, I have kept her updated. After your arrest yesterday, I kindly informed her that she should watch who she beds down with and not be so willing to take a roll in the hay with anyone who darkens her doorstep."

Mitch slowly rose and fought to maintain his temper. "Living up to your asshole reputation, I see. From what I've heard during my short stay in town, your word means absolutely shit around here." Mitch glanced around the room then glared at the sheriff and his deputy cringing like an abused puppy. "Yeah, maybe I'll give it consideration after all."

The sheriff followed his perusal. "Give what consideration? You're wasting my friggin' time, Allen. Make your point and get the hell out of here before I arrest you for trespassing."

Mitch laughed, letting the sound shake his body. "Trespassing in a police station where I've come for help? Tsk tsk. That would make you look like a bigger ass than you already are."

"Allen," Ridgeley snarled between clenched lips.

Mitch smiled. "Seems you're up for re-election soon, Sheriff. I suggest you don't get too comfortable with your office. Never know when good competition will arrive."

The sheriff roared with laughter. "Boy, you are stupider than you look if you think I'd worry about a prick like you ever winning an election over me. This is my fucking town. You'd be wise to never forget that." His eyes were dark and menacing. Another man may have flinched, Mitch only grew more interested, understanding that he'd hit a nerve in the bastard.

Mitch stepped closer, looking down at the fat man inches away. He spoke calmly. "You need me in your jail cell. Marly needs me with her. Don't think for one minute I'm stupid enough to give you your wish."

"Don't think I won't lock your ass up again. You're on my radar, Allen. I suggest staying out of my sight."

Mitch leaned on his cane held steadily in front of him. "Good luck on the murder case, Sheriff. Maybe if you stopped wasting your time busting my balls you'd actually make an effort to find the real killer. Then maybe the townspeople would have a little faith in your abilities as sheriff."

"Hmpff."

Mitch walked to the door, stopped, and faced the sheriff again. "One more thing, Sheriff. When can I get a look at Marly's gun that you say you found by the body?"

The color drained from Ridgeley's face. "I already told you, boy. You'll get to see the evidence when I get a goddamn chance. Now get the fuck out of here."

Mitch smiled, getting the answer he searched for. The gun didn't exist. Another bullshit story. "Sheriff," Mitch said quietly and left slowly but not before hearing the bastard yell, "Deputy, get me some damn aspirin."

****

Mitch had accomplished the simple task he had hoped to by visiting the sheriff——rattle him on the non-existent evidence. He'd called the man out to do his job. A job he was sworn to do to protect the citizens of his town. Now let's see how well he does it, thinking everyone had him under a microscope. And if the sheriff didn't want to keep Marly informed, then Mitch would.

He found Seth's law office and parked in front. Looking through the large windows, he didn't see Marly. When he entered the front door, a little bell rang.

"Be right there," Marly's voice yelled out.

Mitch waited in the tiny reception area until Marly appeared with Seth a moment later.

"Hey, Mitch. This is a nice surprise," she said.

"Hi, Seth. Long time no see."

Marly glared at her brother. "Seth! I told you to mind your business." She slapped at his arm. "Just for that I'm taking an extra long lunch."

"The hell you are. I'll dock your pay," he teased.

Marly gathered her pocketbook and put on her coat. "Go ahead and I'll tell Mom."

Seth complied instantly. "One hour. Not a minute

more."

"Come on, Mitch. Before the slave driver changes his mind." They stepped outside into the cool spring air. "So Seth came by the house to give you the third degree? You can ignore him because he's been doing that to every man that's ever looked my way."

"I didn't mind. That's what brothers do. He had made up his mind pretty quickly that he liked me. But then again, all I care about is what you like."

"Right now, I would love a big glass of wine but since I have to return to work maybe a diet soda and a Caesar salad will do."

Mitch had developed an appetite after walking into the little bistro a block from Marly's work. His knee hadn't even complained about the short walk.

Once again, he felt everyone's eyes on him. But Marly ignored them so he would too.

They were seated and ordered their lunch.

Marly leaned over the table and spoke softly. "So what really brings you by?"

"That obvious, huh?"

"Uh huh. Are you here to tell me that everyone in town is shocked I put my property up for your bail, potentially leaving my son and me homeless for a man I barely know? Or are you here to report that we're having an affair?"

He sipped his water and almost choked. "The first. Who knows about the second?"

Marly laughed, her lips curved enticingly. "No one and everyone. Or at least they think they know. Small town gossip travels like wild fire."

Looking around, he caught eyes watching them still. "I'm beginning to find that out. So you've been getting the third degree about making my bail?"

"Yes. This morning when Mrs. Smiltson came in to settle her husband's will. Seems it's all over town how it was my gun used to kill Howie." She sipped her iced tea. "Then, without missing a beat, she added that she was happy I landed myself a handsome lad."

"I see. But I'm hardly a lad at thirty-five."

She waved her hand in the air. "Wouldn't matter if I denied it or not, her mind was made up and she'd spread whatever gossip she felt would get her the most attention. So I added flames to her fire."

The waitress served their food and left them alone again.

"Flames?" Mitch asked, thoroughly enjoying her spitfire attitude.

Shrugging her slender shoulders, she giggled. "Yeah. I politely told her I was only keeping you around as my sex slave and so far you have been extraordinary."

Did she just say that? "You did not."

"Bet your gorgeous ass I did." Marly laughed with an edge of naughtiness. "Mitch, you should see your face."

Forget his face. His balls ached for her touch. "I guess I've been called worse. That explains all the stares I've gotten. Has nothing to do with the murder just the sex."

She crunched bits of salad onto her fork and kept talking. "Oh, yeah. In the chain of importance in small towns, sex reigns at the top of the scale. Then murder."

"I'll keep that in mind. Hey, any place around here I can get a haircut?"

Her wide eyes mesmerized him. "Sure is. Mr.

217

McField back near the center of town. I have to bring Jeremy for a cut so I'll bring my sex slave, too."

Swallowing the last bite of his burger, he washed it down with a long drink of water. "Tell you what. I'll take the kid with me. It'll save both our dignities than to have his mommy bringing us. No offense."

Marly laughed, the sound tightening his gut. God, he wished they were alone. "Okay. I think I can give up control of that battle," she agreed. "But don't let him get any wacky haircut. He'll try to talk you into it."

"I'll get him a mohawk."

She gasped.

"Don't be silly, darling. The kid's getting a high and tight like me."

"Oh, military style. Perfect."

Running a hand through his hair, he couldn't wait for that appointment. "I've never worn my hair this long. When I was laid up, the hair grew wild. Can't wait to chop it off."

"I think it's kinda sexy." Her foot rubbed his leg under the table.

His gaze caught the mischief in hers. "Forget about it. It's getting chopped." Although he didn't mind any effort to convince him otherwise.

"It's your hair. But I can't wait to see Jeremy's. Be prepared to hear him complain the whole ride home. He hates haircuts."

He grabbed the check from her. "That's okay. He can always walk home."

Instead of walking her back to work, he wished they could sneak away for some hot loving. It was about time he had something to look forward to.

Chapter Seventeen

Jeremy came home in a bad mood. He dumped his backpack on the floor and ignored Jack who jumped around waiting for some affection.

"Hey, kid. Bad day at school?" Mitch asked as Jeremy stomped by.

Jeremy glared like his mother would when her temper was riled. "Were you arrested for murdering Howie?"

Aw shit! The one time Marly was willing to share the burden of control, her plans get scratched because the kid found out ahead of time. They should've known he'd find out at school.

"Your mom and I wanted to talk with you about that tonight."

"No. I want to hear it from you," Jeremy demanded.

His temper impressed Mitch. Like mother like son. "Ah, your mom really wanted to be here to talk about it. It's pretty complicated."

"The kids at school talked about it all day because it's the coolest thing to happen in this town since forever. I want to know, Mitch. I want to know the truth. *Please*."

Staring into those boyish eyes, his heart cracked.

Concern, disbelief, and wonder stared back at him from brown depths. Mitch prayed that Marly would understand that he had to answer the boy here and now. "Yes, Jeremy. I was arrested for Howie's murder. But the sheriff, being the jerk that he is, did it because he hates me for whatever reason. I didn't kill Howie." Truth is, he never wanted to kill again.

"I know you didn't do it. I just can't believe you were arrested. Mitch, are you going to live in jail forever now?"

He bent down to be eye to eye with Jeremy. "No, buddy. Hey, listen, this will all be fixed. You'll see. The truth will come out and whoever did this to Howie will be caught."

Jeremy sat on the couch and pouted. "How if you're already charged? When that happens on TV, the case is over and the bad guy goes to jail."

Mitch sat next to him. "Yeah. But I'm not the bad guy and I'll find out who is so the charges against me will be dropped."

"Really? Can I help? I want to help you, Mitch. I want to help."

"I'll tell you what. I'll keep that in mind. But it's really secret work so you can't tell your friends. Not even Danny. Deal?"

"Deal."

"Now let's go. We're getting haircuts." Mitch stood and was amazed no shooting pains came from his knee.

"You're taking me for a haircut?" Jeremy exclaimed with wide eyes.

"Yup. Got a problem with that, kid?"

Jumping up, he cocked his head to the side.

"Would it matter if I did?"

"Nope."

Jeremy walked out the front door with Mitch following. "Didn't think so. But I'm good with it. Uncle Seth took me a few times. It was better than going with my mom. Don't tell her I said that."

"Okay." Mitch studied him as they got into the car and drove off.

"It's just that every time I go with Mom, I end up seeing kids from school and then the next day they make fun of me because my mom has to take me. I can't help it if I don't have a dad to do those things."

Getting to town took only a few minutes.

"No you can't, kid." The picture formed in Mitch's mind. "Tell me. These kids that do the teasing, are they the reason you've been trying to learn wrestling moves?"

Jeremy hesitated first, then spoke. "Yeah, I guess so. But they started it."

"Easy, buddy. I'm on your side." Mitch parked a block away from the barber's. Once on the sidewalk, he placed his hand on Jeremy's shoulder. "Tell you what we're gonna do. Get our haircuts then race home to get that homework of yours out of the way. I'll show you some easy moves to really kick butt if these kids mess with you again."

Jeremy's face lit up. "Really? Awesome! Come on then, hurry up." He all but dragged Mitch into the barbershop.

"Have a seat, you'll be next," the barber ordered.

"How long, Mr. McField?" Jeremy asked.

"When I get done."

Mitch patted his shoulder. "Plenty of time. Plenty

of time."

Jeremy complained how it seemed like hours before the barber called out "next." Mitch pushed Jeremy to go first.

"High and tight," he told the man who went right to work. Mitch was next and got the same treatment.

"This haircut is the best! It's so cool." Jeremy rubbed his head where shaggy hair had been only a few minutes before.

Mitch smiled as they walked back to the truck. "Now that's a real man's haircut."

"We kinda look alike now," Jeremy said, innocently.

Something in Mitch's chest constricted, but he brushed it away.

"Mitch? Do you have any kids?"

"Nope."

"That's too bad. You'd be a great dad."

The compliment shocked Mitch. He really never thought of himself as a dad. "Really? And why's that?" Curious. That's all he was.

Jeremy climbed into the car. "Because you don't mind spending time with kids. You treat me good even if you've hardly known me for long."

"Guess you grew on me. I don't mind hanging around with you." Mitch backed out of his parking spot and headed home. *Home?* Christ, he had to stop thinking like that.

"I wish you could stay forever."

Mitch's heart flipped. He didn't have an answer for that.

"But I know you can't. Mom never lets any man stay. You've been the longest."

Now that caught his attention and stirred some jealousy. "You don't say."

"Not that any man has ever lived with us. Since you've been here, I haven't heard her cry at night," Jeremy admitted, his voice full of concern.

"She cries? Why?"

"Grandpa and Uncle Seth say it's because she misses my dad and that she gets lonely. Which I don't understand, since I'm always there and she's never alone."

A lump formed in Mitch's throat. "You mean the world to her. Maybe she's just lonely for some company from someone her own age. It's a good thing she has a strong man like you to take care of her though."

Jeremy beamed with pride. "Yeah, but you're the one who got her to stop crying."

Mitch swallowed hard. "I don't know how, buddy. I haven't done anything special."

Jeremy kept his gaze on Mitch while Mitch stared between him and the road. "Just being there must do it. Kids at school said you and my mom are having an affair."

Mitch frowned. Damn nosy kids. "Oh, they did, huh? Sounds like they should be doing their schoolwork instead of wondering what your mom and I are doing."

"What's an affair?"

Aw shit! He didn't want to go down this road again with the boy. *Stall.*

"Is it like playing baseball? You know. First and second base?"

They pulled up in front of the house, but neither

made a move to exit the car. Mitch looked at Jeremy who was waiting patiently for an answer.

"Look, kid. I won't lie to you. But maybe you should ask Mom this question."

"No. She's my *mom.* I can't have guy talk with my mom."

"No, I guess you can't." Mitch blew out a breath and rubbed his hand through his hair, forgetting that he'd just cut it all off. "I like your mom and she likes me. So while I wouldn't call what we're doing an affair, you could say we're romantically involved."

Jeremy stared at Mitch with a blank expression.

"Aw, Christ, kid. Yeah, your mom and I have played baseball." That was the only way Mitch knew how to explain it to Jeremy.

Jeremy's eyes grew wide and stared at Mitch. "Eeww. Gross."

"Shut up," Mitch laughed, relieved Jeremy didn't freak out on him. "Someday you won't think so. One day you'll want the girls playing baseball with you. Now get out of the car."

They went inside where Jack greeted them.

"Thanks, Mitch. For being honest with me."

"Yeah. Now forget about what your mom and I do and go get that homework done."

****

Marly arrived home to see her living room reorganized and Mitch instructing Jeremy on how to punch. They hadn't heard her come in since music blared from the stereo. She watched the two interact and her heart fluttered. Mitch kept angling Jeremy's hands into position, showing him how he wanted him to land a punch. Mitch was limping. Of course he was. This kind of regimen was certainly not good for his bad leg. But she didn't have the heart to interrupt. He was a grown man and should know when he's had enough.

"Good job, Jeremy. Now hit me. Here." Mitch pointed to his midsection.

"No way. I can't hit you."

"Oh, please, kid. Do you really think you're gonna hurt me? Now hit me."

"Okay. But you asked for it." Jeremy landed a solid punch, right in the middle of Mitch's gut.

Mitch's abs tightened and he feigned pain, which had her son jumping up and down, fists in the air, screaming he was the champion.

Mitch dragged Jeremy to the floor, rubbing his knuckles over his head. "Holler Uncle! You don't get up until I hear it."

"Uncle," Jeremy said between gasps of glee.

"Can't hear you. Say it."

"Uncle," Jeremy screamed, then laughed harder.

"Oh, I'm sorry. What was that?" Mitch continued the torture.

"Uncle. Uncle. UNCLE! I'm gonna puke. Stop!"

Mitch released him. "You puke, you clean it. Just remember who's the ultimate champion."

Mitch stood first and extended his hand to help Jeremy up. Only when they both stood, did they notice Marly watching them. They both froze as if waiting to be scolded.

"Ah, we'll put the furniture back. Just needed some room to move around," Mitch said.

"Uh huh. See that you do. I'm going to cook dinner."

"Pasta's already cooking," Mitch shouted after her. "I'm sure she'll figure it out once she looks in the pot. Come on, kid. Put your muscles to work and help get this living room back to normal before your mom kills us both."

****

During dinner, Jeremy was his chatty self.

"Jeremy, I think you need to tell your mom what you heard in school today and what we talked about when you came home," Mitch said, casually.

"What did you hear, honey?" Please don't let it be about sex talk, she thought to herself.

"The kids were saying how Mitch was arrested for Howie's murder and asked me if he was still living here."

"Oh no," Marly gasped.

"But I made Mitch explain it to me. I knew he didn't do it."

"Of course not. Eat your veggies," Marly said.

"I'm sorry, Marly. I know you wanted to talk to him together. I tried to tell him that, but the kid is pretty persistent. Wonder where he gets that from?" He raised an eyebrow.

"Guilty," she said, waving her fork.

"I wanted to wait, but he was pretty upset."

"Not upset," Jeremy corrected. "I was mad."

"Okay. He was pretty mad so I was honest with him."

"Of course you were. I appreciate it, Mitch. And

Jeremy, I'm glad you talked to Mitch about it. It's important to ask questions."

"The kids also said you were having an affair."

Marly almost choked. Damn! She was afraid sex would come into the conversation. It was, of course, the natural order of gossip in small towns.

"They did, huh?" She took a long drink of her iced tea.

"Yeah. But I talked to Mitch about that, too. You know. Guy talk."

"I see." Marly glared at Mitch who kept his head down and his fork busy on his plate. She caught the smirk on his face.

"Just so you know, Mom, I don't care that you play baseball with Mitch since he's really cool and all."

Marly's face burned. She needed to end this now. "Thank you. I appreciate your support. Homework done?"

"Yup."

"Good." She stood, got some ice cream, and put a dish of it in front of Jeremy.

"Eat your dessert. Since it's getting close to bedtime, you need to get in the shower. You can watch half an hour of TV before bed."

"Slow down, kid, or you'll end up with a brain freeze," Mitch warned but was too late. Jeremy pressed his palm against his forehead and complained about the pain. Mitch laughed and Marly couldn't help join him. Her son knew better than to gobble down ice cream.

Sometimes she wondered if he did it just to be dramatic.

Chapter Eighteen

With Jeremy tucked into bed and Jack snuggling with him, Marly dragged Mitch into her bedroom to dig out the paperwork he needed. "Here's a copy of the police report I filed when my gun was stolen."

"It's dated only three months ago," Mitch commented.

"Yeah. That's when I noticed it missing. I don't know how long it was gone. I would never have removed it from the box."

Mitch scowled. "Sorry, but if you have a gun in the house, you really need to know where it is at all times."

She held her hand up to him. "Save the lecture. I've already heard it from my father, my brother, the deputy who came to take the report, and the sheriff."

"Okay. The report says there was no sign of forced entry. Doesn't surprise me since you have the very bad habit of leaving your doors unlocked. Who would have known where you kept the gun?"

Marly stood at the end of her bed. "Of course they thought it was Jeremy, but he didn't know I had it in the lock box."

Mitch folded the report and stared at her. "They took the whole lock box?"

"No. They left the box. Only took the gun."

"Okay. At the risk of asking a stupid question, was it locked?"

Her chin shot up. "Of course it was. The lock was picked and mangled. That's why I knew I hadn't removed it. I had already touched the box, so getting fingerprints wasn't an option."

"Said who?" Mitch demanded.

"The sheriff."

"Of course. Is he always so lazy when it comes to doing his damn job?"

"Yes. But what can be done? He was elected to the job until he either gives it up or retires."

Mitch looked around the tidy bedroom. "Do you still have the box?"

"Um, yeah. I do. The lock was only broken so I didn't want to throw it out. Figured I could replace the lock."

"How many people handled it?"

"Just me."

"The sheriff or his people didn't touch it?"

She shook her head, annoyed. "No. They weren't interested. Just took the report. When I followed up a couple times after that, they said nothing turned up. They figured someone who knew I had the gun took it."

"They went back to blaming Jeremy?"

Her eyes darkened with temper. "Yes, and my family. Sheriff suggested my father or my brother took it, thinking I shouldn't have it here."

"He really lives in the dark ages, doesn't he?" Mitch asked, not surprised at the sheriff's insult.

"Yeah. But not everyone around here is like him.

When I was widowed, I was only twenty-three. So everyone just wanted to help. He's really the only one who treated me like a helpless female."

Mitch smiled. "He doesn't know you very well."

"No, he doesn't. I gave him a piece of my mind after the missing gun incident. He didn't care to be put in his place by a woman, but I didn't care to be spoken to in that way by a man. My dad never did it and my brother never dared. Even Rick, a macho army soldier, never treated me like a helpless female. So no way in hell was that piece of shit sheriff gonna do it."

He dared to smirk. "Does that happen all the time?"

"Does what?"

"When something gets you pissed off, does your temper flare up so quickly?"

Her cheeks blushed a sexy pink. "Sorry. My dad says it's the Irish in me."

His hand rubbed her arm, appreciating her soft skin. "Nah. I'd say it's more of the woman in you. You're a strong woman, Marly. Stronger than most men I know. You've got fight in you and that's important. Means you won't lie down and take any crap."

"No, I won't. It took me a long time to get this way. After Rick died, I was a bundle of nerves and I hated that. I hated feeling lost and scared. But I had a baby to raise. Jeremy depended on me. There's an incredible sense of worth when you have another life depending on you."

Or an incredible sense of guilt. His thoughts drifted back to Boston and that horrible day.

"Mitch, something wrong?" Her fingernails dug

into his forearm.

"No. Sorry. Just know what it's like to have someone's life in your hands, and I don't like that responsibility."

"Is that why you left your job? Stopped being a police officer?"

His body stiffened. "What?"

"I know about the hostage situation. Tell me about it." Her voice was gentle, so caring.

"No need if you already know." The words were sarcastic even if he didn't mean it.

Her hand caressed his arm. "Mitch, I want to hear from you what happened."

Abruptly, he stepped back. "Hell, Marly. What good will it do to stir up bad memories? I left all that behind."

"No, you didn't leave it behind. That's the problem. It's still with you. And running won't help. It's funny. I would never have guessed you to run from a problem."

"There is no problem. It's all over."

She crossed her arms and stared at him. "Is it, Mitch? Because from where I'm standing it looks like you're still haunted by the past. I can speak from experience that, until you face your ghosts, you'll never live like you should."

She slipped her arms around his waist and laid her head against his shirt. His hand caressed her back while he buried his face in her hair.

His words came out so sharp, so painful. "I've never been able to talk about that day. I don't think I want to."

"Try me," she whispered, stepping back to look

into his eyes.

"I don't think I can."

"Take your time. I'm not going anywhere."

He did take his time. Marly waited patiently.

When Mitch spoke, his voice was low. "I've had years of training in hostage situations. I was speaking to the robber to get him to surrender. We had been five hours into the talk, which is still considered early. We'll let hostage situations take as long as necessary until the person gives up, as long as they keep talking to us and we think we have the situation under control. But that changed so quickly."

He took a deep breath and Marly waited for him to continue.

"The robber began making very strange demands. He had two teenage girls as hostages and he was a loose cannon. He was a known drug addict with a history of mental instability. He wanted a helicopter to land on the roof to take him away. Imagine requesting a helicopter to land in a Boston neighborhood. I got a bad feeling instantly. I tried to talk sense into him and give him the option of another form of transportation, like a truck or something. But he insisted on the helicopter and a million dollars cash. The cash wasn't a huge problem, we'd just fake it, but the helicopter sure was. Before I could reason with him, gunfire erupted, forcing us to go in."

The memories came flooding back. The images, the smells, the sounds. He didn't want to relive it, but something inside him forced out the words. Marly didn't look at him with pity. No…she just stood there, giving him her full attention. Must've been why the words and memories he'd hidden from all those months ago were bubbling to the surface to be heard.

"I entered the front door with my team. There were six of us. I could smell liquor. It reeked of liquor from the broken bottles lying around. But it was the silence that disturbed me. Something was terribly wrong. We made it to the backroom. I yelled out for the guy to show himself and drop his weapons. Before I finished speaking my last word, the guy opened fire. I ordered my guys to take cover. I felt a burning feeling in my shoulder but ignored it. I was stuck in a small closet area in the hallway and tried to figure out how the hell I'd get out of there. He shot again and emptied his clip. I could hear the empty echo."

Mitch took a deep breath before continuing. His body trembled. Sweat covered his forehead in a cool, clammy film.

"I slowly left the closet area and walked to the backroom where they were holed up. I was hoping to catch him reloading, but he wasn't giving up easily. He had hidden at the end of the hallway with a baseball bat. He slammed that bat into my knee and the flash of pain that followed stole every breath from my lungs. I went down, fighting the urge to blackout. We struggled for my gun. That's when I saw the two girls crumpled on the floor covered in blood. The sight of it made my stomach sick. I hadn't been able to save them. With the last bit of energy I had left, I grabbed the gun from him and shot him point blank in the chest. He died instantly."

Mitch ran a shaky hand through his short hair.

"I don't remember what happened next. I woke up two days later in the hospital. My captain told me that one girl survived, but her friend hadn't. They had

233

been in there trying to buy liquor with fake IDs and it costs one of them her life and the other will have nightmares forever."

"Why did you leave the force, Mitch? Was it because of your leg injury? Did they say you couldn't work anymore?"

He shook his head. "No. They said the door was open anytime I wanted to return. I had been cleared of any wrongdoing. But I couldn't get that girl out of my mind. I wasn't able to save her and I should have. That's what I was trained to do."

Her slender hands rubbed his arms. The simple touch tightened his gut. "Mitch, why beat yourself up? You did everything you could. He was crazy."

"I should've talked him down. Those girls were counting on me to save them."

"No. They were counting on everyone with you to save them. You couldn't do it alone."

"But I led the team. It was the only time I ever lost a hostage. And the first time I killed a man. I had shot perps before, but never had to take a life."

"Add to that your recuperation from your injury. You probably wanted to jump right back into work and bury yourself up to your ears to forget, right?"

"I couldn't do that. My damn knee was shattered. I had to have one surgery after another. Three in total, each time to remove scar tissue and decrease inflammation. I hated the surgeries because I hated being knocked out. Hated being vulnerable."

"Big, strong man like yourself being vulnerable, well, shit, that must make you, ah, what is it? Human?"

He stared at her.

"Isn't that what you told me I was, Mitch. Only human. But you wanted to be more and it killed you not to get back into the action at work. You needed to prove to yourself that you could save lives. But that damn knee wouldn't let you do it, right? At least not as soon as you wanted."

His mouth dropped. "Damn. You sound just like my captain and the doctors."

Her soft eyes touched his heart. "I know I do. Because I've been there. Someone, everyone, had to tell me that it was okay not to be strong all the time. To feel sad and horrible was the easy part. To be happy again is the hardest thing you can ever do after life altering situations. I felt guilty when I smiled or laughed. I felt even guiltier as the years passed after Rick's death and I slowly felt alive again. I felt guilty when I wanted to feel the touch of a man again. But Rick would've wanted me to be happy. If you don't allow yourself to live and be happy, then that robber took two lives that night, yours and the girl's." She moved closer to him. "The best way to honor her is to live. Live like today was your last day. Enjoy every minute. You deserve it. Because you fought for her."

"But I didn't win damnit!" He trembled, the emotions inside him overwhelming.

"We're not meant to win every battle. We're just meant to fight for life. And you did that. At the cost of your knee, your career, and almost your life. If that doesn't convince you that you did 100% of your job that night, then I'm afraid nothing ever will."

He stared at her for a long moment. She was a breath of fresh air. Her words lifted his spirits…and wasn't that about friggin' time?

"Give me a towel. I'm sending the lockbox out to be tested for fingerprints. If the sheriff doesn't want to do his job, I will. I'll mail it this week."

"There. Now that's better." She leaned up and kissed his cheek.

"I hope you can say that as the days go by because, if the sheriff gets wind that I'm doing his investigation, it's bound to piss him off."

"Good. Then maybe he'll get off his fat ass and do some work."

"I'm going to break into Howie's house," he stated casually and grinned when she stared at him.

"What?"

"I want to know who had it in for him more than anyone else in town. Someone who was pissed off enough to kill him."

"I don't like the sound of this, Mitch. If the sheriff catches you, he'll never let you out of jail."

Mitch chuckled. "He'll never catch me." He hushed her when she went to protest again. "You've inspired me, Marly. The way you talk and live life. I'm beginning to feel alive again myself. Let me."

"I'm trying," she whispered.

"I'm specially trained or I wouldn't take the chance. He'll never know I was there. I need to do this."

"You mean you need to prove to yourself that you still got it."

He thought for a moment. "Yeah. I guess so. But it's more than that. I need to treat this like a second chance."

Her eyes searched his. "What do you mean?"

"Like I've been given a second chance to right a

wrong. To put my talents to good use and clear my name, your name, and put a killer behind bars."

"I think I understand."

"Good."

"But it won't change the past, Mitch."

He breathed deeply. "I know. But it can change the future, and that's what I'm concentrating on."

"Just be careful. Be very careful."

Marly got a towel for Mitch to pick up the lockbox. She turned back to him. "I like your haircut, Mitch. And Jeremy's, too. I can't believe how much older he looks now. He likes it, so I'm very grateful."

"You can make it up to me once we pack this up."

"And how would you like me to do that?"

He grinned wickedly. "All night long."

****

Marly entered her bedroom after checking on Jeremy who was fast asleep. Having Mitch sitting on her bed, waiting for her, made her belly dance with butterflies. She was a grown woman for Christ's sake. Still, having Mitch undress her with his eyes did something to her thought process. She couldn't remember a single thing from her To-Do list that had re-played all day long inside her head.

As soon as Mitch scooted off of the bed and walked toward her wearing only his jeans, she was a goner. His chest beckoned her lips to lay sweet kisses across the bare flesh. Standing beside her, his head dipped, his warm mouth found the tender spot under her ear.

Marly stretched her neck giving Mitch total access to her flesh. His lips left a trail of kisses along her jaw, down her throat, and back up to her jaw. The tiny stubble from his day's beard growth left a prickly sensation as his lips moved over her skin. It thrilled her.

His hands roamed along her arms to her waist around her back, pulling her closer to him. His hand fisted in her hair, angling her head for him to devour her mouth.

With flawless movement, Mitch removed her shirt and bra and feasted on her breasts. Her heart was pounding, her head was spinning. She wanted all of him. She wanted to kiss every inch of him. To explore him. To tease him.

He flipped her onto the bed, his weight pinning her beneath him. He leveled his weight on his arms and his good leg.

"Mitch, no, your leg."

"If I can't handle it, you'll be the first to know. But right now, I want to feel you moving underneath me. *I* need control."

His mouth took hers in a flash of fury. The need was so animalistic, she was thrilled with the pleasure it brought. He couldn't get enough of her, couldn't touch her enough. His breath increased and the golden hue of his eyes darkened to cool brown. He was the hunter, she was the prey, and she was captured. She surrendered to his touch, to his needs.

When his kisses continued to trail from her lips to her jaw, she arched to meet his mouth. After he feasted on her breasts for what seemed like hours, she was sure he was ready to take her. But as he continued the lovely trail of hot, impatient kisses down her navel aiming lower, she tensed.

"Mitch. No. Wait."

"Control," he said, stopping to look up into her eyes. "I want it, Marly. I need it. I need to taste you. All of you."

When he didn't wait for a response, and the objection that was stuck somewhere in the back of her throat didn't surface, she gave in. It was exhilarating to lose herself in the moment, to surrender to the slow exquisite torture he bestowed upon her.

With her mind filling with a misty fog, she closed her eyes and focused on the attention Mitch gave her body. Lowering himself between her legs, he tenderly placed kisses on the inside of her thighs, instantly sending a bolt of heat to her core. He moved without stopping. She was a limber mess of bones lying on the bed, awaiting his next strategically placed kiss.

It was only when he rested his head inches above her most sensitive spot did she realize she never experienced this intimacy before. Had Rick ever wanted to? The question flitted from her mind as Mitch's touch demanded her full attention.

It delighted her, scared her, worried her. She was afraid he'd leave her wanting more of this bliss, something she was fearful few men could deliver like Mitch Allen.

All thoughts were stripped from her mind as his mouth closed over her pussy and slowly feasted. Despite herself, she moaned and arched up to meet his heated onslaught. What a wonderful, decadent pleasure. Her body pulsed like never before, like heavy fingers of pleasure dancing along her skin, teasing her.

He licked and laved at her swollen pussy lips. His thumbs strummed along her tender flesh, gliding through her wetness to caress her clit. The fire tearing through her womb built until it felt like an inferno. Breathing became difficult as her head wobbled from side to side.

"Yes, Mitch. Oh, God, it feels so…good."

His glorious mouth never stopped its exploration. Raking his tongue over her sensitive flesh, he licked at her juices, never slowing in his manipulation. Soon the fire building within her core edged toward the surface. It was all she could do not to bolt off the bed.

The wave of pleasure slammed into her hard and fast, furious and strong. Her body bucked wildly, but this was one ride she didn't want to miss. Mitch never stopped even as she clasped the bed sheets into her fists.

Did he know she was exploding with the most wonderful orgasm of her life and it was all because of his darling mouth? Then it hit again, not as strong as the first but just as sensational. It was impossible not to writhe like a mad woman. Only then did he remove his lips, replacing them with a strong finger in her pussy that toyed with her spasming muscles, making her beg for more.

"Mitch, now! I need you inside me. Oh, God. Now," she said in gasps.

He entered her so gently, so carefully, keeping his eyes on her face. His care only made her want him more. His concern for her comfort was about to undo her, and she moved her hips to entice his to thrust into her. Soon she was moving under him, fast and furious.

The familiar feel of the latex couldn't dim her arousal.

"Oh, Marly," Mitch whispered.

"What?" She stopped instantly. "Am I hurting you?"

His expression did look pained but not because of his leg. "God, no. Keep going."

"Say my name again. Say it," she demanded.

"Marly. Marly. Marly." He came with her when the shudders wracked her body again. Her already sensitive pussy quivered with more waves of pleasure, so much that she doubted that she could remember her name.

His body stretched over hers with shaking muscles as he held his weight off of her. With each thrust, he held his cock deep inside her before thrusting again. His hips pumped relentlessly, stroking her intimate muscles over and over, extending her orgasm until a final shiver from his heated body signaled his completion.

Collapsing together, they lay there, catching their breaths and embracing each other.

At dawn, Mitch crawled out of bed even as Marly reached for him. "Where are you sneaking off to?" she whispered, her voice groggy with sleep.

Mitch stood to pull on his pants and shirt. "Got to get back to my room before the kid wakes up."

"Okay. I guess it's probably for the best until we can talk to him about us. It'd be awkward to explain you sleeping in my room."

"You'd just tell him we played baseball."

"Huh?"

"Sorry. It's a guy thing. Remember, I told you he and I had a little talk?"

"Oh, yeah. So if he asks about us then I should tell him we play baseball?"

He shrugged his shoulders. "Unless you have a better idea for telling him why we're lying naked in your bed."

"Nope. Baseball's good."

Mitch stole one more kiss before leaving her lying there completely sated. She closed her eyes and pulled his pillow to her face and inhaled deeply. What in the world was she doing? What would she do when he left? Her sleepy mind refused to dwell on the inevitable. Instead, it concentrated on the very vivid memories of their lovemaking. The smell of sex clung to the air, thrilling her more.

She could still feel his touch along her skin. His touch was strong and possessive but not hurtful. It made her hunger for more and more until she thought her breath would forever escape her lungs. Dreamily, she drifted off with thoughts of Mitch in her mind.

Chapter Nineteen

Mid-week Mitch met Marly for lunch needing to break up his day, but when he arrived at her office, she nearly plowed him over.

"Sorry, Mitch. I can't do lunch. The school called. The principal asked me to come right in."

"Is Jeremy okay?" he asked, following her to her car.

"Yes. But I guess he was involved in some kind of disruption."

Without asking, Mitch climbed into the front seat of her car. She stared at him. "Mitch, you don't have to come along."

"I don't mind." He fastened his seatbelt.

"Fine. I don't have time to argue about it." She peeled away from the curb. "I've been doing this by myself a long time, Mitch, so please don't feel like you have to be a knight in shining armor and come to my rescue."

"Okay." Somebody's temper was firing up.

"Okay? That's it? Just okay?" she yelled.

"Look, if you want to argue then we can argue, but I'm not trying to be anything. I'm worried about Jeremy, so I want to tag along. If you think I'm being nosy, or will interfere with your motherly duties, tell me and I'll stay in the car."

"No. I don't think any of that." She blew out a breath. "I'm sorry. Didn't mean to be rude. Jeremy never gets in trouble. I can't wait to hear what this is about."

Once in the school parking lot, Mitch didn't make a move to exit the car. "Come on. Jeremy may need you to rescue him if I don't like what I hear from the principal," Marly said.

Mitch tried to keep up with her quick pace but fell about ten paces back. He walked up behind her as the principal came out of her office to motion her in. Jeremy sat outside her office with his hands crossed.

"Hey, kid," Mitch said, rubbing his hand over his head before following Marly into the office. Poor kid looked scared to death. Mitch remembered those days well.

"Mrs. Weston, this is a family friend, Mitch Allen. I would like for him to sit in on our meeting."

"I don't have a problem with that. Actually, I'm glad you brought Mitch in seeing as he's the topic of our discussion today."

Both Marly and Mitch stared at each other then at Mrs. Weston.

"Oh? How's that?" Marly asked.

The principal sat with her hands folded. Why did they all do that? It made them seem so impersonal, so mean.

"Jeremy and Mark got into a fist fight an hour ago. Jeremy explained to me that this gentleman, Mitch, had taught him how to fight."

Mitch squirmed in his seat when Marly gasped and stared at him. "Now wait a minute. You've got it all wrong," Mitch began.

"Have I, Mitch? Then please explain why one of my finest students punched Mark in the face, giving him a black eye?"

Marly looked shocked. "He did what?"

Mitch bit back as pride wanted to burst into a smile. For some reason, he didn't think Marly would understand a smile right now.

"That's right. Mark is icing his eye as we speak."

"What did Jeremy say made him do this?" Mitch asked.

"He said you taught him how to fight these clowns. That's all he would say."

"Mitch! I told you that this fighting stuff was no good."

"Marly, don't have a fit. Ask Jeremy what this was about."

"Obviously to show off the moves you taught him. Mrs. Weston, I am very sorry for this. Please let me—"

Mitch cut her off. "Mrs. Weston, please have Jeremy come in. I think we need to hear his side of the story."

"I think we've heard enough from Jeremy."

"No, you haven't." Mitch rose and opened the door. "Jeremy, get in here."

"Mitch," Marly protested but stopped when she saw Jeremy's shirt covered in ketchup and grease and his head hung down in shame.

"Jeremy," Mitch said, with his hand on his shoulder. "I think it's time you came clean about fighting with Mark. You need to tell your mom and Mrs. Weston or you're going to be the only one in

245

trouble."

"What happened to your shirt?" Marly stood and went to her son.

"That must've happened when the fight was broken up," Mrs. Weston stated.

"Or it's what caused the fight," Mitch insisted. "Go ahead, Jeremy. If you tell the truth, it can't hurt you."

Jeremy sighed. "The other kids, especially Mark, have been teasing me. Bullying me. They pick on me because I don't have a dad to do things with. Today at lunch, Mark smeared his cheeseburger all over my shirt and asked if I was going to get my mommy after him. So I whacked him."

"Fighting solves nothing," Mrs. Weston stated sternly.

"And what does bullying solve?" Marly asked, whirling around to face the old lady. "My son is being bullied. Where the hell were the teachers and why aren't they doing their jobs to keep him safe?"

"That kind of language will solve nothing—"

"Screw it! I'll tell you what will solve this problem. You will. My son will not be penalized for standing up for himself. In fact, he will continue to get self-defense lessons from Mitch. Isn't that right, Mitch?" She whirled on him, her eyes menacing. Damn, she made him proud.

Mitch raised his hands. "Absolutely."

Marly whipped around to face the principal again. "And if another one of these snot-nosed kids wants to pick on my son because his father is dead then you better make sure I don't hear of it or I'll make them run home crying to *their* mommies. And if *their* mommies have a problem with that then I'll deal with them, too. Come on, Jeremy, you're taking the rest of the day off."

At the door, Marly stopped and continued in a calmer voice. "I trust that this will be the last time we have to speak of this nonsense. These kids are here to learn. See that they do just that."

Out in the parking lot, Mitch walked with Jeremy, both of them eyeing Marly.

"Wow, Mom. You were great back there. Thanks for sticking up for me."

"Oh, honey." She hugged him fiercely. "I'll always stick up for you. Why didn't you tell me these boys were picking on you?"

"I tried to handle it myself. Besides, that's what they expected me to do—run to my mommy." His young voice sounded broken.

"That's why you got into the wrestling shows."

"Yeah. But I didn't know the moves right until Mitch showed me. One pop to the face was all it took and Mark cried like a baby."

Mitch and Jeremy exchanged hi-fives. Marly glared.

"Of course, Jeremy, your mom's gonna want me to tell you that fighting isn't always the answer. But I think your mom, of all people, understands that there are times you just have to take care of yourself."

Marly's expression softened. "Come on, men. I think ice cream will solve this problem."

Walking to the car, Mitch whispered in Marly's ear. "I'm a whipped cream guy myself."

"Good to know since I think whipped cream is absolutely sinful."

****

Marly, Mitch, and Jeremy enjoyed pizza and ice cream before heading to the post office to mail the lockbox to Mitch's contact in Boston. Marly gave in to her son's wish to rent a video so they stopped at the local movie rental place.

"This one looks cute," Marly said, referring to a movie about a boy who searches for his lost dog.

Mitch and Jeremy eyed each other and made a face.

Mitch spoke up first. "Ah, men don't do cute. We're going to the blood and guts section."

They walked away together.

"Yeah, no cute stuff, Mom."

Marly opened her mouth in shock and then shut it again. "There's nothing wrong with cute."

Defeated, Marly roamed the shelves of the romance movies. She was in the mood for romance and, since she had to wait to be with Mitch until Jeremy went to bed, she'd find a good romantic movie.

On the ride home, Mitch and Jeremy dominated the conversation, each demanding to watch the movie they picked out first. In the end, Jeremy conceded since Mitch's movie sounded very interesting.

"Mom, you're not going to watch it with us, are you?"

"Jeremy," Mitch scolded. "That's not nice. If she wants to watch it with us she can."

"Aw, you won't like it, Mom. It's scary."

Marly understood when a woman wasn't wanted. "Then I'll pass. But if you have nightmares, you better not let me know or there'll be no more of these manly movies. Got it?"

He hissed out a breath. "I don't have nightmares. Nightmares are for babies."

Mitch wished they were for babies. He'd tried to find a movie he could watch that wouldn't trigger his bad memories, but everything had a cop story or something. For the kid's sake, he'd suck it up and just deal with it. Jeremy was so excited about watching a movie with him that Mitch couldn't help but look forward to it, too.

Once in the house, Jeremy made a beeline for the TV until Mitch walked over to him and turned it off. "Homework first. Bath second. When you have everything ready for school, we can watch it."

When Jeremy would've protested, Mitch just raised his hands and walked away. "Sorry, buddy. Rules are rules. If you don't get that stuff done, guess I'll have to watch the movies by myself."

Jeremy flew up the stairs with his backpack. "Come on, Jack. Come on, boy." Jack did as commanded.

"He's probably hoping Jack eats his homework," Mitch said.

Marly walked into the kitchen. "You're really good with him, Mitch. He listens to you without a fight. I'm getting spoiled."

"He's a good kid. Likes to push buttons, but is smart enough to know when to back off."

Marly opened a water bottle and handed it to Mitch. "So you have two movies to watch, huh?"

Mitch spoke after taking a long sip of the water. "Yeah. I promise they're not bad movies. You're welcome to join us."

"And mortify my son? No, that's okay. But I do appreciate the offer. I have some bills to write out, a cute movie to watch, and a nice long bath to take."

Mitch growled low. "Wish I could join you for that bath." His lips touched hers to quickly steal a deep kiss.

"Will I see you after your movies?" she asked softly, resting her hands on his chest.

His knuckles skimmed her cheek. "Absolutely. Unless you'd rather sleep."

"Yeah, maybe I should catch up on my sleep," she teased.

His teeth scraped against her neck and she squelched a screech. "Oh, really?"

Through giggles, she pushed him back. "Okay. You convinced me. I'll be waiting for you. Right now though, I'm pouring myself a glass of wine and taking a long, hot bath."

Breaking free of his embrace, she got a glass and poured the wine before placing the bottle back into the fridge. As she strutted past him, her hand brushed across the front of his jeans.

"That was just cruel," he complained.

"That'll teach you for biting my neck." She raised her glass to him as she walked up the stairs.

****

Once the movie ended, Jeremy went to bed. Excitement filled Mitch as he walked down the hall to Marly's bedroom, hoping she was awake for him to seduce her. To his disappointment, the room was dark when he peeked in. Of course she would fall asleep waiting for him to finish the movie. The adorable woman was exhausted.

Mitch walked slowly to his room and shut the door before turning on the light. On his bed, dressed in a sexy frilly nightie slept Marly. Yup, he was right. She had fallen asleep waiting for him. But she had come to *his* bed. His heart did somersaults and his cock stiffened instantly when she stirred, awakened by the light.

He sat on the edge of the bed, just wanting to watch her. He couldn't touch her yet. Then he'd have to bury his cock deep inside her tight pussy. But first, he needed to remember her just like this. Sprawled out on his bed in her white nightie, her long, blond hair flowing over the pillows, her eyes sluggish with sleep.

Damnit! When the hell did he fall in love with her? God, what he wouldn't do to have her love in return. But the ghost of her husband still seemed to have a hold on her heart. Mitch shook his head to rattle his thoughts. Dreamy ideas like that were for teenagers, not thirty-five-year-old men having a midlife crisis.

"Hey you," she said, her voice husky with sleep.

His knuckles skimmed her soft cheek. When her head turned and her lips pressed into his palm, he needed no further confirmation. He was totally, unequivocally in love with Marly, with her temper, her stubbornness, hell even with her damn control issues. He wouldn't change a thing about this amazing woman. Well, maybe he'd keep her in his bed, naked and sated. But nothing else.

"Make love to me, Mitch. Just like I've dreamed about for so long."

He slowly stripped, not taking his eyes off her beautiful body as he memorized every curve, every freckle and beauty mark.

When his hands lifted her nightie, he was thrilled to see she wore no panties. Glancing at her face, her innocent smile hid the temptress he knew very well.

Her eyes danced with lust. "I wanted easy access for tonight."

"And I want you, Marly," he whispered, climbing over her to claim her mouth.

Her lips were soft, her touch so tender. His tongue edged its way inside her warmth. No matter how many times they kissed, he'd never get enough of her sweetness. Everything about her was remarkable, but it was the way she kissed him that rocked him to his soul. She stole his breath with each sweep of her tongue over his. The soft purrs escaping from her throat added to his arousal.

Breaking the kiss was necessary if he wanted to maintain his concentration. She was just too damn potent. The soft skin of her neck beckoned for his attention. Not able to deny himself a nibble, he sank his teeth onto her delicate flesh and nibbled until she squealed in delight.

"Oh, Mitch. You're tickling me with your whiskers."

"Sorry, I should've shaved first."

Her body trembled under his hands as they roamed up and down her sides.

"Mmmm. I'm not complaining. Just need you."

Mitch didn't need further prompting. Hell, he needed her just as bad. Climbing off of the bed, he ripped open a condom and sheathed his cock in the hated latex, Mitch steadied himself over her as his cock nudged her pussy lips. Her moans grew louder with each new stroke as he worked to hold his body weight off her slenderness while burying himself so deep into her tight pussy that his cock throbbed with every stroke. Never had a woman felt so damn good.

There was no rush to the finish line. Not tonight. With their gazes locked, Mitch pumped his hips into hers slowly, making every stroke count and as memorable as the previous one. When her tight sheath clamped around his cock, when her eyes shadowed with desire, when she yelled his name, only then did Mitch enjoy his release, an explosion so powerful that emotions rode his heart until he thought he'd beg for mercy.

After disposing of the condom and pulling on his jeans, Mitch lifted a listless Marly and walked silently to her room. He tucked her under her covers before kissing her forehead. His lips lingered for a moment until he gathered the strength to pull away and return to his room.

Sleep would be damn difficult tonight when the woman he loved slept down the hall, dressed in that sexy nightie, when she needed to be in Mitch's bed.

Chapter Twenty

The next two weeks passed with a blur of constant activity at the Hampton household. Between working, housework, and keeping on top of her son's homework, Mitch didn't know how Marly kept on top of things.

"Seth," Marly said, opening the door after dinner. "This is a surprise. Everything alright?"

"Sure is. Going into town for a drink. Thought I'd invite Mitch to join me if it's not too late," Seth said, stepping into the living room.

"That's up to him," Marly replied.

Seth walked to the couch where Mitch stood to shake his hand. "How about it?"

"Sure. It's only eight. Early enough for me."

"Have fun," Marly said, kissing Mitch's cheek. "I want the whole scoop when you get back."

Mitch feigned confusion.

"I wasn't born yesterday. Seth is a workaholic not an alcoholic. He's only asking you for a beer to talk about something he wants to protect his baby sister from hearing. And for that," she said, turning to Seth and pinching his nipple. "You get that."

"Ow!" Seth protested, his hand covering his chest to protect himself from any more abuse. "I told you before not to do that, Marly, or I'll hold you down and shave your head."

She leaned up and kissed his cheek. "Go ahead and try."

Seth picked her up in a bear hug and dropped her down fast. "Give Jeremy a smack on the head for me. Okay?"

"Get out of here." She shoved them both out the door.

Seth drove them to J's Tavern on the far end of town. They took seats at a booth in the corner of the room. Someone had a sad country song playing on the jukebox.

"I dragged you out tonight to give you some information that came my way today about Sheriff Ridgeley. Thought you might be interested," Seth said, before taking a drink of his beer.

"You have my attention," Mitch said, toying with the label on his beer bottle.

"Seems Ridgeley made some unusually large withdrawals of cash from his bank account six months ago."

Mitch raised an eyebrow. "And that interests me because?"

"Because the next day, thirty thousand dollars was deposited by Howie Singleton into his account."

Now wasn't that interesting? "How'd you find this out?" Mitch asked, ignoring his beer.

"Melinda, a young lady I'm romantically interested in, works at the bank. While we were together early this evening, she relayed some information I may have asked her to discreetly look for."

Mitch smirked. "Probably won't be admissible as evidence since there was no warrant and she violated both men's privacy." Mitch's attempt at a scholarly voice earned him a laugh.

"Please. You're preaching to the choir here. Remember, I'm a lawyer. I knew that. But that's not why I wanted to look into them. Thought the info could be of use to you. You're going to use your expertise to solve this homicide and fix my sister's life, right?"

"You could say I'm looking into a few things."

Seth leaned forward and talked quietly. "Good. So if this kind of info comes your way, no matter how it was found, it can only help."

Mitch nodded, sipping his beer. "Is she cute?"

"Who?"

"Melinda."

Seth smiled and sat back. "Gorgeous. Great ass. We've been off and on for a while. And my parents adore her."

"You thinking of settling down?"

Seth roared with laughter. "Hardly. Though she'd like that. Not in my life plan, though. Too scary. Being with one person forever and ever. The whole 'death do us part' stuff freaks me out. That could be a long time."

Mitch had never given forever any thought either until Marly entered the picture.

"Besides, I'm married to my work. Like my sister said. I'm a work-a-holic," Seth conceded.

"Be careful. I was once married to my work, too. It got me nowhere. When the career ended, I was all alone." Mitch's heart constricted painfully. He wasn't alone now, well, at least for now.

"Guess it's a good thing I'm a lawyer and not a cop. My career will last for however long I want it to."

"Tell me why Ridgeley withdrawing thirty grand and allegedly giving it to Howie is useful. Maybe he borrowed the money and was paying it back."

Seth hissed. "Yeah, right. Howie wouldn't lend his own mother money let alone a cousin he despised."

"Can't understand why he'd despise Ridgeley. He's such a peach and all."

"That is one fucked up family," Seth confirmed, and waved the waitress over. "Another round, please."

She took Seth's empty bottle and Mitch's half-filled bottle he wasn't done with. He'd just wait for the next round.

"Ridgeley and Howie were cousins. His father and his mother were siblings. They were close in age and forced to play together even though they always ended up in a fistfight. They were both messed up in the head but in different ways. Before the grandfather died, he sold the land Marly has to our dad. The remainder of the land stayed with Howie's family, which he inherited when his father died."

"So Ridgeley got screwed out of the deal."

Seth grunted and swigged more beer. "In today's standards, yes. But, years ago, his father was compensated with cash for what land might have been his."

Mitch shook his head, looking around the small tavern with its scratched tables and chairs. "Interesting. Why'd I believe small towns would be boring?"

"Hey, we have our share of nutcases just like the

city."

"We can rule out Ridgeley paying back a loan. And we can rule out Ridgeley stealing any money since he was withdrawing, not depositing."

"That's right."

"Another interesting piece of gossip around town is that over the last six months, probably around the same time of this withdrawal-deposit thing, Ridgeley and Howie had become best buddies, although Ridgeley didn't smile about it."

Odd. "Do you think he was blackmailing the sheriff?"

"I don't think Ridgeley would've kissed his ass for nothing."

"Damn. It's a shame I missed the ass kissing. Must have been a sight to see." Sarcasm was good therapy.

"I'll never see the same out of my left eye," Seth confessed and laughed.

"Did Howie have any family other than Ridgeley? Was he married?"

"Nope. That bastard was as mean as they come. No woman wanted him unless he paid for her. Another piece of town gossip." Seth lounged back in the booth lazily.

"I met Howie once and could tell he was mean to the core," Mitch said, wishing he had punched the bastard when he could have.

"It'll be interesting to see who gets his land since there's no will."

Mitch took a long swig. It was nice to sit and enjoy a beer again with a friend.

"Talk is that Ridgeley will get the land since he's

next of kin."

"Are you shitting me?" Mitch asked, shocked. "So Marly goes from one asshole neighbor to another? Shit!"

Seth leaned forward again. "Listen to me, Mitch. This is my specialty. There was a note against the land and it has to be paid off before it can be inherited. Ridgeley doesn't have that kind of money since his house is already mortgaged."

Finally some good news. "That's promising. Isn't it?"

"Maybe. But who's to say an outsider looking to settle down in a nice little town like Courtsville couldn't buy it?"

Mitch saw where this was leading. "Sorry. I'm not planning on staying."

"You could've fooled me."

"Stop. It isn't what you think."

"Tell you what I think," Seth offered. "I think you and my sister are happy together and Jeremy adores you. Not to mention there's an ideal job in law enforcement coming up for re-election that you'd win by a landslide, so employment wouldn't be an issue. But I think you're a chicken shit when it comes to commitment."

Mitch glared. "You don't know me."

"I know your type."

"Really?"

Seth was very cocky. "Yup. You're me. Never wanting to settle down. First, it was your work. Then it was the open road and you were determined to run away. But then Marly came along. You weren't expecting her to grow on you so fast."

Mitch was silent. Was he that transparent?

Seth was as serious as Mitch had ever seen him. "You never had a chance, Mitch. Marly's a great person. Getting stuck in town doomed you. Don't have to admit it, certainly not to me. But just try to deny you're in love with my sister. You can't."

Before Mitch could be defensive, Jerry interrupted them as he swaggered to their booth, slurring his words. Mitch could smell the whiskey before he stopped in front of them.

Bloodshot eyes stared at Mitch. "Somethin' gots to be done 'bout that ol' sheriff. I dragged my sorry ass down to his orrffice and tald him I killed Howeee and ya know what that son of a bitch did? Wells. I'll tells ya. Nothing."

"Maybe you should switch to coffee, Jerry, before you head home," Seth said.

Jerry laughed and then coughed heavily. "Already dids thats hours ago."

Mitch focused his eyes on the drunk man. "Appreciate you trying to get me off the hook, Jerry, but you shouldn't take the blame for something you didn't do."

"But I dids it. In my heads, I dids it for years." He banged a finger on the side of his head. "I drinks a lot so who's sayings I didn't shoots him finally?"

"You wouldn't stoop to something like that. You're a good man," Seth added, not taking the man seriously either.

Jerry wandered back to the bar where he had left his coffee. Mitch watched as Jerry lit a cigarette and then Mitch turned his attention back to Seth.

"Any reason the sheriff wouldn't take Jerry's

confession seriously. I mean the man seems to hate Howie—hell, has for years. Why blame an outsider like me?"

Seth glanced at Jerry then back to Mitch. "Maybe cause it's easier. Jerry is well liked around here. He'd not hurt a fly, so the sheriff would have a harder time making charges stick against him than you. And your rep as a cop only adds fuel to his fire. Ridgeley will never have the success you've had and he knows that. Chaps his ass."

Mitch shook his head in disgust. "Success. I lost my last case in the worst way, so I don't see why he can resent me on that."

"Sheriff Ridgeley has always wanted to fire that tanked up gun at his side but people in Courtsville are, for the most part, peace loving and law abiding citizens, so he's never had a chance to take a shot."

Or has he?

"Come on. I better get you home. My sister is going to want to pick your brain about what we talked about. Might as well give you enough time to do so."

They argued over who would pay the tab, but Seth won.

"Yeah," Mitch agreed. "Guess I better be honest with her."

"Now my friend, as a lawyer, I have to agree that honesty is the best policy."

"Yup. And since you didn't let me help with the tab, you'll understand when I tell her I went with you to help you pick out engagement rings for, what was her name, Melinda?"

Seth's face dropped. "You wouldn't."

"I will. Unless you take this twenty and let me

pay half that tab."

Reluctantly, Seth took the money.

At the truck, Seth laughed. "I like you, Mitch. You're all right."

"So I shouldn't tell your sister that you invited me out only to check me out some more on her behalf?"

"Not much gets by you, huh?"

Mitch shook his head.

"Just being a good brother. She'll kill me if you tell her." His puppy dog eyes were so pathetic, Mitch laughed.

"As long as you tell me I've passed your test, then my mouth remains shut."

"You pass. With flying colors."

"No more tests?"

"No more tests."

Chapter Twenty-One

The next day, Mitch waited until Marly and Jeremy had left for work and school before he left on his investigation. If Marly knew Mitch planned to break into Howie's house today she'd worry herself sick or, worse, want to come with him. He couldn't have that. Not that he didn't think she'd make a great cat burglar with her slim, sexy figure. But she had Jeremy to take care of and couldn't risk being caught.

The day was cloudy, gray, and dreary. Kind of how Mitch felt as he walked across Marly's land and into the trees that separated hers from Howie's.

Mitch had been on the antibiotics Doc Peterson had prescribed him for about three weeks now. Never in his life had he taken medicine so religiously. Of course, never before had medicine done him so well. He could walk without his cane for the first time since the injury. He knew a marathon wasn't in his future, but to have the freedom of both hands again was so satisfying to his independence.

Slowly, Mitch walked to the edge of the clearing, employing his police training to scan the area around Howie's house for someone else's presence. He waited a good ten minutes to be sure he was alone before he walked to the side of the house.

Mitch recognized the car parked in the driveway as one of the cars that had sped past Marly the night they'd almost been run off the road. It would be interesting to see what kind of car the sheriff drove. He'd bet any amount of money that Ridgeley was chasing Howie that night. Just created more questions.

Mitch crept to a window and pulled on black leather gloves before he peered inside. It was dark and quiet. Didn't look like anyone had been there for quite some time since there was dust everywhere. Not that Howie appeared to have good housekeeping skills anyway. There was no sign of a house alarm. He didn't expect any, but the city man in him made him confirm before attempting to enter.

None of the doors had been left open like Marly was in the bad habit of doing. He should've figured either Howie locked them or the sheriff came around and did so after his death. It didn't really matter to Mitch how they got locked. He just had to get them unlocked.

From the back pocket of his jeans he pulled out a small metal clip. He expertly opened the gadget that had been his close partner back in Boston. No need for a battering ram when you could quickly and quietly pick a lock and deliver the element of surprise.

Within seconds, Mitch was inside Howie Singleton's house. His lungs immediately revolted from the stink of stale cigarettes and beer. With the back of his hand covering his mouth, Mitch gagged, his stomach filling with nausea.

It didn't take Mitch long to see that Howie had a huge love of porn. Obviously, Howie hadn't cared who saw the magazines since he hadn't made any effort to conceal them. But then again, glancing around, Mitch surmised that Howie probably wasn't the type to have guests. If he did, they were probably scum like him.

Hundreds of lottery tickets and scratch tickets covered every tabletop. Looks like the guy had a passion for gambling and loose women. Mitch wondered which it was that ultimately did him in.

The state-of-the-art computer sitting on a plain wooden desk in the living room surprised Mitch. He wouldn't have thought of Howie as the computer literate type. The perverted, pathetic type suited him, but not the computer savvy type.

Mitch touched the mouse and the screen came alive. No way! This was too good to be true. Was it a trap? Was someone watching him?

He could imagine the sheriff sitting on his fat ass somewhere outside, watching Mitch and waiting to arrest him for breaking and entering. No way would Mitch let him cuff him again. Nope. Even with his bum leg, he'd out run the fat bastard.

Since no guns came charging in, Mitch opened the Internet and checked the history. It wasn't much of a surprise that there was a laundry list of porn sites. Seemed Howie would peruse any porn site and every kind of kinky sex site he could find.

Mitch wasn't interested in viewing porn so he switched to view Howie's email. Again, there was no surprise that the only emails Howie had in his Inbox were porn site receipts for downloaded pictures.

Mitch spent the next twenty minutes quickly searching Howie's computer files for anything of interest. He viewed more tits and ass than he cared to remember and none of it was pretty. He was ready to give up when something caught his eye.

His jaw dropped as his eyes widened at the images in front of him. His stomach turned when he saw a naked Sheriff Ridgeley on the computer screen. And the sheriff wasn't alone but in the embrace of another naked man. The sex was bad enough to watch but to see Ridgeley's face and his flab all hot and sweaty was revolting. Mitch squeezed his eyes shut for a minute, but it was no use. That image was burned into his memory.

Now everything made sense to Mitch. If Howie had these revealing pictures of Ridgeley, that may explain the thirty grand Ridgeley forked over to him. It also meant that Howie might have died over these pictures. Mitch had no proof that Ridgeley killed Howie but every policeman cell in his body was screaming it.

And that made Ridgeley all the more dangerous.

After making sure there was paper in the machine, he hit print. Eleven pages later, Mitch folded the disgusting pictures to shove in the back pocket of his jeans. He looked around the room to be sure he got whatever he needed. The last thing he wanted was to have to come back in here.

The fridge was full of beer and some kind of decaying take-out food. As quickly as he opened the door, Mitch closed it. The stench was a mix between rotten eggs and vinegar. The counter was covered in dirty dishes and unopened mail. Mice shit was everywhere. Nasty.

Mitch picked up a receipt for a hotel called Calling Hours Motel. Scanning the countertop Mitch found more similar receipts. They were dated weekly. Howie had made regular visits to the motel. He folded one of the receipts and crammed it into his back pocket with the pictures. He smelled a road trip coming soon. He'd find out what Howie was doing there, even though he had a pretty good idea just by the name itself.

When Mitch turned to leave, a blinking red light caught his eye. The phone was archaic, but it did have an answering machine. He pressed the play button. The two new messages were automated messages about some kind of truck parts Howie ordered.

Then the saved messages came on. Mitch's body tightened at Sheriff Ridgeley's voice.

"Howie, you stupid son-of-a-bitch! You pick up this goddamn phone now. You don't want to continue this. You piece of shit! This has gone too far. I better hear from you."

The message ended. Mitch waited patiently for the next. With no surprise, Ridgeley came on again.

"Howie. I want everything you have. You promised me, so stop jerking me around. You got what you wanted. The fucking well is dry and now it's your turn to pay up. I expect to have every fucking copy of every fucking picture in my hand by tomorrow evening. Do you understand me? I may have a lot to lose, but if I lose so will you. Don't piss me off any more or you'll see how mean I can get."

Damn! That was a threat but nothing to link him to the murder.

The next message was a female voice. "Hi, Howie, it's Madeline Ridgeley. I got your message. You said it was urgent that you talk to me. I'm home

267

now so when you get this give me a call. I'm going to call Jonas now to see if he knows what is so urgent. I do hope everything is all right."

There were no more messages, but Mitch had a clear picture of what had happened. Howie evidently stepped too far into Ridgeley's business.

If Howie was blackmailing Ridgeley over the pictures Mitch found, then he figured Ridgeley had had enough, especially if he found out that Howie contacted his wife.

After all, Mitch thought as he shut the door behind him and disappeared into the woods to get back to Marly's house, what man would want his wife to see explicit nude sex photos of him cheating on her?

Especially when he was cheating on her with another man.

*****

Marly sat at her desk, staring into space, twirling her pen, and wondering what she was going to do about Mitch Allen. Better yet, she wondered what she'd do without him. How did she let things get this far? She'd always been careful not to fall for another man. Most weren't ready for instant fatherhood.

The familiar anger welled inside her belly. She'd never asked any man to be a father to her son. And she certainly hadn't dated for that purpose.

It was too hard for the men she dated to believe she only wanted some adult companionship and maybe some good sex, not a father for her child. But they always got cold feet and even the prospect of sex couldn't keep some around long enough.

Small towns were especially hard on the single folk. Especially the young, single folk. There were very few single men or women left in town. She reminisced about her trips over the years into the bigger cities surrounding Courtsville. If you were looking to meet someone, those were the places to go. Sitting around a small town like this wouldn't get you a date. This was the type of place where everyone knew everyone. What thrill was there in dating someone when you already knew more than you ever wanted to know about them?

Marly rested her hand on her chin and stared outside into the town through the front office window. People scurried about doing their daily rituals—going to work, taking a break from work. The children were still in school and the little ones outside clutching their mamas' hands were too young for school. Friends stopped to greet one another, offer hugs, and gossip.

Marly sighed. Yeah, all male companionship had deserted her through the years because she was a single mom with a young son.

All but one man. All but Mitch.

Looking back, Marly saw the pattern. She wouldn't have admitted it before now, but it was there sure enough. Hadn't she counted on the men running from her? Wasn't that easier than making a commitment? Easier than giving love another go? Then along came Mitch and he stuck for a while. Not just stuck, but took an honest interest in her son and in her.

But he was only temporary, even if his reasons for leaving would be much different than all the men before him. He was a lost soul searching for his place

269

in life. A place that had been violently taken from him.

She couldn't imagine what it was like when a life depended on you only to lose that life to violence that you couldn't stop. Jeremy depended on her for life and she'd never survive if she ever let him down.

A male voice interrupted her thoughts. "Damnit, Marly! If you're going to stare off into space, take a vacation day. There's work to be done around here," Seth complained.

She looked up at him and smiled. "You know, that's a great idea." She stood and opened the desk drawer to get her pocketbook.

"What? No, that was sarcasm."

"I know and it worked. I'm going for a manicure."

"A manicure? Come on. Who's going to finish the Adams report and court papers?"

She patted his cheek. "Brother, dear. I'm sure with your brains, you can get it done. Or it will wait until tomorrow when I return from my day off."

She stepped outside into the warm sunshine, leaving Seth talking to himself. Once inside her car, she headed home. It wasn't a manicure she wanted. It was Mitch Allen. And he hadn't run off yet, so she planned to enjoy him while she could. A woman had a right to feed a need. And, damnit, she would exercise those rights. Her tires screeched as she pulled away from the curb, leaving a faint trail of white smoke flittering through the air.

She was going to get her some.

****

Mitch had returned home from Howie's house and jumped in the shower hoping to get that God-awful smell off his skin. A good twenty minutes in the hot spray did the trick. Mitch was finally clean. He contemplated burning his clothes, but threw them in the washing machine first to see if that worked.

He'd been in town for three weeks. In that short time, he had forgotten about being on the open road. Forgotten about the urge to get as far away from Boston as possible.

With the Singleton investigation stalled and him as the only suspect, Mitch had a fight ahead of him. He wouldn't mind if it were a fair fight. But being framed by a dirty sheriff to take the fall for his indiscretions didn't sit well with Mitch. He'd be damned if he let the sheriff get away with murder.

Mitch unfolded the pictures he had printed. He needed to get copies to his lawyer immediately and plan a strategy for his defense. With any luck, the charges would be dropped. But Mitch wasn't counting on luck, so he'd find more evidence against Ridgeley. There was a good chance the sheriff would drop the charges and let him leave town if he knew Mitch had copies of the pictures. But then Mitch would be resorting to blackmail and stooping to Howie's level. He wasn't going to do that. Besides, then the sheriff would get away with murder and he couldn't let that happen. Not when the sheriff could easily turn around and frame Marly. Mitch would be a free man soon enough.

And that's what he was waiting for, wasn't it? To be a free man and get on with his life. What life? He had no clue what he would do when he *could* leave.

271

He had left Boston just to drive. Go anywhere. Now that he had the chance to go anywhere again, he wasn't so sure he wanted to. He would miss the hell out of Marly and Jeremy. Shit, the kid meant the world to him. The special bond they'd formed shocked him. The kid had been robbed of a father and still had done well. All thanks to Marly.

And Marly. How could he leave her? It wasn't just her bed he'd miss. No, it was the woman he'd miss. Her smile, her eyes, those curves. And the brains. She was smart and brave and yet so very feminine.

He had never been one for serious relationships, mostly because he'd never had the time to commit to one. But now, spending the last three weeks as part of a family, sort of, he wondered if this was something he'd want in the future. There was nothing forcing him to leave and everything keeping him here. Was he ready for a family? The thought alone filled his stomach with excitement.

If he stayed here, he had to find work. His disability pension would cover him until he could work again, but he couldn't sit around doing nothing. He had been tossing around the idea of writing a book on his hostage negotiation experience. But since the shooting, his interest in writing had all but disappeared. Though, if he could write a book teaching the craft of negotiation, then he'd still be helping in the field.

His cell phone chimed in his pocket.

"Allen."

"You've got good sense, boy," Captain Amory said on the other end.

"Yeah? How's that?"

"That lockbox you sent me. The results just came back."

Mitch leaned against the counter. "You lifted prints? Did you get a match?"

"Nope. Not on the fingerprints. But we got DNA from the blood."

Mitch paced the kitchen floor. "Blood? What blood? I didn't see any blood."

"You weren't supposed to. It had been wiped down. All but one spot inside the handle. Someone was smart enough to wipe off the blood but not smart enough to get it all."

Fucking awesome! "So did you get a match on the DNA?"

"Nothing in the database. The country boy who left this blood behind hasn't been in trouble before or we'd have something to go on."

"You know it definitely was a man."

"That's what the blood results say."

Mitch sighed. "Okay, now what? I'm right back where I was with no one to pin the robbery of Marly's gun on."

"Get me some DNA samples and I'll test them."

"The results won't hold up in court because I don't have a warrant." Maybe the sheriff hired someone to kill Howie.

"Who's worried about court? You're in the backcountry, Allen. All you have to do is know who stole the gun and, more than likely, that's your killer. When you confront him, he'll shit his pants and panic. That'll prove his guilt and you turn him in to the sheriff."

273

Mitch tossed Jack the ball he dropped at his feet. "Okay. It may take me some time, but I think I can get some hair samples from the town barber. He'll keep his mouth shut if I tell him it's part of a secret investigation. The guy's really into cop shows on TV so he'll be more than thrilled to be part of the real thing."

"Go ahead and send me what you get. Then I'll do what I can."

As soon as he hung up the phone, a car pulled into the driveway. Mitch walked cautiously to the window and watched Marly walk up the driveway looking irritated.

He met her at the door. "Hey, there. Everything okay? What are you doing home?"

Her eyes narrowed. "Do I need a reason to be home?"

"Easy. Just a question."

"I'm sorry. I came home for you. Because of you."

He knew he looked so damn confused because that's exactly how he felt.

"Because I want you," she explained.

"Oh." He smiled and gathered her into his arms. "A nooner?" He bent down, devouring her mouth. He could feast on her all day and night and still walk away wanting more. So much more.

She pulled back and threw her pocketbook on the dining room table and faced him with her hands on her hips. "Yes. There I was at work. Couldn't keep my mind off of you. Just kept seeing you naked."

His cock strained painfully in his pants. "I like that. You rushed home to rip my clothes off and take advantage of me."

She laughed, the sound light as a soft breeze. "Yeah, something like that. Was going to get a manicure, but you were more appealing."

He held his arms wide. "Then quit stalling and rip away."

As their lips touched, her cell phone rang.

"Ignore it," Mitch demanded, his breath already ragged and hurting his chest.

"Can't. No one calls me on my cell. Hello?"

Mitch watched the color drain from Marly's face.

"Oh, my God! I'll, I'll be right there."

Mitch froze. "What's wrong?"

"Mitch, Jeremy is missing from school."

"What? What are you talking about?"

"That was the school. They said he was there for first period, but he hasn't been seen since 9:30. Mitch, I've got to find him." Her body trembled in his grip.

"I know. We will. Come on. I'll drive."

"Okay."

They ran out the door and were on the road in seconds. From her cell phone, Marly called Seth who promised to call her father and go looking for the boy.

"Did the principal say if any other kids were missing or not accounted for?" Mitch asked.

"I didn't ask." Her voice broke.

"Call her back while we drive there. Find out who's not in school and get me an address."

Marly dialed. "Mitch? I'm so scared. We have to find him."

"Listen to your motherly instincts." His gaze danced between hers and the road.

"What?"

275

"Your gut. Does it tell you something bad has happened to Jeremy?"

She was silent for a moment. "Well. No. It doesn't."

"Good. Then he's fine. Mother's intuition is stronger than any vibe I've ever known. We'll find him, darling." He held her free hand and caressed her knuckles with his thumb.

"Okay," she sniffled.

"And he better have a damn good excuse or I'm gonna kick his ass." Mitch waited a moment before continuing. "With your permission, of course."

"Don't worry. If he doesn't have a good excuse then he'll need you to save him from me."

Chapter Twenty-Two

"Mom, I didn't think you'd find out," Jeremy complained from the backseat. "I'm sorry."

"Skipping school because you didn't study for a test is unacceptable," Marly lectured.

Mitch drove while Marly gave her full attention to Jeremy.

"I did study. I just didn't get it. What's the big deal? I was okay at Danny's house."

Marly leaned around the front seat to speak with her errant son. "I thought you were in school. I'm your mother. I need to know where you are at all times. Do you understand me?"

"Yeah."

"If you study and don't get something then you come to me."

"You were busy. I didn't want to bother you."

Her voice shook with anger, the fear still in her eyes. "I am never too busy for you, Jeremy. There's no excuse to cut school. You're so grounded."

"Mom!" exclaimed Jeremy. "That's not fair."

"What's not fair is making me worry because you took the day off from school. What if I took a day off without notice from my job? I would get fired."

"Come on, Mom. Uncle Seth wouldn't fire you."

"Sure he would if his business was compromised. What I'm trying to explain is that you not only got in trouble at school and with me, but now you've interrupted my day, your uncle's and granddad's day, and Mitch's and that's not right."

"I agree." Mitch said. "That's why when we get home, Marly, you go get that manicure you had planned. I'll make sure the kid stays out of trouble until you get home."

"Mitch, you shouldn't have to give up your day for this. I'll deal with it."

"Don't worry about it," Mitch said, pulling alongside her car in the yard. "It's not like I have anything to do all day, so I don't mind babysitting the kid." Mitch glanced toward the backseat.

"I don't need a babysitter," Jeremy protested.

"You sure do when you can't stay where you're left. Now say goodbye to your mom and climb up front. I have an errand to do and you're coming with me." Marly exited the truck and walked to the driver's side.

Jeremy did as instructed with a little grumbling.

Marly leaned into the window. "Jeremy—no TV, no video games, no phone, no going outside, no bike, and no anything else that is fun. You got me?"

"Yeah."

"Yes, Mom," Mitch corrected and Jeremy repeated.

"We'll be okay, Marly." Mitch explained. "Gonna have us a little talk since we have the entire afternoon with not much else to do."

Marly looked at Mitch with understanding and trust in her eyes. She totally trusted him with her son or he wouldn't have gotten her to go for the manicure. Mitch drove to town slowly. He glanced at Jeremy and saw the kid had his head hung low and was fidgeting with his hands. Mitch let the silence hang between them for a while.

It was Jeremy who spoke up first. "You mad at me, too?"

"Yes, I am. Very much," Mitch confirmed, keeping his gaze on the road.

"I was going to be in trouble either way, whether it was for cutting school or flunking that stupid math test."

"If you were having trouble, why not ask for help?"

"Because then I wouldn't have been able to hang out with you."

Mitch felt his heart swell with pride but squashed any outward signs so Jeremy wouldn't think he was off the hook. "If I knew you hadn't prepared for your test, you're right. We wouldn't have hung out until you had the homework done."

Mitch drove past the barbershop and pulled over. "Wait here. I've got to go speak with the barber." Mitch got out of the car and shut the door before speaking to Jeremy. "Don't even think about getting out of this car, kid. I looked for you once today and I don't plan on doing it again, hear me?"

"Yeah."

As Mitch suspected, McField the barber was more than thrilled to be part of a secret investigation. He was taking a big chance trusting a local to secure key evidence in a murder investigation. But Mitch simply explained that McField was the only person in town who could help him.

By the time Mitch walked back out to the car, McField was devising how to schedule haircuts for the five men on Mitch's list.

"Mitch," a woman yelled. He turned to see Bethany walking up to him. "How's the leg doing? Wow, you look so much better."

"Grandma!" Jeremy yelled from the car, jumped out, and raced to her.

"Yes, ma'am. How can I ever thank you?" Mitch smiled in greeting.

Jeremy hugged her waist and spoke excitedly. "Can I come over to your house, Grandma?"

Bethany smiled and ruffled his hair. "Not today, darling. When you behave in school, then you can come over." Jeremy's jaw dropped. "Grandma knows everything that goes on around here." She turned to Mitch. "And so does everyone else for that matter." Her laughter was contagious as Mitch joined her.

Her words merely confirmed his suspicions that someone in town knew something about Howie's murder and wasn't speaking up.

"Now, Jeremy, you go with Mitch," she said, kissing the top of his head. "Let Grandma get back to her errands."

"Yes, ma'am," Jeremy agreed and walked back to the car.

"Mitch, I'll tell you how you can thank me," Bethany said, her expression serious, her eyes focused. "Don't let my baby girl chase you away if you'd rather stay. She's very good at that. You'll need to be on your toes or she'll end up running you from town better than the sheriff ever could."

Mitch wasn't in a position to debate the matter on a public sidewalk so he just agreed. "Thank you, ma'am. Appreciate the advice."

She patted his cheek and walked away.

He walked to the car but stopped when she called his name again. When he faced her, the twinkle had returned to her eyes.

"One more thing. If you break my Marly's heart, then you'll deal with me. And you tall and strong types don't intimidate me one bit. Understood?"

Damn, now Mitch knew exactly where Marly got her fiery side. "Yes, ma'am. I totally understand."

Mitch was relieved to be seated back in the car. At least he could handle an eleven-year-old better than a mother's scrutiny.

"What did you have to see the barber about?" Jeremy asked as Mitch merged into traffic. "Doesn't look like you got a haircut."

"I needed his help with something. And don't change the subject. We're still discussing you skipping school. That was a bright idea."

"Oh, come on, Mitch. You can't tell me you never ditched school. Everyone does now and then."

Mitch glared at him. "Does that stupid statement you just made make any sense to you?"

"What do you mean?"

"Just because everyone does something doesn't mean you have to. And not everyone cuts school. And yeah, I did, and when my dad found out I couldn't sit down for two days."

Jeremy's eyes grew wide. "He hit you?"

"Yeah. And it wasn't the first or last time I got a whipping. That's because I wasn't smart enough to keep out of trouble and follow the rules. At the time, I thought I knew everything but, looking back, I realize I knew nothing. So my dad would take it out on my hide for the really bad things I did, like if I put myself in danger by skipping school." Mitch glared at Jeremy, letting his words sink in. "For the rest, I was usually just grounded."

"You're not going to hit me, are you, Mitch?"

When Mitch looked at him, Jeremy was white as a ghost. Good, at least he put a little scare into him to get him to think twice about his actions next time.

"Not my place. But if it were my place, yeah, I'd blister your ass just for making your mom worry the way she did."

Jeremy looked truly repentant. "I'll make her a card to say sorry."

"Good idea. And clean your room, too. That'll really make up for today."

"Mitch, are you going to marry my mom?" His young voice was hopeful.

Mitch swung his head to stare at Jeremy before turning back to the road. "Now why would you think that?"

Jeremy played with the radio. "I don't know. You look good together. That's what Debbie says when you're with someone you like."

Mitch smiled. It wasn't a totally bad thought. "Well, buddy, I don't think your mom and I are heading in that direction, but I promise that if I thought things were serious with your mom, I'd talk to you about it first. Because I think anyone who wants to be with your mom should have your approval."

"Then you'd be my stepdad like my friend, Paul,

has, right?"

"Yeah. That's right."

"Cool. I'm sorry for today and if you do want to be my stepdad, I'd say it was okay since you make my mom happy."

Mitch smiled, his heart pounding hard. "That's good to know, buddy."

"If you were to become my stepdad then would it be your place to punish me?"

"Yeah, I guess it would be. I'd always talk with your mom about it though. Does that change your approval of me?"

"Nah. Just means I have to be more careful about getting caught doing things I shouldn't."

Mitch laughed and ruffled his hair. "I'll tell you what. If you didn't do those things in the first place then you wouldn't get caught and, therefore, you wouldn't be punished. But I know temptation is there for us boys and we can't always stay out of trouble. Now we've got to pick up my truck. Maddy should be done by now with the extra work I asked him to do."

When Mitch picked up his truck, he left Joe's car with Maddy for a tune-up like Joe had instructed.

Back at Marly's house, Jeremy jumped from the truck. "I'm going to clean my room now."

"Good idea." Mitch watched him walk away.

Marriage? Mitch had never thought about getting married. Never thought he was the type, but talking with Jeremy certainly made him think. Yeah, Mitch needed to admit that he was totally in love with Marly. Then he needed to figure out just what the hell he was going to do about it.

And Jeremy was part of that plan, too, of course.

Since he had the kid's approval, it was time Mitch got to talking with Marly.

Chapter Twenty-Three

The next day, Mitch planned to head out early to investigate the motel. After updating Marly the night before on what he'd found at Howie's house, she was nervous about him going.

"Good morning, everyone," Seth said, arriving as Jeremy finished his cereal. "I'm in desperate need of coffee."

"Here you go," Marly said, pushing a mug into his hands.

"Hey, Mitch. Ready to leave?" Seth asked before sipping the hot brew.

Mitch raised his eyebrows then turned to Marly. "You think I need a bodyguard or something?"

"I just thought you'd like some company," she said innocently.

With arms crossed, Mitch stared down at her. "Bullshit. Need I remind you that I used to do this for a living."

"And need I remind you that you used to have backup available. So consider Seth your backup." Her little chin jutted out, challenging him to disagree. The little witch!

"Yeah. Backup," Seth agreed, refilling his cup.

"And I don't have to remind you that, per the

sheriff's orders, you're not allowed to leave town for a minute let alone the whole day." With hands on her hips, she continued to put Mitch in his place. "And certainly not to perform an investigation the sheriff should be doing."

Mitch sighed heavily. "It's pretty hard to investigate yourself, so the chances that the sheriff will do anything close to a real investigation are slim to none."

"At least Seth will be with you if you run into trouble with the sheriff." Damn, was she about to stamp her foot?

"Fine." Mitch turned to face Seth. "But leave the lawyer in you behind. Where we're going, I need a bad ass not a college degree."

Seth straightened to his full height to be eye to eye with Mitch. "Okay. I can be a bad ass. These muscles qualify me as a lean, mean fighting machine."

Marly laughed.

"Yeah, well, you and your muscles get in my truck cause I'm leaving now. Marly, I'll call you when we're headed back."

"Be careful. Please. I know you used to do this for your job, but I'm not used to real life crime drama. Call me as soon as you head home. Promise."

"I never make a promise I can't keep, so I promise to call you." Mitch kissed her lips long and lazily.

"I'll wait in the truck while you have your make out session," Seth announced. Jeremy ran down the stairs and exchanged high-fives with his uncle.

"Kisses like those will make me re-think my schedule for today," Mitch admitted.

"I wish I could help you there. But my mean old boss is taking the day off and leaving me to pick up the slack."

"Right. See you tonight. Jeremy, be good in school."

In the truck, Mitch explained what he knew so far.

"You do know that if the sheriff finds out you were in Howie's house he'll have your ass," Seth declared after adjusting his seatbelt.

Mitch glared. "You promised to leave the lawyer behind. And, yeah, I know better than to get caught."

Seth shrugged. "Howie had always been a compulsive gambler. Shit, I'm surprised he held onto his property since he would lose all his cash on bets."

Mitch put on his sunglasses against the morning sun. "Gambling addiction makes a man desperate. Probably why he blackmailed the sheriff."

"Wonder how he found out about the sheriff's indiscretions."

"Don't know. And I hope to hell I can get those pictures of him out of my head sometime soon."

Seth laughed. "Yeah. They were pretty gross. I'll never look at him the same way again."

For the next forty-five minutes, they drove in silence, listening to the radio as Mitch swerved in and out of traffic.

"Here it is," Mitch announced, pulling into the small parking lot of the Calling Hours Motel. "Place is a shit hole just like I expected. Come on. Let see what we can find out."

As soon as they exited the truck, two scantily clad women approached. "Hey, boys. We can give you a good time."

"No, thanks," they said in unison and walked past the women and through the front door of the motel's small lobby.

Mitch approached a skinny man at the front desk. The man reeked of body odor and tobacco. "What you fellas need?"

"Need to know if you know Howie Singleton," Mitch asked, removing his sunglasses.

"Nope."

"That was an awful quick answer, don't you think?" Mitch asked of Seth who nodded. "Let's try again. Howie Singleton came here weekly up until he was murdered a few weeks ago. Good customer like that is worth remembering."

"Nope."

Mitch was losing patience, even though he'd fully expected not to receive cooperation from anyone. He reached in his pocket and pulled out his badge. "Now does this help you remember anything or do I call my backup to search this place top to bottom and see what kind of contraband we can come up with to close this joint down for a really long time. Seems like that would put a lot of people out of work."

The man hesitated but spoke softly, his gaze darting around the empty room. "Howie was an asshole dirt bag."

"Good. Now at least we're talking about the same guy. Tell me what you know." Mitch stood with his arms crossed, using the familiar routine of interrogation to get the information he sought.

The man spit into a small metal can, the wad of black chewing tobacco stuck in his cheek. "Just like you said. He came in weekly. Spent the weekends here. Gambled at the casino down the street during the days and bought his ladies for the nights."

"Did he ever come in with another man?"

"Nope. He only liked women."

"No. I mean did he travel with any buddies."

The man snorted. "Howie wasn't the likeable sort. He had no friends. Can't say I'm surprised he's been murdered. Wasn't anyone around that liked the bastard. Then again, everyone around here wants everyone dead."

"Ever see this man around here before," Mitch asked, showing a picture of the sheriff.

"Sure. He used to be a frequent visitor. Maybe once or twice a month, but never stayed overnight. Just came in for the day to have some fun, if you know what I mean."

"You said used to. Did he stop coming?" Seth asked.

"Yeah. Just like that." The clerk snapped his dirty fingers. "I figured he either got caught by the missus or dropped dead."

"How'd you know he was married?" Mitch asked.

"I didn't. But most of these men who come here are. This one," he said pointing to the sheriff's picture. "He was too well groomed not to be married. And he only came during the day. Never overnight. Another sign."

"When was the last time he came here?" Seth asked.

"Months ago."

"Would you say about six months?" Mitch spoke.

"Yeah. Sounds about right. He dead?"

"Nope. Thanks for the info."

Mitch and Seth turned to leave until the man stopped them. "Just about forgot. Howie had a safety box here. We offer to lock up our customer's valuables for a fee. He hasn't paid his fee this month, so I'm going to ditch them. You can have them."

"Yeah, I don't think Howie will be making any more payments," Mitch confirmed.

The man went into a back room and returned with a yellow envelope. He handed it to Mitch. "Don't know what's in it. And don't care. I need the box freed up to rent. That's all I know, fellas. We never spoke."

"Got it. Thanks."

Mitch and Seth returned to the truck and emptied the contents of the envelope.

"I guess Howie wasn't as stupid as people thought if he was smart enough to stash his blackmailing pictures," Seth said, staring at the original prints of Sheriff Ridgeley in various sexual positions with the male prostitute that were neatly wrapped in an elastic band inside the envelope.

"Let's check out the casino up ahead. See what else we can dig up," Mitch said, taking a right out of the lot.

An hour later, Mitch and Seth headed back home. "Howie owed sixty grand. That's a lot of money. He was a severe gambling addict I guess," Mitch said.

"That clerk was probably the only person sorry to hear Howie was dead," Seth said with a laugh.

"You kick the bucket owing someone sixty grand and they're bound to miss the shit out of you." Mitch dialed Marly's number as promised. "Everything went well. We should be home in time for Jeremy to get home from school. Yup. See you tonight."

"Do you know how easily you two interact?" Seth asked, cocking an eyebrow.

"She's a great person. I'll admit it. She's grown on me." Mitch merged onto the highway, trying not to speed to get back to Marly sooner.

"Any plans to stay?" Seth's tone was concerned.

"See, that's why I hate you lawyerly types. Always asking questions."

"Can't find out anything without asking. And avoiding the question won't work because I can ask questions all day."

"And I can ignore you all day. But since I don't want to be cross examined on the ride home, I'll tell you that I don't know exactly what I'm going to be doing."

"Fair enough."

"But I can tell you that my plans aren't as cut and dry as they were the day I drove into town and ended up at Marly's house. I guess you could say that I have a lot of thinking to do," Mitch admitted, his stomach tightening at the thought.

"Far be it for me to keep you from thinking. I'll just rest my eyes here and leave you to your thoughts. Wake me when we get back."

As Seth dozed in the passenger seat, Mitch let his thoughts wander to Marly. He had to admit that he missed her when they were separated and looked forward to hearing about her day and Jeremy's day. Most of all he enjoyed being part of the Hampton household and all the craziness a family brings. Losing that sense of belonging scared him almost as much as belonging to something that special.

Mitch's cell phone chimed. When he answered, Mr. McField was excited. "The project will be completed in two hours. Stop by to see me at your earliest convenience."

"I'll be there by the end of the day," Mitch confirmed before he disconnected.

First things first. He needed to clear his name before he could even think of offering it to Marly.

****

After dropping Seth off at his office and briefly visiting Marly, Mitch headed home to piece together what he had so far on the investigation. But first, he was stopping at McField's to see what the barber-turned-detective had for him.

"Hi, McField," Mitch said as he entered the shop. "Hi, Jerry."

Jerry was in the barber chair getting a haircut. "Jeez, Mitch. How many times you gonna get your haircut?" Jerry asked.

"I admit it. I'm obsessed."

"Have a seat," McField said. "Be with you in a minute. There you go, Jerry. Seven dollars."

Jerry paid quickly, grabbed his hat, and left after nodding to Mitch.

"Last piece of hair," McField stated, handing Mitch a couple of sealed plastic bags with a single strand of hair in each.

On the outside of each bag, written in perfect penmanship, was the owner's name.

"This is great. You did a fantastic job."

McField beamed ear to ear. "I did some research and they say it's best to use a strand of hair with the root ball attached for DNA analysis."

"Looks like you did just that." Mitch studied the bags and sure enough, each strand of hair had the root ball attached. He didn't even want to know how McField had managed to pull it out without them questioning what the hell he was doing. All that mattered was that he got it.

Mitch shook McField's hand.

"Don't mind helping you out."

"Remember though. This is top secret, totally confidential. You can't tell a soul. Not even your wife."

McField laughed. "I wouldn't say a word to that woman unless I wanted it all over town. You have my word."

Mitch placed the bags in his glove box for safekeeping. The last thing he needed was for the bags containing Maddy's, Jerry's, Ridgeley's, a deputy's, and Amos' hair to blow out the window. When Mitch turned from Main Street to a side road headed to Marly's house, sirens sounded behind him. One look in the rearview told Mitch he was pretty much screwed, but he immediately pulled over and waited.

Sheriff Ridgeley approached his truck.

"Good afternoon, Sheriff. Can't say it's a pleasure to see you again."

"Don't get smart with me, Allen. You're not in a position to piss me off."

"That's right. I'm out on bail, wrongly accused of murder. But we both know that, don't we? What did I do this time?"

"One of my deputies says he saw you coming back into town a little while ago. You're not supposed to leave town, remember?"

Mitch shrugged. "Wasn't me. Maybe your deputy is due for an eye exam."

"Where have you been this morning then?"

"At my attorney's office." Mitch kept his voice casual.

"No you weren't."

"Yes, I was. Call Seth McFadden, he'll tell you." Damn, this wasn't good.

"Seth isn't your attorney."

Think fast. "He is for my real estate transactions. You see, I have a whole team of lawyers for different purposes."

Mitch enjoyed the look of concern that flashed in Ridgeley's eyes. But Mitch had to tread lightly. The last thing he needed was Ridgeley searching his truck and finding the samples of hair. He'd never explain his way out of that.

"What the hell do you need a real estate attorney for? Marly finally come to her senses and kick your sorry ass out?" The sheriff's pudgy face was covered in sweat thanks to the blazing sun.

"Hardly. But I am interested in some property that should be coming on the market soon. Looks like I could get a great deal."

"Where abouts?"

"Now, Sheriff, I can't give away my secrets. You may try to steal a good deal out from under me. Is there a reason you pulled me over, other than to discuss my morning errands?"

"I'm watching you, Allen. Stay out of my way."

"Glad to. May I go?"

"Yes."

Mitch pulled away slowly, keeping an eye on the rearview mirror. Ridgeley turned around and headed in the opposite direction. Mitch was no fool. He was already calling Marly to inform Seth of his attorney-client privilege regarding their fake meeting this morning.

Chapter Twenty-Four

At the house, Mitch played with Jack for a while. No matter how many times he threw the ball, Jack obediently fetched it to lug it back. But then he wanted to play tug-o-war until Mitch was able to free the ball from his mouth and throw it again.

His cell phone rang. "Allen," he said, throwing the ball as far as he could for Jack to run after. "Hey, Captain, what do you have for me?"

"For starters, I can tell you that this Sheriff Ridgeley guy is no angel."

"I'm listening."

"Appears he was arrested six months ago not too far from where you are now."

"Let me guess. Was it in Jasper City, small little town about forty miles from here?"

"Yeah, that's right."

"And would it be at a seedy little place called Calling Hours Motel?"

"You know about this arrest already?"

"No, but it's making sense how the victim was able to blackmail this guy." Was Howie there when Ridgeley was cuffed?

"Sheriff Ridgeley propositioned a female prostitute for sex but didn't want the sex from her."

This was so confusing. "Then from who?"

"From a male prostitute. Looks like Ridgeley could always find them, but not that weekend. According to the police report, he was pretty desperate to find a male prostitute. The sheriff knew where to look for one, but couldn't find any this weekend with good reason."

"Which was?"

"The local police were working a sting operation to catch johns and prostitutes. The prostitutes got wind of it and took off, leaving only the johns to take the heat."

"Shit! That must've fried the sheriff's ass being arrested and putting his career and family on the line." This case was more dangerous than Mitch expected.

"Says here in the report that the sheriff wasn't a big fan of, and I quote, big-city-fucking-know-it-all-dickless cops."

There it was spelled out in a police report for Mitch to finally understand why the sheriff resented him so much. It wasn't personal. City cops busted the sheriff so he hated them all. Didn't matter from how far away Mitch came.

"I wonder how come he got to keep his job as sheriff." Mitch couldn't imagine the good people of Courtsville allowing that.

"I've got that answer. You see, part of the sting operation was a quick slap on the wrist, fine paid, and he was released on personal recognizance. No one ever found out."

"The cops did the sting as a deterrent to keep the johns away, hoping to cut down on the prostitution. Typical," Mitch said.

"With the case of the sheriff, it looks like it worked since he hasn't been back, according to my sources."

"That's what I found out, too. I'd say that's fair enough motive. Man's being blackmailed over sex and stands to lose everything—job, reputation, family— he's bound to go off the deep end and kill the one person who knows. Howie Singleton."

"You need proof of the blackmail and need to place the sheriff at the scene. I bet he has an iron clad alibi," the captain advised.

"You think he had someone do his dirty work?"

"Would make the best sense. Don't you think?"

Mitch recalled Jerry drunkenly admitting to the murder. He was a gullible person. Sheriff could have easily got him to do it. But you needed the guts to actually take a life and Jerry was too weak. He didn't fit the part, but then neither did the sheriff, and he had to prove otherwise.

"How's the DNA coming?"

"You know how that takes. My guy is trying to move it along. And as for Howie Singleton, he was arrested for drunk driving twice, paid the fines, nothing more. I'll keep in touch and you watch your back."

"I've got some hair samples I'll mail out today. See if any DNA matches the blood on the lockbox."

"Send them along. I'll take care of it and be in touch."

"Thanks."

Jack barked and when Mitch looked toward the road he saw Jeremy racing to the house.

Mitch smiled. "Hey, buddy. How was school?"

Mitch walked to the kitchen to get them milk and cookies while Jeremy complained about his homework. For the first time in his life, Mitch actually felt like he was home.

While Jeremy worked on his homework, Mitch spent the hour mowing the lawn. For such a mundane task, he utterly enjoyed himself. He couldn't have done this a few weeks ago when he his cane was a constant companion. Now his knee protested when he overdid it, but not for simply moving around, which was fantastic in his world. Which reminded him that he needed to make a follow-up appointment with Doc Peterson.

Mitch was sweaty and tired but didn't that lawn look picture perfect. He went into the house for a cold glass of water and found Jeremy sitting at the TV playing video games.

"Don't think you're supposed to be doing that, buddy," Mitch stated as he walked to the kitchen.

"Why not? My homework's all done."

Mitch returned with his drink. "I remember your mom revoking your fun privileges until further notice. Remember? You're grounded."

"Aw. Come on. That's not fair."

"You go ahead and keep playing. She'll be home soon from work and I'm sure she'll remind you."

Jeremy immediately turned off the TV and plopped onto the couch. "Now what am I going to do?"

The phone rang.

"For starters, you can answer that while I go put away the lawn mower."

Moments later, Mitch was walking back to the

porch when Jeremy raced out of the house. "Mitch!"

"What? What is it?" Mitch saw the alarm on Jeremy's face.

"There was a guy on the phone and he said to tell my mom and her boyfriend to mind their fucking business or I'll be sent to a new home and will never see her or you again. I don't want a new home." Jeremy was breathless.

"Okay. Calm down. Come on inside and we'll figure out who's making prank calls."

"Sorry I swore, but that's what he said."

"You did a good job, buddy, coming to get me right away. Come on."

Mitch walked with Jeremy right beside him, keeping him close to his side with his arm across the kid's shoulder. He scanned the area but nothing appeared out of the ordinary.

Inside, Jeremy repeated the brief phone call again for Mitch.

"Did you recognize the man's voice?" Mitch asked.

"No. It was really strange."

"Strange how?"

"I don't know. Like it was rough. An old voice. He was mean."

"Yeah, he was. But don't you worry because your mom and I aren't going anywhere. Whoever called was just being a loser, trying to scare me from investigating Howie's murder. Obviously, I've ticked someone off. Sorry you got that call because of it, buddy."

"But didn't you get arrested for it?"

"Sure did, but just because someone is arrested,

doesn't mean they're guilty. I didn't kill Howie and I'm trying to clear my name. To do that, I have to find out who is the real killer." Mitch sat on the couch next to Jeremy.

"Can I help with the investigation? I can help."

Mitch studied him. He was so eager to be part of it. His big eyes were fixed on Mitch's face. "We'd have to ask your mom about that. Then when I think of what I can use your help with I'll let you know."

"Ask his mom what?" Marly said, carrying two bags of groceries, her pocketbook, and the mail as she entered the living room.

"We're going to tell you something, but you can't panic. We have it under control," Mitch said, standing then following her into the kitchen with Jeremy in tow.

"Yeah, Mom, we do."

"Uh, huh. Start telling me."

While Mitch and Jeremy filled Marly in on the call, Jack walked the kitchen floor looking for food.

"Jeremy, I don't want you answering the phone until this has been resolved. Mitch, I've just about had it. First, a man is murdered on my property. Then my guest is falsely accused of murder. Now my son is being threatened. Whoever this person is must be pretty damn stupid to mess with a mother and her child. Pretty damn stupid."

Guest? He was only a guest? That was something to ponder another time.

Marly put the groceries away, talking the whole time. Mitch and Jeremy moved out of her way.

"We'll get to the bottom of this. But can I help you put the groceries away since the milk doesn't go in the cupboard and the cereal doesn't go in the

301

fridge?" Mitch grinned, clearly bemused by her actions.

Marly looked at her errors. "Shit!" She looked at Jeremy. "Sorry. Guess my brain is too busy being pissed that someone is messing with my son."

"And you have every right to be pissed. But I promise you that I will clear my name and find the real killer so your lives can get back to normal. I'm not one to make promises I cannot keep."

"I'm going to help him," Jeremy injected.

Marly's face paled. "You most certainly are not. This isn't a game, Jeremy. This is a very dangerous situation. One that I don't want you to have any part of."

"Mom! That's so unfair. You're treating me like a baby. I can help, Mitch. Please." Jeremy's temper mimicked his mom's.

Mitch interrupted. "He's already a part of it and he lives here. We're going to need to keep him close to us at all times. It wouldn't hurt for him to help out with little stuff." Mitch winked so that only Marly could see.

She was silent for a moment then spoke. "Okay. But, Jeremy, you do exactly what Mitch says. If you don't, you're off the case."

"Got it."

Mitch leaned down to be eye to eye with Jeremy. "Not a word of this investigation to anyone. Not Danny or any other friends. Part of your very important job will be to keep all of this top secret. The more information we find out, the more you'll have to keep secret. Think you can handle that?"

"Yup. Sure can. I won't say a word unless it's to

you or Mom."

"Good. Because if you screw up once, just once, then you will be off the case for good. No second chances."

"Okay."

A loud knock came on the front door. Mitch immediately moved in front of Marly and Jeremy. "Marly, are you expecting anyone?"

"No," she said softly, holding Jeremy close.

"Stay here. I'll see who it is," Mitch said and walked to the door.

"Sheriff Ridgeley, two visits in one day," Mitch said through the screen door.

"Need to talk to you, Allen."

"Go ahead."

Mitch made no move to open the door.

"You can come out here or I'll come in there."

Mitch opened the door and stepped out. "This is bordering on harassment, you know."

"It's not harassment when I'm investigating a crime. A break in at the Singleton house."

Mitch remained calm and unconcerned. "This has something to do with me how?"

"Were you in Howie's house, Allen, snooping around?"

"Do I look dumb to you, Sheriff? First of all, if I had been I'd never tell you. Second, how the hell would I know where Howie lived when I didn't even know him?"

"Come on, now. You know he's Marly's neighbor. Have you been in his house?"

"No. Are we done?"

"Seems someone was on his computer. Left a

date and time from yesterday. I may not be a big city cop like you were, but I'd say a dead man can't start his computer."

"How do you know someone was on it yesterday, Sheriff? Have you been snooping at your cousin's house?" Mitch countered, hoping to fluster the man.

"I'm his kin and have every right to be there. It's up to me to keep an eye on his property until it's dispersed to his heirs."

Mitch kept his eyes on his. "Heirs meaning you. I know you're going to inherit his property. Oh, but first you have to pay off the mortgage. Kind of hard to do that on a small town sheriff's salary. Guess it will be going up for sale."

"If you think for one minute I'll allow you to buy his property, you're crazy."

"You'll have no say in what I do."

"The hell I won't. Besides, you're not going to need a house when you're in jail."

"You know, Sheriff, I hear Howie frequented a motel called Calling Hours in Jasper. You may want to check it out. Maybe someone from there snooped in his house. Can't imagine the interesting things Howie could possibly have." Mitch enjoyed watching the color drain from Ridgeley's face.

"What are you getting at, Allen? Just spit it out instead of beating around the fucking bush." Sweat rolled down his flushed face.

"I think you're a smart man, Sheriff, and can figure things out without having to be told. If we're done, I'd like to go have my dinner."

The sheriff walked away without another word.

Mitch was satisfied. Ridgeley knew that Mitch

was on to him. Now Mitch could sit back and wait for the sheriff to panic and incriminate himself. Criminals usually tried to cover their tracks.

Mitch would be watching closely.

****

After dinner, Mitch cleaned out his truck. He had to keep busy. Had to keep his hands moving. Jeremy hadn't left his side since they included him in the investigation.

"Look, kid, part of doing an investigation is having a lot of patience. What I want you to do is to let me know of any rumors or stories you hear from friends. Kids always hear the things adults don't want them to, and they love to talk. When your friends talk, you listen and then tell me."

"Okay. That's easy. Hey, what's this?"

"What?" Mitch looked at the small pocketknife Jeremy held. "A pocketknife. Careful its razor-sharp. Good to have for small repairs or if you're in a jam and need a sharp tool."

"That's really cool." He studied it for about five minutes, opening all the gadgets before he tossed it back into the toolbox. "I like how it has everything from scissors to screwdrivers and knives."

Time to teach the boy how to work on a car. "Here. Take this rag and follow me. I'm going to show you how to check the fluids under the hood."

"Cool." Jeremy listened attentively as Mitch explained the parts of the engine and how to check fluid levels.

"You need to take care of your vehicle, like your

bike, if you want it to be dependable."

"Then how come you didn't take care of yours?"

Mitch grimaced. "What? I always take care of my truck."

"Then why'd you break down and end up here?"

"The hose was old and didn't work right damaging the radiator. I had no control...you know what, smart ass?" Mitch grinned. "Shit happens sometimes no matter how good you take care of things. All I could do was try to prevent problems by regular maintenance."

Jeremy shrugged and hitched his thumbs in the pockets of his shorts. "Better try harder to keep this truck running. You looked silly driving Granddad's car." Jeremy squealed with laughter.

"Is that so?" Mitch said, ruffling Jeremy's hair, then closed the hood. He replaced the rag in the toolbox and took out the pocketknife. "Here," Mitch said, tossing the red knife to Jeremy. "It's yours. But if I see you doing Kung Fu shit with it, I'll take it back."

"I can really have it? Awesome. Thanks." Jeremy hugged him around the waist unexpectedly, Mitch's arm wrapping around his shoulders. Mitch felt the last flip of his heart. Hell, he loved the kid.

"Let's go see what Mom is up to."

"Okay. Hey, Mitch, look!" Jeremy pointed to a large plume of thick black smoke billowing over the far edge of Marly's field. Howie Singleton's house was on fire.

"Come on, buddy, inside now," Mitch demanded, practically picking him off his feet as they ran into the house.

"Marly," Mitch yelled.

"What is it?" she asked, running into the room.

"Call the sheriff. Howie's house is on fire."

She dialed quickly and the three of them watched from the porch. Sirens wailed closer. Within half an hour, all of the smoke was gone, but the smell lingered in the air.

It nauseated Mitch but he had rattled the sheriff. "We're all going to be very careful until I can gather the proof I need to put the sheriff behind bars."

"You believe he's the one who killed Howie?" Marly asked.

"I definitely do now. The sheriff is in panic mode. That makes him very dangerous. Let's go inside. I'm pulling together my file and calling my contact in Boston to get the proper authorities involved so we can end this. I want you and Jeremy to feel safe again."

Wrapping her arm around Mitch's waist, they all walked back into the house. "You're here with us, Mitch. We feel safe."

"Marly, call Seth and your parents over. Might as well update them all at once."

Chapter Twenty-Five

The next day, Marly was exhausted after leaving work and driving home. It had been a long day and an even longer night last night after the fire at Howie's house was finally extinguished. The last thing Marly wanted was to dwell on murders, arson, and threats. Let Mitch and Seth worry about that crap. She had to balance her checkbook and get some laundry done. She went over her list of chores for the evening in her head. There was always something that needed to be done.

Jack was chasing the ball Mitch and Jeremy were throwing to each other in the front yard when she pulled up. As soon as Jeremy saw her, he ran over and gave her a big hug.

"Mom, since it's Friday, can we go out for pizza?"

She winced at her aching feet. "I brought pizza home and then we can watch some movies. I have some things I need to get done around the house."

Mitch wandered over. "Hey, there." He kissed her lips in that lazy, carefree way she had grown accustomed to.

"Oh, brother," Jeremy complained and snickered.

Marly ignored her son's comment and leaned into

the backseat to grab the food.

Mitch took the pizzas and walked to the porch. "Remember, kid, some day you'll be kissing girls and liking it."

Jeremy ran away, making gagging noises, with Jack right on his heels.

"Rough day?" Mitch asked, following Marly into the house.

"Yeah. My brother was on a tear about some missing files until they turned up in his briefcase. Then a pipe leaked in the back room and threatened to damage our files so we had to scurry around moving files. My shoes are water stained and ruined."

Mitch pulled her into a strong hug after placing the pizza boxes on the counter. It felt so good to be in his arms. Very good. Should she tell him that her mind had been preoccupied with him and where their relationship was headed? Should she confess how deeply in love with him she was? And how worried she was for all their safety?

Listening to his heart made her imagine hearing the sound every day for the rest of her life. She wanted him. Needed him. She begged the words to come out of her mouth.

He lifted her chin up and kissed her lips. "I think you need to go soak in the tub while me and Jeremy set the table for dinner then we'll set up a movie and relax."

"Mmmm. A nice, hot bath sounds wonderful. But you're not going to make me watch some creepy movie, are you?"

"Nope. As long as you don't make us watch some girlie movie."

309

Us. That simple word meant so much to her. Did Mitch realize that he included Jeremy in almost everything he did? Did he know that meant so much to both of them?

"Deal."

Marly soaked for half an hour in the tub. Once dressed in sweatpants and a T-shirt, she followed the smell of the pizza downstairs. Her stomach growled in protest.

"I'm starving. Pizza never looked so good," Marly said. "But first I have to go take the clothes off the line. The weatherman said showers were heading this way. Save me some." She disappeared into the backyard while Mitch and Jeremy sat at the table eating.

When a car pulled into the driveway, Mitch jumped up to look out the living room window, Jeremy following him. The sheriff drove his own car. "Damn, that was the one chasing Howie's car that night," he said under his breath. "Fuck!"

Mitch grabbed Jeremy's arm gently. "Jeremy, listen to me carefully. Go upstairs now and hide. Do not come out until I say it's okay, understand?" Mitch instructed.

"Okay." Jeremy did exactly as told.

The sheriff walked through the door with his gun already drawn before Mitch could do anything to protect himself.

"Evening, Ridgeley. What do you need the gun for?" Mitch asked, standing with his arms crossed.

Sweat beaded on the evil man's face. "Came to take care of some loose ends. Where's the other two?"

Mitch stepped closer to the pistol aimed at his

heart. "They're not here. Leave them out of this. It's me you want. Always has been."

Ridgeley walked past Mitch to the kitchen, saw the three plates and yelled for Marly and Jeremy.

"I said leave them out of it." Mitch shouted. *Not again!* He refused to allow another innocent person to die if he could help it. "I'll make damn sure I don't lose this time. Do yourself a favor and leave now, Ridgeley."

The sheriff yelled their names again, ignoring Mitch.

Marly came running in. "What's the matter? Oh." She stared at the gun now pointed at her.

"Get over there with your lover. Where's the kid?"

"No! You leave him alone," Marly warned, stepping closer to Ridgeley until Mitch pulled her back.

"Jeremy, get down here now!" Ridgeley's voice shook the house.

"Jeremy, you don't come out until I say so," Mitch yelled louder.

Ridgeley swung around swiftly, pistol-whipping Mitch three times before he hit the floor with a loud thud.

"No!" Marly screamed, kneeling beside his motionless body. "What the hell do you want from us?"

"I want peace. And I can't have it. First, my idiot cousin tried to take it from me and now your lover is. I'm not giving up my life just because I took care of a few urges."

"Get the hell out of my house now," Marly

demanded.

Ridgeley laughed dangerously. "I'll be leaving soon. After I finish you all off. Ain't leaving any trace of my past to be uncovered. I'm ending this now. Once and for all."

The sheriff took out his handcuffs and dragged Marly up to her feet. She struggled, but in the end the sheriff proved to be too big for her to handle and handcuffed her to a dining room chair.

Ridgeley hauled a still unconscious Mitch up and fastened his hands behind his back with rope he took from his front pocket then leaned him against the leg of the dining room table.

Marly wiggled against the metal on her wrists. "He's bleeding. How could you do that to him?" she demanded.

"Don't worry. He'll be bleeding a lot more real soon. Now call your brat down."

"Fuck you!" she screamed, her legs kicking out frantically.

He slapped her hard across the face. The blood from her split lip pooled in her mouth and ran down her chin.

"I'll never let you near my son," she said between clenched teeth. Her wrists were raw where she tried to pull her hands through the metal cuffs.

Mitch started waking up, shaking his head, and blinking furiously. As soon as he looked at Ridgeley, he struggled to stand but the rope kept him in place. "You won't get away with this, Ridgeley. I've already made phone calls. You'll be arrested for Howie's murder. Do you really want to add to that number?"

"Boy, ain't no one arresting me for shit.

See…when I'm done here, it's going to look like a murder-suicide. The little lady here should've thought twice about letting a stranger in her home. Especially a psycho ex-cop who's a loose cannon. Shame the kid will get knocked off too. But not my problem."

"You can't possibly think you'll get away with this." Mitch said each word slowly.

"Oh, I do and I will." The sheriff paced like a rabid dog, looking up the stairs then back at his two hostages.

Marly's breath hitched when the sheriff became distracted by Jack's barking outside and, while he peered out the window, Jeremy snuck down the stairs and crawled along the floor to hide under the dining room table. This couldn't be happening. Jeremy was only a boy. There was no way anyone would hurt her son as long as she still had a breath left.

When Jeremy's small hands touched Mitch's bound ones, he flinched slightly before turning to Marly. The pained expression broke Marly's heart. They were both incapacitated and unable to protect poor Jeremy from the sheriff's wrath. Tears ran silently down Marly's cheeks until Mitch's face blurred.

Marly blinked away the tears. In her peripheral vision, she watched in horror as Jeremy, barely hidden under the tablecloth, used a small knife to cut Mitch's binds. She wanted to scream for Jeremy to run, to save himself.

Marly's head was about to explode from the years of emotion buried deep inside her and now ready to erupt. If her hands were free, she'd choke the life from Ridgeley.

Without realizing how hard she struggled against her binds, Marly froze when the sheriff studied her. She couldn't bring attention to herself if it would give Jeremy's location away. Her body stilled, her fingers flexing from numbness, her wrists on fire, but surprisingly she felt nothing other than grief swallowing her. Like black claws digging deep into her gut, fear consumed her.

"Why kill your cousin over a few pictures?" Mitch demanded.

Good thinking, Mitch. Keep the sheriff talking until Jeremy can free you. Stall.

"Pictures. What pictures?" Ridgeley asked.

"The ones of you and the prostitute that Howie used to blackmail you. I saw them and know all about your arrest." Mitch spoke slowly. Stall.

The fat man laughed with pathetic arrogance. "I didn't kill Howie over those stupid pictures. Although, I could've easily because he pissed me off. I gave him those pictures."

Mitch appeared really confused. "You gave them to him? Why would you give such revealing pictures to a man who wouldn't care who saw them?"

"Because he was making me money. He posted them on websites and got paid for it. I found out I'm in the wrong business. Shit, there's no money in law enforcement. The money is in porn. Internet porn. It's big bucks. Not many people around here use computers, so I didn't think twice about selling some very nice pictures of myself to make extra money on the side. Always made sure I couldn't be identified."

"Sheriff, you are hardly poor. Why would you need extra money?" Marly asked.

"I enjoy my fair share of gambling. But it can be an expensive habit if you hit a dry streak and don't win." The wretched man talked as if he expected sympathy for his plight. "Then he stopped making me money with the pictures and I wanted them back."

"If not for the pictures, then why kill Howie?" Mitch asked.

"Because he blew the casino deal. That would've made me the most powerful man in this town. I had invested my savings—thirty grand—because Howie said he had sealed the deal and the casino would be coming. Naturally, thirty grand seemed like a perfect little investment for me, since in the long run, I'd be making it back and much more when the casino was operational."

"How did he blow the deal?" Mitch talked slowly as if trying to figure out what to do.

"The bastard banged the wife of the casino developer who then pulled out of the deal. Howie had blown my thirty grand already and I saw red. I was tired of being shit on. Howie didn't give a shit. He laughed at me."

"So you killed a man."

Stall. Marly could barely breathe, holding her breath in fear of losing her son, her most treasured gift.

"I did. Felt real good, too. That asshole had it coming. And what better time to do it than when a stranger comes to town? A stranger who is familiar with guns and had already killed before. That's right. I know how you got injured. Guess being a big shot cop didn't help you save that poor girl. You sucked at your job I guess. Sorry, but it was very easy to frame you."

Marly's blood turned to ice in her veins. Never

315

Christina James

had she wished ill of someone, but this man wasn't human. He was a snake. He deserved to suffer like those around him had suffered at his hands. If he touched one hair on Jeremy's head, he'd never see the light of day again. Never would she have thought of spilling another person's blood, but doing so to this man would be justice.

"That wasn't very nice, Sheriff," Mitch said, sarcastically.

"Then this woman here posts your bail when I was going to let you escape and you'd leave town and the murder would be history. But you stuck around like a fool, chasing pussy around like a puppy."

"I happen to enjoy pussy, thank you."

Marly dared to look out of the corner of her eye again. Her heart pounded when she realized Jeremy had one of Mitch's hands freed. His little hands worked feverishly on the other.

"Now you see why I can't let you go." The sheriff's voice vibrated with his escalating temper.

Jeremy scooted back farther under the table as Mitch flexed his fingers then wiggled them. Jeremy placed the small knife in his hand and Mitch closed his fist.

"Hey, Sheriff. Let my mom and Mitch go," Jeremy yelled from behind Marly as he stood.

"There you are, you little shit."

Marly's heart stopped. Before her stood a monster who would kill her son. Fuck no! "Jeremy! Run!" she screamed, kicking out at Ridgeley as he advanced on her boy.

Without hesitation, Mitch leapt off the floor and charged the sheriff. The sheriff fell backward with

316

Mitch on top, the pocketknife sliding across the floor. A loud whoosh filled the room before the sheriff gasped for air.

Marly's eyes widened as she watched Mitch's fist connect with the sheriff's jaw, his head slamming to the side. Mitch straddled the sheriff's massive stomach as his fists smashed into Ridgeley's face, the sounds of bones crunching nauseated Marly.

Where was the gun?

Both men rolled over and over across the living room floor as the sheriff gained momentum and took swings at Mitch. One particular crushing blow to Mitch's face stunned Marly as a two-inch gash opened wide on his cheek.

"Jeremy!" Marly screamed. "Take my purse and run outside. Use my cell phone to call Uncle Seth. He'll know who to call for help. Then you run far away from here. Go!"

Jeremy moved quickly to the side of the room, grabbed her purse, and stopped at the door, horrified at the fight.

"Jeremy! Get out of here. Now." Marly yelled.

"Listen…to…your…mother…kid. I've…got this…asshole…under…control," Mitch said breathlessly, wrapped in a wrestling hold with Ridgeley.

Jeremy hesitated another few seconds then disappeared through the door. With Jeremy finally safe, Marly's head spun as she wiggled in the dining room chair she was still tethered to and offered a silent prayer.

Marly focused on the brawling men. Both were sweating and bloodied, the smell sickening. Curses were hurled, some she'd never even heard.

"Mitch!" Marly screamed, struggling against the cuffs, warm liquid oozing down her hands. More blood.

Exhausted, she resigned herself to witnessing the man she loved be beaten bloody, and there was nothing she could do about it. Tears streaked down her cheeks, slight warmth against her icy skin.

Her eyes widened in shock as the sheriff's hand inched toward the gun on the floor. "Mitch! The gun."

Mitch's hand reached for the gun at the same time Ridgeley's did. Both fingers fought for control before the skirmish forced it out of their grasp.

Marly let out the breath she had been holding. She forced her eyes shut, not wanting to watch the man she loved be killed in front of her, in her home, in the home she had thought of sharing with him. She could still hear their groans and grunts, still hear the vicious sounds of fists pummeling bodies and bones crushing. Opening her eyes again, it appeared as if the overweight and out of shape sheriff was finally getting exhausted as his movements began to slow while Mitch kept pounding on him.

Flashing lights and screaming sirens encouraged Marly to keep her eyes open. Oh no! Were the police pulling up outside good cops or the sheriff's crooked deputies? Fatigue consumed Marly. At least Jeremy was safe.

Loud gasps caught her attention. When she looked, the sheriff's hands were around Mitch's throat from behind with Mitch elbowing him in the ribs. Ridgeley looked like the devil himself, with his black, hollow eyes and devious smirk.

"Mitch!" Marly screamed, watching Mitch struggle for air.

With amazing strength, Mitch pulled the sheriff's arm from his throat. His body flipped over to latch onto Ridgeley's throat and gave him the same treatment, choking him while the man's fat hands fought against Mitch's. The way Mitch scrambled around the floor, his knee must've been killing him. Marly cringed, feeling the pain from his battered body. His determination amazed her.

Seconds later, glass shattered and wood smashed.

Policemen, not the sheriff's deputies, surrounded them, guns drawn, yelling commands. "Get down, both of you," a large man pointing a fierce looking rifle ordered.

Marly breathed a long sigh of relief. These were the good cops. Thank God!

Jeremy rushed back in hollering. "No! Not him. Not Mitch. He's not the bad guy."

Mitch gasped, lying on his stomach, arms outstretched as the police dressed in riot gear assessed the situation. "Go with the policemen, Jeremy, and listen to them," Mitch said with a gravelly voice.

Another policeman grabbed Jeremy around the waist and hauled him from the room as he struggled. "It's okay, buddy," Mitch said. "They'll let me up when they figure out what's going on." Still, Jeremy yelled and cursed as he was dragged back outside. Mitch smiled slightly.

Marly's eyes stung from unshed tears as she watched her son defend the man she loved.

"Ma'am, we'll free you in a moment," a tall man said to her. "Mitch Allen?"

"Yes," he replied. "I'd like to get the fuck up if I could."

"Of course, sir." The man extended his arm and assisted him to his feet. "Captain Amory said to tell you he still has your back." Mitch shrugged him off and limped to Marly's side, taking the key from an officer and undoing her cuffs.

"Jonas Ridgeley, you are under arrest for the murder of Howie Singleton, and the attempted murder of Mitch Allen, Marly Hampton, and Jeremy Hampton. You have the right to remain silent…" an officer said as he escorted a handcuffed Ridgeley from the house.

As soon as she was free, Marly bolted for her son, pushing past Mitch to run outside. She came back into the house seconds later, holding Jeremy tightly.

"Easy, Marly. The kid's got to breathe," Mitch said, gathering both of them in his arms.

Seth and her parents ran through the door next as the police cleared out.

"We're okay, Dad," Marly said, arms still around Jeremy, while Seth shook Mitch's hand.

Doc Peterson rushed in with Maddy. "Good Lord, is everyone okay?" Doc asked, faded black medicine bag in one hand.

"Yes. I think so," Marly whispered, her hands checking over Jeremy for injuries. "But Mitch needs looking at."

"The hell I do," Mitch complained, the blood already drying on his face.

Before Marly could speak, Bethany spoke. "Sit down, Mitch. Doc Peterson, he'll do exactly as you tell him."

Wow. Did Mom just effectively put Mitch in his place or what? Marly smiled as Mitch obeyed Bethany. It was times like this that Marly appreciated having some backup. Men and doctors were a sour mix.

Chapter Twenty-Six

"I'm not into making house calls at my age. We were at the diner when we heard about this ruckus." Doc was visibly shaken as he swabbed and cleaned Mitch's wounds with what felt like fire instead of antiseptic.

Small towns used to irritate Mitch with their close-knit communities but, with the show of support in the room, he understood what made small towns so special and why so many people chose to live in them.

Mitch shook Jeremy's hand then gathered him into a bear hug. "You did real good back there, buddy. You saved our lives."

"I learned it all from you."

Mitch's heart swelled with an emotion so strong it stole his breath. "But we have to talk about this problem you have with not staying put when you're told to stay put."

"Sorry. But you gave me this pocketknife because you thought I was old enough to use it properly. Before you came here, I was man of the house. I had to protect my mom any way I could."

"Yes, you did. In my opinion, you're still the man of the house, buddy." Mitch held him tight for a long while. "You protected her just fine."

Mitch's cell phone rang. "Allen."

"Did the calvary arrive?" Captain Amory asked.

"Just in time too. You sent them?" Mitch asked, walking away from Marly and Jeremy to hear better.

"I did. Got a bad feeling about the sheriff when I got your message about Howie's house burning down. Made some calls to the Tennessee State Police when I couldn't reach you tonight."

"Sorry, was a little tied up…literally."

"It took some convincing, but the state police took my concerns seriously and sent in their team to find you."

"Good call. Thank you."

"Finally found the gun thief in a sealed juvenile database and his DNA matched that on the lockbox. Daniel Bennington. Small time thug as a teenager. Been clean since he was nineteen and was charged with breaking and entering."

"Doesn't mean he's been an angel since. Just means he hasn't been caught yet."

"True. But he moved from that area a few months ago. Moved to Texas and hasn't left that state. Probably stole Marly's gun and sold it for a few quick bucks."

Mitch sighed. "At least with Ridgeley in jail and charged with the murder, Marly can rest easier. I can tell her the stolen gun wasn't part of a bigger scheme. Just some screwed up kid trying to make a fast buck."

"Make sure you keep in touch, Allen. Let me know if I can ever help out again. Felt good to be on a case again."

Mitch never felt happier. "Well, no offense, but I hope I never need your help again. I'll be sure to be in touch. I'll be putting you down for a reference when I apply for the sheriff's job."

"That's one phone call I look forward to."

Mitch disconnected and joined Marly and Jeremy in the kitchen. He explained what the captain had told him.

"It's all finally over." Marly's words hung in the air.

"Yeah, finally," Mitch whispered.

****

"Mitch Allen?" a state trooper asked as he entered the kitchen.

"That'd be me," Mitch responded, standing to face the officer. "Jeremy, go in the other room with Uncle Seth and your grandparents."

Jeremy looked at his mom, hesitated, but then backed slowly from the room.

"Allen, the charges against you have officially been dropped now that Ridgeley has been charged."

"So he's free to leave town any time?" Marly asked, standing beside Mitch. Her stomach lurched and her heart ached. *He's leaving town.*

"Yes, ma'am. You're a free man. We're done here, folks." The trooper left them alone. Jeremy came back into the kitchen and sat quietly at the table.

Marly's stomach tightened so she pulled on all her inner defenses to help her be strong and do what she had to do. "I guess you'll be leaving now that your name is cleared."

Mitch faced her, his eyes searching hers. "I actually planned to stay in town a little longer for some unfinished business."

"You've been in town only a short time. What business could you have?" Maybe her words were sarcastic. She didn't care. The less they talked, the quicker he could leave.

He shrugged, the red marks on his face not distracting from his handsomeness. "Some odds and ends."

When he moved closer to her, she pulled back, not wanting to hear him say goodbye. "You're a free man now and can leave and get back to your life. Or the road."

Mitch frowned. "I could've left the very day I got here or three days later or yesterday. No one was forcing me to stay here."

The nasty fingers of her temper were tickling her throat. She fought to keep her voice calm. "Oh, you stayed by your own choice?"

"Of course I did."

"That's bullshit. The sheriff forced you to stay because you were a suspect."

His broad shoulders shrugged under his blood-splattered T-shirt. "I could've left any time. I could've made arrangements to come back when necessary."

"You would've forfeited my property?" Shock assailed her. The jerk!

He folded his arms and watched her. "Never. I would never have done that and you know it. The sheriff had no legal right to keep me in town. I could've given him a new address and he wouldn't have been able to do shit as long as I was where I could be found."

"Then maybe you should've done that."

His jaw tightened. "I stayed because I wasn't ready to leave."

Her heart pounded. "Well, you got to play cop again and solve the murder, which I'm grateful for, but I really have to ask you to leave now. Leave tonight. I've got to get this house back to the way it was before you came."

Her body trembled with nausea. She couldn't believe she had gotten the words out and took control of the situation. She was the one asking him to leave, not giving him the chance to leave her.

Control. God, Mitch was so right. She always needed to have control. But that's how she kept her life together. And she needed it now more than ever. Anything to keep her from throwing herself in his arms and admitting how he was breaking her heart by leaving.

But that was no way to keep a man. Nor was any other reason other than true love. He should stay only because he wanted to. She'd never force him to stay when he didn't want to.

Mitch looked around. "Looks exactly like it did the first time I walked in that front door. Well, except for some blood in the living room and a broken door frame."

She blew out a breath. "That's not what I mean. You have to leave and I have to help Jeremy when you go because he's going to miss the hell out of you."

"And what about his mother?"

"I'll be just fine." Her chin jutted up so she could look him in the eye. A big smile was plastered across his face. He was happy? What the hell?

"I see. You'll just build up another wall around

your heart and live for everyone else but yourself. Is that how it goes, Marly?" His question reeked of cockiness.

She stepped toe to toe with him. "You son of a bitch! You don't know me."

His hands gently gripped her arms. "The hell I don't. I may have only known you for a short time, but I know you like to take long, hot baths with a glass of wine, eat chocolate cake for breakfast, you bite your lip when you're in deep thought, and blush when I tell you how beautiful you are."

Her breath hitched before she spoke. "There's more to me than that."

"You're right. There's a lot more. You have a great head on your shoulders that you use to support you and your son. You have a vicious backbone when someone threatens someone you love. You're stubborn as all hell and dig your heels in when you're ready to fight, like now."

She threw her hands up in the air and pushed past him. "This conversation is over. Leave." She used every bit of inner strength to fight back the tears. How could there be any tears left after earlier?

Mitch pulled her back in front of him. "Oh, yeah. Did I also mention you have control issues?" he said with heat. "You want to control everything around you so you don't get hurt again. Which is totally understandable, but not fair to you or to Jeremy."

How dare he lecture her? "Get off of me." She jerked her arms out of his hands but he caught hold again and held tighter.

"You're also beautiful and sexy and make my mouth water every time I look at you," he continued.

"I've been enjoying learning something new about you each day. I want to continue to learn about you each day for the rest of my life."

"You…can't do that…from…the…road," she snarled through clenched teeth, wishing she had the strength to break free of his grasp. The swine!

"No, I can't. I never said I was leaving, Marly. You just assumed I was. I'm staying. As long as you'll have me, I'll stay."

She froze. Did she just hear him right? "What are you saying, Mitch? That you'll stay until you're done playing house? Forget it. I'm not about to play that game."

"That's right. You go ahead and try to push me away. Your parents warned me you'd do that."

Her eyes narrowed. "My parents? You've spoken to my family about us?"

"Yup. And Jeremy, too."

Her temper was on the edge as she glanced at her son sitting a few feet away taking in the argument with interest. "How dare you get his hopes up that you'll be around forever when a few months ago you were traveling the road looking for God knows what in God knows where?"

His lips inched up into a smile. "Now I know where I'm supposed to be."

"That's nice, but it won't be here."

"Yes. It will."

"You arrogant—" his mouth covered hers, effectively cutting off her words.

He broke the kiss but stayed close. "Marly, you are the only woman I've ever fallen in love with. And, yes, I spoke to Jeremy because it mattered to me what he thought."

Tears streamed down her face, but she remained silent.

"If I'm going to marry his mother then I sure the hell need his blessing, don't I?"

"Mitch." Her voice was barely a whisper. Afraid to close her eyes, fearful that she'd open them again to discover that she was only dreaming. She just stared.

He silenced her by placing his finger over her lips. "I wish I could get down on one knee, but you'll have to take this from me standing up."

When he held her hand, she was trembling but there was no stopping it.

Caressing her knuckles with his fingers, he spoke slowly. "Marly, I love you. If you give me the chance to spend the rest of my life with you, I'll promise to spend every day proving my love to you. I'll never try to replace Jeremy's father, but I promise that I'll treat him like he was my own and love him every bit as much as I love his mom. How about it, Marly? I have to get you a ring, but will you be my wife?"

She stared at him. The silence hung in the air. Tears streamed down her face following the same path as the ones she'd shed earlier. But these were different. These were happy tears. Tears of joy. The vice around her heart loosened and she could breathe again. Dizziness swarmed in her head but deep breaths took care of that.

"I've wanted you since the day you walked in my door, Mitch," her voice was so soft. "I'm afraid to take the chance. I love you, but I'm afraid to be left alone again."

"You won't be alone. You'll have me and Jeremy

and hopefully some more little ones. I won't let you push me away, Marly. I love you. You said you love me. Now prove it and be my wife."

She stared at his fingers caressing her knuckle where she'd wear his ring. She saw hope. And finally saw the future and all that she had ever wanted. All she needed to do was get the courage up to say one word.

One little word to take her into the future and beyond.

Suddenly, that one word didn't seem so scary. "Yes," she said softly. "Yes. I will be your wife."

With a big smile, he picked her up off of her feet in a huge hug before kissing her lips. "Okay, Jeremy," Mitch turned to her son. "She said yes."

Jeremy jumped up and down, yelling and exchanging high-fives with Mitch. Jack jumped around barking.

"How would you feel about finally becoming that big brother that you've always wanted to be? Would you like that?" Marly asked.

Jeremy shrugged his shoulders. "That'd be cool. Wait. I wouldn't have to change diapers, right?"

"Nope, kid. Just the shitty ones," Mitch said, laughing.

"I think you'd make a great big brother, honey," Marly said, the tears threatening to spill over again.

"We'll start trying for a baby as soon as we get married. How's that sound?" Mitch asked her, kissing her lips gently again.

"Sounds perfect," she sniffled.

"Kid, you see me sweating here trying to convince Mom to marry me?" He ruffled Jeremy's hair. "This calls for a special celebration," Mitch said. "Jeremy, you get the cereal and I'll get the chocolate milk."

The three sat and ate the cereal at the kitchen table with Jack at their feet.

Mitch raised his spoon. "To the three of us."

"To all of us," Marly agreed.

"And Jack, too," Jeremy said.

"Of course, Jack, too," Mitch said.

"Thanks…Dad," Jeremy said with pride.

Marly never knew how much impact one word could have. She never expected to see the day when her son could call someone Dad. She had given him everything over the years except that one word. Now only Mitch could give it to him and, from the expression on Mitch's face, he enjoyed every bit of it. Looking forward to life with Mitch gave her a new outlook on love. For once, she had something to look forward to.

"I figured I'd apply to be the next sheriff of Courtsville. How's that sound?" Mitch asked.

"Sounds good to me," Marly said, facing the fear of losing him to a dangerous job. "I know you'll do a great job and be safe."

"Always, darling."

She leaned closer so only he could hear her. "All I want you to wear to bed is the badge, Sheriff Allen. Just the badge."

"Now that, my dear, can be arranged."

"What'd she say?" Jeremy asked.

"She wants to play baseball," Mitch confirmed.

"Eeww. Gross. Come on, Jack." Boy and dog ran upstairs.

"That's what you get for being nosy, buddy."

Mitch and Marly laughed, finishing their cereal with chocolate milk.

A Place To Call HOME

CHRISTINA JAMES

Chapter One

Now, Hannah O'Leary had been in many dangerous predicaments in her twenty-six years, but nothing compared to the situation she found herself in at the moment. Her fingernails clawed the surrounding dusty plywood floor, desperately trying to pull her long, slender body from the hole through which she dangled helplessly.

The dank air in the old attic mixed with the inch thick grime that covered every foot of the very cluttered room. Her nose wrinkled every time she breathed, the smell reminding her of soiled socks and wet newspaper. Surely if she could grasp one of the many antique furniture pieces around her, she could crawl out of the gap she'd blindly fallen through while inspecting her new house.

Hannah reached with all her iron-will toward a large dresser but fell inches shy of success. Her legs flailed on the underside of the splintered hole and sheared lumber. Alone in this big, deserted house, she'd give anything to have even the boogeyman rescue her.

Exhaustion quickly settled deep into her bones—her very sore bones. Her head throbbed from the stifling heat in the large, dark room. Her long hair shrouded her shoulders and back, its thickness providing a blanket of warmth she certainly didn't need or want. The muscles in her arms twitched and spasmed in protest from holding up her body's weight. Oh, how she wished to have solid ground under her feet again. And her poor leg burned from what she guessed must be one hell of a scraped knee.

A squeak penetrated the silence. What was that? She scanned the area, her ears strained to listen for the noise to come again. Slowly, she twisted to see behind her. *Please don't let there be rodents, or worse, creepy crawly things in here,* she prayed. There was no one but her in the attic.

What could she do to save herself from dropping to the floor below? Daring to peek down where her waist disappeared through the floor, she surmised she had to be some fifteen feet in the air. Letting herself fall wouldn't do.

Scream. That's what she'd have to do. Someone would hear her from the street. Right?

Oh, please, she begged the gods.

Then she screamed. And screamed. And screamed.

Her parched throat, raw and painful, begged for water. Her voice cracked, but she promised herself she'd not stop until rendered mute.

"What the hell is going on up here?" a man's voice boomed through the room.

Help is here. Thank God!

"Over here. Help me. Help," Hannah yelled toward the doorway.

"All right already. Quiet down." The massive man marched into sight, scowling. When his gaze found her, he stopped short. "Just what the hell do you think you're doing up here?"

"Getting a manicure," she said sarcastically, her nails digging into the floor deeper. Didn't he know when someone yelled for help it was serious? "What the hell does it look like? Now would you please get me out of here?"

He muttered an oath, dropped a plastic clipboard, and kneeled. "Well, I certainly can't leave you like this. Hold still. Moving around like a fish out of water ain't gonna help you."

"Just please get me out of here," she said, biting her lip to keep from sobbing.

His large, strong hands squeezed through the broken wood and slid over her waist, down her hips, and over her bottom.

"Hey! Must you do that?" she demanded, wiggling from his touch, wedging herself further.

He sat back on his heels, rested his hands on his knees, and leaned over her. "If I don't touch you, how do you figure I get you out of this fine mess you've got yourself into?"

"You don't need to cop a feel while doing it." Embarrassment flowed through her from head to toe. Her cheeks heated with her mortification. It'd been years since a man had touched her, and this wasn't exactly romantic.

His face rested inches from hers. In the limited light, Hannah could just make out the hard angles and planes of his features. Their gazes locked, a glint of amusement in those dark eyes of his.

"Now as appealing as that sounds, sweetheart, I'm a busy man. But once we get you out of here, maybe I can adjust my schedule to cop a feel. Now do you want my help or not?"

"Of course I do. Please. I can't hang here all day."

"Then hold still."

She jerked her head up, irritated by his demanding tone. Who was he to boss her around? "Who are you anyway?"

"Looks like your hero. Now quiet. Let me work here."

He placed his arms through the hole and once again his hands roamed her waist, hips, and bottom. She bit down on an oath. She wouldn't admit how good those strong arms felt maneuvering over her body.

"Put your arms around my neck," he commanded and cupped her bottom.

Shaking her head, she panicked. "No. I'll fall through."

"No you won't. I've got a good hold of you."

"Yeah. I've noticed."

"Damn it. I said put your hands around my neck. Now."

She huffed and did what he told her. "Don't drop me," she demanded nervously.

"Don't give me a reason to. And don't hold my neck so tight. I like to breathe."

With his face so close to hers, his warm breath tickled her cheek with each word. A tingle ran down her spine. Probably just a reaction from her fright.

"Just hold on. I'm going to lift you up. When I tell you, hold your knees to your chest as high as you can. Got it?"

"Yes."

"Okay." His fingers dug into the curve of her bottom where it met her thighs.

Oh, God, how embarrassing to have a strange man's hands holding her in such an intimate fashion. And damn she didn't want to notice, but he was so strong, his arms solid, his fingers long and brawny, and currently massaging her buttocks thoroughly, while he lifted her slowly, angling her through the jagged wood. Breathing heavily with fear, she pressed her face against the curve of his neck and inhaled his scent. She couldn't miss the smell of his skin, the scent of soap and heat.

"Okay. Now," he ordered.

She raised her knees even though they felt as heavy as logs. And then she stood on solid floor again, held tightly around the waist by his arm. He bent, grabbed his clipboard, and hauled her with him, lifting her and carefully and crossing over the wooden planks. Just like she'd done—before she'd lost her footing and crashed through the floor. Each stair creaked as the tall stranger walked her down to the second floor. Hannah squinted at the bright sunshine pouring through the dirty windows.

"You can let go of me now." The demand was stronger than necessary, but she could no longer hide her embarrassment.

"You sure? I don't mind helping hold you up. Well, until you can stand on your own."

His smile should be outlawed for the danger it presented to a woman's state of mind. To *her* state of mind. Between the heat, humidity, and him watching her so closely, she swayed not knowing which to blame. Southern men may be known for their manners, but never had she seen a smile that intoxicating. With his slow drawl, he must be born and bred Southern.

"I think I can handle it now. Thank you."

Slowly he removed his arm from her waist. "Sure now?"

Before she could answer, she staggered.

His hand grabbed her elbow. "Stay still."

"I'm trying. Don't forget I just finished hanging from the damn ceiling. Have to get used to my feet again." Her knees protesting her weight, she froze when his hands purposely roamed her body. She brushed him away. "What the hell do you think you're doing?"

"Checking for injuries. Stay still."

"I will not. You did your good deed for the day. Now stop."

He ignored her protests and continued to run his hands over her arms, legs, and back. "You're dirty, but you'll survive. You're not injured. No broken bones."

Before she knew what he planned to do, he grabbed his clipboard, lifted her into his arms, cradled her to his chest, and walked to the stairs.

"Hey! Put me down." Why be so nice to her when he didn't even know her? Accepting his help needed to be done earlier, but she could take care of herself now.

"I will when I get you downstairs. Don't think you should tempt fate with a header down the stairs on those wobbly legs. And the next time you inspect an attic, use a flashlight. If you had, then you would've seen that floor is riddled with dry rot."

"Thanks for the lesson. I can walk fine. Now please put me down." She wiggled against his hard torso needing him to stop holding her so close. Her body heated, and she knew it had nothing to do with the summer temps.

"No," he said simply, starting down the winding staircase. "Hold still, lady. Unless you want to kill us both."

When she turned to see how close they were to the bottom, he lost his footing, and they tumbled down the last of the stairs with her landing under him.

He called out a string of curses. "What part of 'hold still' did you not understand, lady?" He sat up next to her and rubbed his lower back.

She sat up as well, her body smarting in too many places to console.

He continued to yell. "I need my body in one piece to earn a goddamn living."

She flinched, guilt consuming her. "I'm sorry. It's not like I planned to make us fall."

"Had you listened to me and stopped moving, I wouldn't have tripped."

He was right, of course. How did she tell him that being held in his arms had made her too nervous to think clearly? She sighed, wishing she could rewind the entire morning.

He stared, still sitting on the floor with her. "Okay. Maybe you didn't mean to nearly kill us. You okay?"

She shrugged and straightened her shirt, offering a shy smile. "Yes. Thank you for rescuing me from the attic."

"And you repay me by lying to me?" he said, frowning. "You're hurt and won't admit it. I know some first aid. Let me look at your leg."

"No. I'm fine really. Just a little scrape." She inched back from him. "So what are you doing here anyway?"

"Sorry," he said, extending his hand. "Name's Mac. You called me for a bid to renovate this place. MacDevin & Sons Construction at your service. It's Ms. O'Leary, right?"

"Hannah."

"Hannah," he repeated, her name rolling off his tongue to serenade her ears.

"Do you have a bid, Mac?" She let go of his hand.

"I do. You're not getting it, though," he said and gestured toward her injured knee. "Not until I look at that cut on your leg."

She frowned. "Now that's not playing fair."

He shot her that killer smile again. Thank goodness she wasn't standing. Her knees would've weakened instantly. Damn, if a smile could have that kind of effect on her, then she needed to get laid.

She scooted up and sat on the bottom stair. Her injury throbbed, and when she glanced down, she found her pant torn and a jagged gash sliced across her knee. Mac's large hand covered her calf and tugged until her leg straightened then he slid his callused palm up her shin. Dear God, why did that have to feel so good?

He studied the knee, released her, and stood. "Be right back. Don't move," he directed and walked out the front door.

Too bad Mac didn't know Hannah took orders from no one. She struggled to her feet, retrieved her purse from where she'd left it near the door, and grabbed a wad of tissues. However, trying to hold the tissues over her knee and hobble back to the stairs proved to be difficult. With her injured leg bare from knee to ankle, she eased back down onto the stair step and looked up when Mac returned.

He grimaced. "Thought I told you to stay put."

"You did. I didn't want to."

"You have a hard time with listening, don't you, Hannah?" Mac popped open the first aid kit.

"You'd be wise to learn I don't follow orders or take demands."

"Yeah? Even when your safety is concerned? That's just being stubborn." He reached for her, and she pulled away.

She held the makeshift bandage over her bloody skin. "I'm fine, really."

He ignored her, bent down to study her leg. "This is pretty banged up. Needs to be treated. Let me see."

Did the guy ever give up? Never had someone paid this much attention to her. If he would just leave her alone, she could handle it herself. But no. He wanted to play doctor. "I think it's time you left."

He pried her hand to survey her scrape.

"Why won't you listen to me?" she demanded.

He grabbed her leg before she could pull away. "I promise I won't hurt you. Let me help you before you get an infection."

"So, now you're a doctor?"

"Hardly. More like I have plenty of experience with scraped knees."

With a sigh, she relented. He only wanted to help—no harm there—and her leg did throb something awful. After she'd traveled ten hours from Tennessee and drove through the night, utter exhaustion consumed her since her arrival in town two hours earlier. She'd been too excited to see her new house, so she hadn't bothered to get a hotel room. Her real estate agent had assured her the small apartment attached to the house remained habitable, so she could stay on-site and monitor the renovations.

Hannah studied the man leaning over her to clean her injury. He stood tall, at least six feet four and a solid two-fifty. His gray T-shirt fit snug over a muscular frame that boasted long arms and a narrow waist. Jet-black hair, short and thick, created a striking contrast with his tanned skin. His eyes held the deepest blue, bright and serious.

His firm thigh brushed against her leg. The simple touch unnerved her, creating delicious visions in her mind of her legs entangled with his. Decadent chills prickled her warm flesh. With him this close, the angles of his face shone clearly. The high cheekbones, the stern jaw, the slightly crooked nose, the freshly shaven skin, the thin lips now set in a grim line.

"Are you done checking me out?" he asked.

Her cheeks warmed, and she turned her attention back to her leg. "Don't be so full of yourself. I wasn't checking you out. Just thought I should be able to give the police an accurate description of you, should I need to."

"How about you just thank me for saving your pretty ass?"

Did he just compliment her ass? "I've said thank you." Time to change the subject from her anatomy. "Can I see your bid now?"

Those gorgeous eyes snapped up to meet hers

briefly. "When we're done." His voice didn't hide his impatience. "Hold still, will you? I don't have all day to play nursemaid."

She wanted to slug him. "I can take care of it myself."

He chuckled. "What with your fancy tissues? All you managed to do was get paper bits in the wound."

"Ow." Pain caused her to pull away, but he held her calf in a vise grip and poured peroxide over her scrape. "You did that on purpose," she accused.

"No, but I am going to keep doing it until it's clean. Now hold still."

Struggling proved useless with his strength. "I don't need your help."

"Too bad. You're getting it. I've enough to worry about than a clumsy woman causing herself an infection."

"Don't call me names."

"Sorry." He recapped the peroxide bottle. "But you have to admit you're pretty clumsy. Not to mention stubborn," he added. Using a cotton ball drenched in peroxide, Mac brushed across the wound, clearing away small white bits of tissue. His firm grip kept her still.

When he released her to separate gauze, she tugged her leg away. He eyed her before his large hand clamped around her calf and hauled her back toward him. "Do I need to tie you down to finish?"

Something in his voice and his glare had her believing he'd do just that and take immense pleasure in it. The swine! "Listen, Mac. I appreciate your help. Really I do. But I happen to be a big baby when it comes to pain. And this hurts like hell. Please stop."

He glanced up and smiled. His hand rubbed her leg with long, slow caresses. "I promise we're almost done."

Dear God! Forget the fire in her knee. If he didn't stop rubbing her leg like that, he'd set her entire body aflame. He smudged on some kind of antibiotic cream and covered the red, swollen area with fresh gauze, taping it in place.

"Okay. So maybe it does feel better now," she admitted when finally allowed to move her hostage leg.

"Told you. Big baby." Mac grinned and replaced everything into the first aid kit.

She smiled. "Hey, in my defense, you weren't very gentle."

"I can be very gentle when needed, Hannah." That slow, Southern drawl sang to her like a lullaby, the blue of his eyes twinkling with mischief.

When he stood, he offered a hand to help her stand, totally interrupting her thoughts of how gentle he could be. She couldn't miss Mac's long perusal of her body. This certainly had ended up being a better day.

"If you think you'll be okay now, I do have to get going. I'm falling behind on my very busy schedule."

She cleared her throat and wished she had some water. "Of course. Thank you again."

After picking up his clipboard and scribbling on the top page, Mac handed her his prepared bid. "Here you go, Ms. O'Leary."

She accepted the papers. "I'll be in touch, Mac."

He leaned down to talk softly into her ear. "I do hope so. It's not every day I get to rescue pretty ladies hanging from holes in the floor. Stay out of the attic, Hannah. And please listen."

She laughed. "Promise."

With one last flash of that killer smile, Mac left her to admire his retreating back as he stepped out into the blazing sun. She considered it a treat to watch his hips sway in that rugged fashion of a man on a mission, his long legs eating up the ground to the driveway.

While getting into his truck, he looked back at her, his inviting smile holding promise. Now she would have to decide whether or not to accept the invite to what would definitely be a very interesting encounter.

But first, she needed to check his references. And while she did that, she'd have her head examined for considering anything more than business with the smooth talking, sexy Southern contractor.

****

Three hours later, with the humidity rising and her silk blouse clinging to her sweaty body, Hannah stared at the bid in her hand. The two other contractors she'd scheduled had failed to show for their appointments. Hannah had bought the property, thinking it would be fun to restore an old Civil War era house to its original luster. But boy, had she been mistaken. After calling one of the no-show contractors and being told outright that it required too much work and wasn't worth it, disappointment filled her.

Mac's bid was all she had to go on. She admired the neat penmanship and professional appearance of the document. Compared to previous bids, which had taken her forever to decipher the writing and understand the construction lingo, Mac's was a dream. Precise, legible, everything broken down into concise detail for each part of the job—electric, plumbing, and carpentry. She had no trouble understanding his proposal.

She sat on the stairs, the same place where Mac had thoughtfully cleaned her wound. When memories of his large, strong hands on her slender legs surfaced, she quickly banished them. She would not, absolutely would *not*, be distracted by his outstanding physical appearance and sexiness when there remained business at hand. Although, the wetness between her legs said differently.

With each of her new business adventures, Hannah had gained measurable knowledge of the construction and renovation industry—except obviously how to walk in attics, her throbbing knee reminded her. The layman terms Mac had used were easy to follow, so his proposal helped her understand what kind of massive project she actually faced. When she looked at his total price, pleasant surprise jolted through her. Mac's proved more than reasonable, and he could start in two weeks.

Hannah looked around, trying to envision her new restaurant, but the house was in too bad shape. Holes covered the walls, the scratches marred the floors, the paint peeled from the ceilings. When she'd bought it, the realtor had advised her that the house hadn't been looked after for years, but she never imagined this. No wonder it had been a steal.

Her belly growled, reminding her she hadn't

eaten lunch. She'd go into town, find coffee and food. Then with her full stomach and caffeine-energized brain, she'd get back to work.

Hannah retrieved her luggage from her car and hauled it upstairs to the small apartment above the main house. The real estate agent had explained the apartment served as servant's quarters years ago. At least it stood in better condition than the main house. While the apartment needed serious renovations, updates, and redecorating, it wasn't falling down around her.

Hannah changed into denim shorts and a white cotton tee and enjoyed instant coolness. Opening the front door, the afternoon heat and humidity asphyxiated her once again. The air hung thick while heat rose from the ground. She trudged to her car and turned the AC on full blast, reveling in the icy air stream before she drove away.

Large, old houses lined the narrow streets. Beautiful gardens beautified many front yards. Seeing a gas station, Hannah stopped for fuel and directions to a decent place to eat. A few minutes later, Hannah entered the Daylight Café, which was crowded with lunch patrons.

The charming restaurant boasted large windows, allowing the sunlight to shower the inside with bright rays. The large u-shaped countertop situated in the middle of the single room filled the space, and smaller tables sat scattered around the remaining area. Tantalizing aromas of grilled meats and veggies clung to the air. The noise level astonished her with everyone talking, laughing, shouting. For something that appeared chaotic at first, the café turned out to be a well-run establishment with lively customers and an ambience that screamed Southern hospitality.

A plump waitress approached her. "Honey, just take a seat. There's room around the end of the counter."

Trudging to where the woman had indicated, Hannah realized how exhausted she'd become, her legs feeling more like tree stumps. The only available seat sat between an elderly man and another guy with his back turned to her while he spoke with the person next to him.

A young waitress set down a menu in front of her along with a white ceramic cup and saucer, which she sloshed coffee into. Taking tiny cream containers from her apron, she dropped them next to the cup and walked away.

The man next to Hannah swung around. "Well, my day just got a hell of a lot better."

Hannah immediately recognized the voice. Turning toward the husky sound, she confirmed she'd parked herself right next to Mac. Her heart skipped a beat. "Oh, really? Why's that?"

He leaned closer and whispered, "Because I didn't expect to see you here."

The way his warm breath tickled her ear sent a delicious chill down her spine. "Well, it's nice to be recognized. You're the only one in town I know so far."

When the waitress reappeared, Hannah turned her attention. "Could I have a chef salad, please? And keep the coffee coming."

The waitress scribbled in her notepad, took the menu, refilled the coffee, and disappeared.

Hannah couldn't help but squirm from the heat emanating from Mac's body. With him practically on top of her, she wanted to push him aside, like that would even be physically possible. She wasn't used to such closeness, and when his hard thigh brushed against her leg and his elbow bumped her arm, she spoke up. "Could you please move over? You're squishing me."

He raised an eyebrow and moved a millimeter away. A millimeter! The man was an ape! Couldn't he see her distress at being overcrowded?

"It's no wonder you're so skinny," Mac said. "You can't live on salads."

"Just how do you know what I live on? And by the way, it's rude to comment on what a lady chooses to eat." Why was his cologne so noticeable and sexy?

"I'll be sure to keep that in mind. You don't know what you're missing with the chicken salad club. Should have had that."

"I'll take my chances, thank you. Has anyone ever told you how pushy you are?"

He laughed. "Yeah, quite often. It comes natural to me. Like your stubbornness does to you."

"You know, for a contractor you sure have a lot of time on your hands right now or else you wouldn't be sitting there leisurely. Thought you were a busy man."

He frowned. "I am. But I do like to eat. Unlike some people, I eat well to keep up my strength. I never skimp on my lunch time, my breakfast time, my dinner time." He grinned wickedly, leaning closer to her ear. "Or my bed time. A man needs to feast."

She bit her tongue, refusing to be sucked into his

sexually suggestive conversation. But she also didn't miss the twinkle in those deep blue eyes when he sat back. His eyes fascinated her too much, so she worked on her PDA, a perfect distraction to his hot body. Ogling the man in public wouldn't be wise.

To her relief, Mac said nothing else but greeted everyone who passed by, obviously a very popular man. At least two young women smacked his cheek loudly with kisses, which for some reason unnerved Hannah. She wouldn't call it jealousy, precisely, but more a sense of missing out on something amazing. After all, she couldn't help but remember his strength, being pinned under him briefly after their unfortunate tumble down the stairs, and how those hands had roamed over her body. It had been so many years since she'd been intimate with a man, she couldn't remember how long. Too long. But her sex life had never been amazing, so how could she miss something she'd never had?

Her chef salad arrived, and the waitress topped off her coffee. She hardly realized how hungry she felt, but the first bite tasted heavenly. Mac continued greeting people and making small talk with everyone. The café started to empty when people finished their lunches and went about their business. When Mac turned his attention back to her, she'd just taken the last bite of her salad and sipped her coffee.

Oh, how those gorgeous eyes studied her the moment they landed on her face.

"So, what did the other bidders have to say?" he asked.

"They were no-shows." Not to mention they'd wasted her time.

"So, does that mean I get the job?"

She shrugged. "Not until I check your references."

"Fair enough. You can ask anyone here if you'd like."

She looked around the small café. "You provided some I plan to call this afternoon. I really do appreciate you placing a bid. Looks like you're the only contractor around not afraid of a little hard work."

"It's one of the biggest projects I've worked on, but I do enjoy a good challenge." His words drawled slow and sexy, and his lips curved slightly at one corner.

Damn, how would she ever work with him if she couldn't even manage to sit on a lunch stool next to him without getting spikes in hormone levels?

"I can give you a call tonight if that's okay." She watched him closely, hoping that her tone didn't give away her desire for him.

"Sure. Call me any time, Hannah."

Now, why did it sound like those words held more promise than she wanted to admit?

Clearing her dry throat didn't help her voice, so she sipped some water then spoke. "Would you mind telling me where I could find some industrial appliances to check out? I'm used to big cities with access to every kind of store."

"You'll get the same around here, but just got to travel a bit is all." He wrote out some quick directions on a napkin and handed it to her. "This is where I suggest you order any appliances and fixtures. It's only about a twenty-minute drive out of town. Tell them Mac sent you, and they'll take good care of you."

Hannah could think of some ways for Mac to take good care of her. They all involved their naked bodies, sweat, and lots of tongue action. Oh God, why did she want to fuck the one man able to help her with her restaurant? No way could she screw this up. Then she'd just be horny *and* stuck without a contractor.

"Thank you, Mac. You've been very kind to me. I think I'm going to like my stay in Charleston," she said and smiled.

When he stood, the loss of heat from where his thigh had touched her leg was immediate. Looking down at her, his baby blues melted her on the spot. "You will enjoy your stay, Hannah. I promise."

When his hand squeezed her elbow, she jumped. What was it about his touch that electrified her skin?

Mac bellowed goodbye to the remaining café customers before he walked to the door. "If any of y'all would like to do me a favor, I'd be mighty appreciative. It seems the lovely lady," he said, letting his Southern drawl drag out the words, "right over there is looking for some confirmation on my references as a contractor. Maybe y'all could enlighten her on my work ethics and save her some time. Have a good day."

After that speech, he whispered to the waitress and then winked at Hannah. He left the café without another word.

All the customers stared at Hannah. She quickly busied herself with preparing to pay the bill, but when the waitress returned, she only cleared the dishes.

"May I please have my check?"

"It's paid for."

"Paid for? By whom?"

"By Mac."

"Of course," she sighed, shoving her money back into her wallet. He'd already done too much for her. That act of kindness had been totally unnecessary.

The old man sitting next to Hannah spoke. "Mac's the best contractor in this part of the world."

"You can say that again," another man said from down the counter. "Ain't nothing that boy can't fix, and when he fixes it, it stays fixed."

Suddenly, Hannah grew interested in the conversations surrounding her.

Another man spoke up. "They don't make boys like Mac anymore. His mama beams when she speaks of him doing so good for himself and all by himself too. Nope. Boy was never one to take a hand out, not even when God knows he deserved one."

Hannah sensed a tight-knit group. "You mean he's legit?"

"Legit? What's that?" the old guy next to her asked.

"Well, I, um, mean is he trustworthy? Is he a legitimate businessman?"

The crowd around her laughed and made inaudible comments.

The old man next to her responded. "Mac is too honest to be a businessman, but he is one hell of a contractor. He's got the best prices in the state and works so hard and so quickly he makes the rest of us look like bums."

"Yup," another man confirmed. "He's a man of his word. Very particular about keeping his reputation pristine. But he has nothing to worry about since he's the most recommended contractor around. Hell, I don't know where he ever finds the time to sleep. Seems he's always working."

"But you'll never hear that boy complain."

"Got that right," someone seconded.

"If you don't mind me asking, pretty lady," asked a guy seated down the counter.

"The name is Hannah O'Leary."

"Okay, Ms. O'Leary. What's your business with Mac? You ain't from around these parts."

Everyone in the café instantly fell silent, all eyes fixed on Hannah.

"Well, sir, I'm the new owner of the former Brigman house on Jackson Street. I'm opening a restaurant catering to breakfast and special functions, and well, Mac had stopped by to make a bid on the necessary repairs."

"The ol' Brigman house, huh? Everyone in town knows only Mac is capable of fixing up that heap of wood. He'll do a mighty fine job for you, Ms. O'Leary. Just you wait and see."

Hannah swallowed hard. Working with the sexy contractor appeared to be inevitable. She politely excused herself, and with flaming cheeks and a nervous belly, she stepped out into the blazing heat of the South Carolina midday.

About the Author

Award winning, multi-published author Christina James lives in a Massachusetts suburb with her two children. When penning stories, she enjoys writing of romance and heartache and of characters who overcome the odds. Passion is at the heart of every tale, and she strives to create realistic characters, so the reader can fall in love with them as much as she does. A sucker for a good love story, Christina writes hot, sensual romances with a little sarcastic wit and some humor in a contemporary setting. Look for her naughty Operation Series to continue featuring the other Navy SEALs. For naughty and wicked romance with no strings attached…read a Christina James novel.

Other titles by Christina James:
A Place to Call Home
Make a Wish and Blow
Operation: Spank Me
Operation: Tempt Me
Web of Lies

www.christinajamesauthor.com

Join Christina on Facebook
http://www.facebook.com/#!/profile.php?id=10000301
9022368&sk=wall